THE PRICE OF CASH

What Reviewers Say About Ashley Bartlett's Work

Dirty Sex

"A young, new author, Ashley Bartlett definitely should be on your radar. She's a really fresh, unique voice in a sea of good authors. …I found [*Dirty Sex*] to be flawless. The characters are deep and the action fast-paced. The romance feels real, not contrived. There are no fat, padded scenes, but no skimpy ones either. It's told in a strong first-person voice that speaks of the author's and her character's youth, but serves up surprisingly mature revelations."—*Out in Print*

Dirty Money

"Bartlett has exquisite taste when it comes to selecting the right detail. And no matter how much plot she has to get through, she never rushes the game. Her writing is so well-paced and so self-assured, she should be twice as old as she really is. That self-assuredness also mirrors through to her characters, who are fully realized and totally believable."—*Out in Print*

"Bartlett has succeeded in giving us a mad-cap story that will keep the reader turning page after page to see what happens next."
—*Lambda Literary*

Dirty Power

"Bartlett's talents are many. She knows her way around an action scene, she writes *memorably* hot sex, her plots are seamless, and her characters are true and deep. And if that wasn't enough, Coop's voice is so genuine, so world-weary, jaded, and outrageously sarcastic that if Bartlett had none of the aforementioned attributes, the read would still be entertaining enough to stretch over three books."—*Out in Print*

Cash Braddock

"There were moments I laughed out loud, pop culture references that I adored and parts I cringed because I'm a good girl and Cash is kind of bad. I relished the moments that Laurel and Cash spent alone. These two are really a good match and their chemistry just jumps off the page. Playful, serious and sarcastic all rolled into one harmonious pairing. The story is great, the characters are fantastic and the twist, well, I never saw it coming."—*The Romantic Reader*

Visit us at www.boldstrokesbooks.com

By the Author

Sex & Skateboards

Dirty Trilogy

Dirty Sex

Dirty Money

Dirty Power

Cash Braddock Series

Cash Braddock

The Price of Cash

THE PRICE OF CASH

by
Ashley Bartlett

2017

THE PRICE OF CASH

ISBN 13: 978-1-62639-708-8

THIS TRADE PAPERBACK ORIGINAL IS PUBLISHED BY
BOLD STROKES BOOKS, INC.
P.O. BOX 249
VALLEY FALLS, NY 12185

FIRST EDITION: NOVEMBER 2017

CREDITS
EDITOR: CINDY CRESAP
PRODUCTION DESIGN: SUSAN RAMUNDO
COVER DESIGN BY MEGAN TILLMAN

Acknowledgments

There are no moral absolutes. No one, nothing is ever entirely right or wrong. We don't tend to reach that realization until we are far past childhood, far past the decisions we might have made otherwise if we had known.

This book is about stasis. The moment when you realize that some people will never understand you, never empathize with you, never entirely see you. It is about the panic that washes through you and suddenly you think the only solution is to freeze. If you don't move, then maybe you'll never have to admit that you are misunderstood. That your concept of right and their concept of wrong have aligned and one of you must falter. As Cash finds in this book, the truly paralyzing moments are those when someone else has the relative high ground.

I spent a lot of time avoiding writing this book while I was supposed to be writing this book. My haiku game has certainly improved, which is entirely unhelpful in novel writing. Carsen, you're the reason I finished writing (not the haiku, the novel). Between the numerous pep talks, your inexplicable need to use the telephone, and your talent for finding inventive ways to break the law, you saved me. Thank you.

Bold Strokes has been my home since I was a tiny tot. Every time they send a contract, I think they've lost their damn minds. So thanks, Rad and Sandy, for not being sane. Cindy, I'll probably never forgive you for inflating my ego. I'm not sure what you were thinking.

And you, my audience. Thanks for coming back even when logic and propriety suggest you should go the other way. Cash and I couldn't do it without you.

Dedication

For my wife.
My moral center might be off,
but at least it's the same as yours.

CHAPTER ONE

Laurel's hands were under my shirt. The tips of her fingers dug intricate, meaningless patterns across my stomach. Her thigh pressed between my legs in the most delicious way. My neck tingled where her lips brushed against my skin.

"We need to make the deal out back. It's too crowded in here. The audio will be worthless," she whispered in my ear. Detective Kallen had a way of really killing my pseudo mood.

I did my best to make it look like Laurel was whispering dirty, sexy plans for the evening. Jason was staring at us from across the table. He was grinning in that bro way. Like he was about to break out the high fives. Our act was clearly working.

It wasn't difficult to play the lie when Laurel had me so turned on that my boxer briefs were soaked. The hard part was convincing her that my arousal was just an act. When I was finished with that lie, I planned on convincing myself.

"Babe, babe. Slow down." I gripped her wrists and pulled her hands out of my shirt. "I think we need to cool off."

Laurel grinned at me. "You're too easy."

"You're cruel." I kissed her. Softly. The kind of kiss that was a promise. She groaned, then stifled it. "Let's head outside. I can't think in here."

Laurel rolled her eyes and led the way out back. Jason grabbed his backpack and shook his head. Laurel kept my hand firmly in her grasp, which had a lot more to do with staying in range of the wire she was wearing than intimacy.

"How do you do it?" he asked.

"What?"

"Get chicks to want you like that?"

"Secret lesbian power. Can't tell you." I bumped him with my shoulder. I almost felt bad. But I was selfish. Better him than me.

Laurel chose a table on the far end of the patio. It was darker, quieter out here. She sat at the far side of the table. I slid to the back, which left Jason sitting with his back to the next table and a Latino guy in his early forties. Lucas Reyes. Kallen's partner.

I reminded myself that Jason had screwed me over once. Years ago, when I was just getting started. I hadn't gotten a solid supply line yet. He offered to hook me up with a doctor at a clinic in Elk Grove. After the first few shipments, I realized he was taking a finder's fee he hadn't mentioned. I was paying three times the street rate. When I confronted him, the supply suddenly dried up.

It wasn't an uncommon business practice. I'd been pissed at the time, but that faded. My dirty sheriff, Henry, became much more adept at stealing from the evidence locker. That was before he lost his shit and tried to kill Kallen. And me. Henry was a dick.

Now, Jason stuck to the south side of the county. I stuck to the north. And we didn't mess with each other's supply lines. Until tonight. He'd been cool when I called to explain that my guy had disappeared. Offered a rate born of belated mutual respect.

I tried to recapture my earlier anger, but it was worthless. I couldn't dilute my guilt with a grudge that was half a decade old.

Jason settled into his seat, leaned forward a little. Enough for privacy, but not enough for intimidation. "Tell me what happened."

"Honestly, I don't know," I said.

"I thought your guy was solid."

"Same. He was off the last few months. Just jumpy, you know? Nervous. And then, gone." I snapped my fingers.

"And you don't know why?" Jason seemed intrigued, not skeptical.

Laurel sighed and gave me a look. I sighed and sent the look right back to her. "No."

"What?" Jason asked.

I waved my hand like it was her show. "Whatever."

Laurel leaned closer to Jason. "I think he was supplying someone else."

"That's cold." Jason shook his head. "You sure you didn't off him?" He grinned at me.

I laughed. "Believe me, I'd love to smack the shit out of him, but no. He'd be much more useful to me alive. Asshole left me in a tight spot."

"I feel that." Jason set his backpack on the table. "This will hold you over, but it will take a while to set up something steady."

"You mind?" I pointed at the bag. He shook his head. I unzipped it and looked inside. It held three quart-size Ziplocs filled with pills. Blue and white. Another bag was half-full of faint orange.

Jason outlined his terms. He was still overcharging me a little. I pushed back to make it look real, but I wasn't trying very hard. Laurel played the role of bored girlfriend beautifully. So beautifully I had to remove her hands from my body three times before stopping my conversation with Jason.

"Babe." I gave her a stern look.

She knocked off a couple of IQ points and pouted. "What?"

"We're having a discussion." I nodded at Jason.

"Wrap it up." Kallen leaned close and placed a line of delicate kisses down my throat. Clearly, we had gathered enough evidence to satisfy her.

"Sorry, man. Would love to stay," I said to Jason.

"No worries." Jason grinned. I slid an envelope across the table. Jason counted the money and pocketed it. "Pleasure doing business with you." He held out his hand. I shook it and shouldered the backpack of drugs.

"Come on." Laurel tugged my shirt to pull me toward the gate leading to the street.

Before we could open the gate, a uniformed officer stepped into view on the opposite side. Kallen shot me a look. Jason hesitated. I just opened the gate and kept walking.

"Excuse me." The officer stepped in front of us.

Laurel and I looked at each other. We shared a moment of perfect understanding, then sprinted in opposite directions.

Jason took off half a second behind us. He shouted a stream of curses as the uniform tackled him. There was a dull thud as another cop landed on top of them.

I took a quick right down an alleyway. Pounding footsteps echoed behind me. They were moving a lot faster than I was. Running had never been my thing. I wondered briefly how much they had told the uniforms on this detail. The chances that they had been told I was an informant were slim. This was going to hurt. I spared a glance at my pursuer. It was Reyes. I stopped running.

"Christ, Braddock. Why are you making me run?" Reyes bent at the waist and did some heavy breathing.

I leaned against the fence that ran the length of the alley and worked on my own breathing exercises. "I didn't know it was you." I dropped the backpack of evidence between us.

"You're lucky. The guy chasing Kallen just failed his detective exam and is pissed." He straightened and shot me a grin.

"Does he know she's a detective?"

Reyes nodded. "He went through the academy with her brother. They didn't get along."

I laughed, then felt mildly guilty. "It will look realistic, at least."

"On that note." He spun his finger in a circle. "Hands behind your back."

"Can't you punch me first? I have a reputation."

"I'm not punching you."

"Please?"

"Not a chance." He pulled a set of cuffs from under the back of his jacket.

I shook my head. Cops were such assholes. "Give me a sec." I rubbed my palm against the side of my head until the pomade loosened up. When it felt sufficiently disheveled, I spun and put my hands behind my back. "All right, Detective."

"You're a jackass." He tightened the cuff on one of my wrists.

"I respectfully disagree." A curl fell onto my forehead. I blew it off. The second cuff clicked shut. "Don't go so tight."

"Sorry. Authenticity." Somehow, I doubted his reasoning. Reyes grabbed the backpack in one hand and gripped the handcuffs with the other to guide me.

By the time we got back to the bar, Jason was already in the back of a cruiser. Kallen and two uniforms were half a block in the other direction. She looked small between them. Every few steps, she would jerk her arm out of the grip of the blond cop on her right. Her nose was bleeding. Blood was smeared across the forearm of the guy she was clearly trying to get away from.

"Looks like they went a little too realistic," I said quietly.

"Yeah. I think I'll go intervene. Can I hand you off to a uniform?"

"Don't. She wouldn't want you to." I didn't take the time to analyze why I cared about Laurel's feelings. They weren't my business anymore.

Reyes sighed, but didn't hand me off. He opened the back door of his Crown Vic. I was about to duck in when Reyes went stiff. I followed his gaze. The blond cop was on the ground. Laurel was smirking as the other cop dragged her away.

"What the hell is she doing?" Reyes asked.

I looked around. The other uniforms were hustling to help get Laurel into a car. Jason caught my eye. He looked a little terrified, but he was laughing his ass off. He mouthed "badass" and started shaking his head. I grinned at him and shrugged. Reyes put his hand on my head and shoved me the rest of the way into the car.

A few minutes later, Reyes got behind the wheel. He waited until the cruiser carrying Jason had a decent start before turning on the car.

"You want me to drop you at home?" We pulled into the street.

"I don't need to stop by the station?" Not that I was complaining about getting these cuffs off sooner rather than later.

"We will need your statement, but it can wait. I have a feeling we'll be tied up for most of the evening."

"Is Kallen going to have issues with that blond cop?"

Reyes shrugged. "Oakley didn't like her before. So no more than usual."

He was lying, but I didn't want to push it. No, I didn't need to push it. Laurel wasn't my concern. "You want to drop me on Twentieth? I'll walk from there."

We cut over a few blocks and Reyes pulled into an alley. He opened the door and I slid to the edge of the seat. I stood against the car while he loosened the cuffs.

"Either Kallen or I will call you in the morning. Try not to get arrested tonight."

I turned and leaned back on the trunk. Reyes huffed and rolled his eyes when I rubbed at the red mark ringing one of my wrists. "Generally, I try not to get arrested. It's not my fault you guys have all of these standards."

"They're called laws. When we call, answer."

I decided not to respond. He knew I was going to pick up. "Have a good night, Detective." I walked down the alley, finger combing my hair back into place.

He climbed back in his car and took off. I had participated in a few smaller busts already, but this was the first time he cut me loose before we got to the station. Maybe they were starting to trust that I wouldn't run. It didn't seem likely. Trust wasn't high on their list of motivations.

❖

Grab a drink with me?

I sent the text without much thought. Going home felt lonely. It never had before. Now everything there seemed to carry Laurel. It was weighted with the potential for what could have been. Memories we would have made. Instead of hope, I had the lies we'd told each other. Wading through my disappointment every time I opened the front door was wearing on me.

So I walked to the gay bars that were huddled on one corner as if separating would dilute them. Mercantile Saloon spilled across its patio, over the disused parking lot, so that the noise enveloped the street. Thumping music, contrived laughter, the squeals of straight girls granted access to the sanctum. I rushed past the spectacle and slid into the overt darkness of The Depot. I ignored the corner where Laurel had once waited for me. I had made it so easy for her to seduce me, to entrap me. A quiet, low voice in my head reminded me that Jason was being booked into County and I wasn't. His freedom for mine.

Then again, I wasn't free either.

I felt heat against my back and breath across my neck. "Hey, stranger, come here often?" Kyra's voice was low and warm and enticing.

"Hey." I turned to let her slide between me and the press of bodies lined at the bar. "You got my text." I put my hand low on her back. It wasn't possessive. Intimate, maybe. It felt like a shield. If I was here with someone, I wasn't here alone. I wasn't anywhere alone.

"I was staring at the walls, the ceiling, out the window. Basically, doing everything I could to avoid actually painting."

"So I saved you from yourself?"

"You're my hero." Kyra leaned in and kissed my cheek.

The press of her lips was smooth and soothing. A promise without the weight. She expected nothing, demanded nothing. She stayed close as we tried to get the attention of the bartender. The bare skin of her midriff seemed to radiate heat. She was wearing big boots and slim jeans with a flannel tied below her waist. I liked the brush of cotton against my bare forearm. I liked the casual press of her body against mine. As if we had done this a thousand times before. Which, to be fair, wasn't inaccurate. I'd known Kyra for years, but I hadn't seen her in years. She'd come back from Los Angeles midsummer. There was a comfort in fucking an old friend. She understood me in a way that I allowed from very few people. She had known me before all of the walls of adulthood were built.

We ordered drinks and made our way to the back corner of the building. It was loud. The TVs mounted everywhere were playing the most recent sexually fraught female pop music video. Two women were grinding suggestively against each other. There were no dudes on screen. MTV was dead, but videos were apparently still the progressive frontier.

"So tell me what you're working on."

That was all it took to launch Kyra. I scooted my bar stool so I could lean against the wall and watch her speak. When she talked about painting, it settled her. Her core went entirely still, but her hands danced. There was a streak of pale green oil paint that stood out in stark contrast to her skin. She started tracing her fingers through the air to sketch the plateau she was working on. She tended to do the same thing when we fucked. My body became an involuntary sketch pad.

"You're not understanding a damn thing I'm saying, are you?" Kyra smiled to let me know she wasn't mad.

"No. But I'm enjoying watching you," I said. She shook her head. "You're all academic and artistic and it's hot."

"Don't fetishize my livelihood." Her admonishment was contrived.

"Then what should I fetishize? All you do is paint and talk about painting."

"You sound like my mother." Kyra's mouth turned down as she realized what she had said. "No, wait. Not the fetishizing.

The painting thing." Kyra sat up straighter. "There is more to the world than painting." She drew out her vowels in an affected Persian accent.

I locked my gaze just over Kyra's shoulder. "Oh, hello, Mrs. Daneshmandan, what are you doing here?"

Kyra spun halfway around before she realized. She whirled back and slapped my stomach. "You're an asshole."

"Why would your mother be in a gay bar in Midtown?" I managed to ask through my laughter.

"I don't know. You seemed so sincere." She shook her head. "You suck."

"I've never even met your mother."

"And you never will. Because you're an asshole." She dropped her hands to rest on my thigh.

"I don't know how I'll ever recover." I almost sounded sincere.

Kyra started drumming her fingertips along the inseam of my jeans. "So Saturday. You're coming? You got the postcard?"

I tried to come up with a coherent response. Instead I mumbled nonsense.

"I'm going to take that as a yes?"

"No, I mean, yes. Probably not though. I don't know if I'm available." This was why I didn't like to lie. I was terrible at it.

"Oh, good. That cleared it right up."

"I'm sorry. It's just Second Saturday."

"An occasion you love. Your favorite part of summer. You never used to miss it." Each point was punctuated by a tantalizingly brief tap against my leg.

"I know. My neighbor and I—she's my best friend, kind of. We always go together. It's our thing," I said. Kyra waited. "We missed the last one." More waiting. "We haven't spoken in over a month. I don't know if I can go without her."

"I'm not following."

"We might be fighting."

"You don't know?"

"No."

"Got it. So continuing to not speak is a great move. And you should absolutely skip Second Saturday." Her hands started their dance again. "Now, there are some people who would suggest talking to this friend, but I think you're making the right move. You've always been super passive, which makes the not talking a highly logical choice."

I didn't think I'd ever heard so much sarcasm packed into so few words. I loved where she was coming from, but I didn't have the energy to analyze it. "Can we not talk about this?"

Kyra stopped her rambling long enough to search my face. She nodded once, then leaned forward and kissed me. Her lips were chapped and warm. The thick curls that tumbled into her eyes tickled my brow. I reached up and cupped the back of her head. Her soft hair was buzzed and shaved closer to the scalp than I'd ever dared. She groaned and pulled away. I watched her study me. Her eyes were ringed in dark makeup, her lashes a long, delicate fan.

"You know I like you, right?" Kyra asked. "I mean, I like this." She squeezed my thigh. "But I like you. As a person. You're not bad like you think you are."

I forced myself to smile. "I know. You're wrong and you shouldn't, but yeah."

She shook her head and grinned. "My place?"

"Yeah." I took a long drink from the beer I had forgotten and stood.

Kyra slid her hand into mine and led me out of the bar.

CHAPTER TWO

It was just after three when I got home. The streets were finally quieting down. The summer heat tended to inspire revelry, not sleep. Kallen's truck was at the curb. It looked faintly green in the streetlight. My SUV wasn't in the driveway. I remembered belatedly that I had driven to the meeting with Jason to prove some point. I couldn't remember what point, but I sure made it. That was going to be a long walk in the morning. I knew I could ask Laurel for a ride when she came to pick up her truck, but I didn't want to.

My porch light was off again. One day I was going to consistently remember to turn it on before I left the house. I climbed the steps and just managed to keep myself from jumping when I saw movement at the far end of the porch. My eyes adjusted and I realized Laurel was asleep on the bench.

A thick wall ringed the edge of the porch. It was about three feet high. Just enough to build deep shadows. The smooth sheen of Laurel's hair caught the moonlight, but everything else was in darkness. As my eyes adjusted, I could see her slouch. Feet planted, the arrogant spread of her legs. Her arms were folded protectively over her chest. She had thrown a red-pink chambray button up over her T-shirt, but I was guessing she hadn't gone home.

I walked over and nudged her foot with one of mine. "Hey, Laurel." Nothing. "Detective Kallen," I said loudly.

She shot upright, grunted, and glared at me.

"What are you doing?" I asked.

She rubbed her eyes vigorously, then shot her cuff and squinted at her watch. "Oh, good. I was afraid you hadn't properly fucked her, but five hours seems like plenty of time."

"I don't know how to respond to that."

"You're not denying it." Kallen carefully arranged the cuff back over her watch.

I shrugged. "I'm not discussing it. I'm not accountable to you."

"You're accountable to our cover."

"I think you'll find that not even the Sacramento Police Department can regulate who I fuck." I turned away from her. If she wanted to sleep on the porch, that was her business.

"You know she's not even a lesbian, right?" Laurel's question was quiet, desperate.

"She's pan. So what?" As soon as I spoke, I knew I shouldn't have. Announcing that Kyra was pansexual was clearly an assertion of dominance, a demonstration of Laurel's ability to gather information. Indulging her wouldn't get us anywhere.

"Yeah, but she's not a lesbian."

"What the fuck is wrong with you?" I spun back to glare at her.

"Nothing. I'm just letting you know." Laurel pushed herself farther up the bench. Her posture was still casual, arrogant, but with a hint of the stiffness of a salute in it.

"What business is it of yours if she's a lesbian?"

"It should be yours." She wouldn't look at me. Just studied the street.

"Are you seriously policing her queerness right now?" I couldn't believe we were having this conversation. I shook my head, but nothing changed. "I don't know why I asked that. You police everything else. Why not sexuality? What about mine? Am I enough of a lesbian? Or am I tainted now?"

Laurel finally met my eyes. "That's not what I meant."

"Yes, it is."

"Okay, fine. It is." Her mouth was set in a hard line. "I didn't mean it though." She unfolded herself from the bench. "Your life is my business now. Your choices affect me."

It was what I wanted. But as soon as she brushed past me and descended the stairs, I no longer wanted it. The door of her truck popped and creaked. I let myself into the house. The air was still, stagnant.

I was staring at the ceiling and trying to convince myself to get out of bed when there was a knock at the door. It seemed as good an impetus as any so I rolled out of bed. I was wrestling myself into too tight jeans and stumbling down the hallway when the back door opened.

"This is stupid. I get it. You're mad, but I'm not sure what you think I could have done. So I've decided that you're wrong." Robin nudged the door closed with her foot. She walked past me into the kitchen and set two cups of coffee on the table. She sat and popped the lid off one cup. "Also, it's Second Saturday and it killed me not to go out last month. I miss you. You're a jerk and you're bad at talking and I should probably feel guilty, but I don't because you're a jerk."

I yanked my hand out of my jeans, buttoned them, and shuffled the rest of the way into the kitchen. I pulled out my own chair and collapsed into it. "You think I'm mad at you?"

"You don't call. You don't come over. Andy said you haven't contacted her. You can be mad at me, but that's not cool."

"I haven't even seen Andy." It was as if she had disappeared. If she was putting that much effort into avoiding me, I wasn't going to push it. Hell, Robin hadn't even asked me to keep an eye on Andy. Not that I blamed her. Drug dealer.

Robin stopped blowing across the surface of her coffee and stared at me. "Andy's been out of town for three weeks."

"Huh?"

"Three weeks. No Andy. That's why I've been working nights."

"You haven't been avoiding me?"

"No. You've been avoiding me."

"I was giving you space. I brought the police into our home. They searched the place. Put up notices and tape." I waved my hand at the front door. "I hid drug paraphernalia in your closet. I put you and your kid at risk."

"Huh." Robin made a face at her coffee. Then she started laughing.

"What? Stop it. Why are you laughing?"

"I thought you were mad that I didn't stop them from ransacking your place." She continued laughing. "I have drug paraphernalia in my closet?"

"In the ceiling. That storage space." This was all very strange.

"Oh my God. I told you to put it there, didn't I?"

I nodded slowly. "Years ago."

"So I've got drugs in my closet?" Robin asked. I nodded. "And you're not pissed that I let the police tear your place apart?" I shook my head. "And you thought Andy was avoiding you?" I nodded. "Oh, Cash. I missed you." Robin leaned over and pulled me into a hug.

I had a lot of questions. I decided to ignore all of them and give into the hug. "I'm glad you decided to tell me I'm a jerk."

Robin shrugged. "I had a shitty shift last night. On my way home, I stopped for coffee and I didn't realize until they handed me two cups that I had ordered for you too."

"Aww, you did miss me." I finally grabbed the coffee. It smelled good. Like coffee. "So tell me about the shitty shift."

Robin nodded once and grinned at her coffee. She told me about getting peed on and a teenager dying from an overdose and another losing a leg and how someone had changed the soap in the locker room to one that she hated. It was all sad, but it felt less so to hear it shared. She twirled her empty coffee cup until I put my hand over hers to keep her still.

We were interrupted by the beeping of my cell phone. I dug it out of my pocket and fought a grimace. Reyes. "Sorry. Give me a sec." I swiped. "Hello."

"Cash, it's Reyes."

As if his number wasn't stored in my phone. "What's up?"

There was a swell of noise that sounded like the squad room. "Sorry. Give me a minute." A door slammed and the rhythmic click of Reyes's boots echoed off cement stairs. "I'd like to meet you and go over our reports from last night. Are you available this afternoon?" I imagined him leaning against the wall in the stairwell, the ankles of his designer pants hiked up just so.

"Sure."

"Good. Two o'clock at Rick's Dessert Diner? That early, we should be able to get a private table."

"Wait. Me and you? What about Laurel?"

"Oh." He cleared his throat. "Her schedule is a beast this week. She asked me to take the meeting."

That wasn't right. I didn't trust the sudden shift in our routine. I could imagine a thousand reasons, few of them good. But I trusted Reyes. Then again, I'd trusted Laurel Collins. I'd have to watch myself. "Fine. Two o'clock."

"Thanks." Reyes hung up.

"Sorry." I set my phone on the table.

"So how is Laurel?" Robin asked. She smiled knowingly and I realized she didn't know.

"Shit."

"What?"

"I...we haven't talked."

"Oh no. Did you break up? Sorry. I thought you said her name. She's been around a fair bit." Robin resumed spinning her cup. I let her.

"No. I mean, yes. You and I haven't talked. Laurel is a cop."

Robin stopped twirling. She pulled her hands back to her lap carefully. The kitchen felt silent and slow. After a minute, she spoke. "She was watching you."

"Yes."

She nodded once with finality. "Can you talk about it?"

"I'm not supposed to. Legally." That seemed like a good point to clarify. "Then again, I'm not supposed to have drugs stored in your closet—which I need, by the way—so I don't mind telling you. Only if you want to know."

"It seems like something I should know."

I nodded. "Laurel's real name is Laurel Kallen, not Collins." Robin blinked rapidly. Like she was struggling to comprehend the incomprehensible. "She's a detective with Sacramento PD. She and her partner, Lucas Reyes, liaise with the local FBI office on narcotics cases. They recruited her because she's very talented at undercover work." I stopped explaining when I realized that Robin was crying. "Whoa, hey. We're past that. It is what it is."

"But she made you fall—She started a relationship with you. That's unforgivable. Oh, honey, I'm so sorry." She put her hand on my forearm.

I shrugged. Then nodded. Then I didn't know what to do so I shrugged again. "She did her job. I did mine. She was better."

"But that's…" Robin searched my eyes. As if I knew the word. "Immoral."

"I'm a drug dealer."

"Illegal."

"Drug. Dealer." I slowed it down.

"Fucked up."

"Okay, yeah." That one I could get behind.

"You breaking the rules doesn't give her the right to do so."

I appreciated her trying, but I had been wrestling that angel for a month. "No, I think the law does that."

"So?" Robin huffed. She was doing a lot of moral stretching to make me feel better. I loved her for that.

"Yeah, I get it. What are laws anyway? Just rules some old white dude wrote down."

"Yeah." Robin clenched her fists.

"But you and I happen to agree with most laws." I kept my tone even.

Robin rolled her eyes. "I'm quite aware of what I believe, thank you."

"I've been having this conversation with myself for a long time," I said.

"What do you mean?"

"Morality. Laws. Whatever. I've been thinking a lot."

Robin laughed. "Did prison scare you straight?"

"Jail." I raised an eyebrow. "And, no. Before that. Since I started dealing."

"Seems like something you've been questioning for a decade might not be worth pursuing." She was gentle, but it was hard for that not to sting.

"But I haven't exactly been debating if it's wrong. It's more like I've been debating what wrong is. I haven't figured that out yet. How do I know that what I do is wrong if I don't know what wrong is?" I asked. Robin was staring at me like I'd lost my goddamn mind. "Okay, back up. I know what wrong is, but think about it. We only know what's wrong situationally. Like each action dictates the potential wrong."

"True." She said it real slow. "At work, I've taken various oaths to guide my behavior. I want to preserve life. That's why I'm a nurse."

"When you drive, you don't want to kill people so you follow laws."

"We don't want to kill people because taking life is wrong."

"Is it?" I asked. Then I laughed. Robin definitely thought I'd lost it. "I don't kill people because the punishment is high. And because I don't want the guilt of having taken a life. That's about me. Not them. Not their potential. Not morals. Maybe it wouldn't bother me. Maybe it would. Testing the theory has a cost that's too high. So I don't kill people. Why don't you kill people?"

She started blinking at me again. "Isn't it too early for you to be this philosophical?"

"Never." I smiled and felt wicked.

"You are strange."

"And you love me."

Robin put her hand over mine. "I do."

CHAPTER THREE

The original Dessert Diner had been on K Street in a narrow, dingy building. It didn't need to be retro; it was vintage. Cracked pink vinyl. Chipped gray Formica. The pink neon sign was actually neon. They were open as late as the bars. Every kid in a thirty-mile radius had ended up there at some point on prom night.

But then the rent tripled and they moved.

Now it was bright white lights. Shiny red vinyl booths. New white Formica tables. Everything seemed clean. It was blinding at midnight. But at two o'clock on a Thursday afternoon, it was whitewashed, glaring. I had never been in during daylight hours and I vowed I never would be again.

Instead of intoxicated twenty-year-olds, the patrons were suburban family types in the big city for an outing. Toddlers inhaled handfuls of sugar. Kids screeched and sprinted. And parents watched their offspring's displays with what appeared to be affection and joy.

Reyes was tucked in a booth at the back. There were two cups of coffee in front of him. He looked out of place, but content until a kid screeched. His jaw tightened. His knuckles went pale. Good. He was regretting this venue too.

I slid into the booth across from him. "This is atrocious."

Reyes nodded. "I'll make this quick. The statement you emailed looks fine. Kallen is processing it right now."

"Then why am I here?"

"I've never been one for tact." He sighed. "Can I just ask you some questions and we will pretend I was subtle?"

"Depends. How serious are you about that?"

He grimaced. "Pretty serious. My partner does our undercover work for a reason. I'm better with straightforward. She says I need to work on it."

I laughed. He was being serious. "How about this. I will swear up and down that we had a conversation and whatever subject you want to discuss happened to come up of its own volition."

"Great." Reyes was genuinely excited at that prospect.

"If you answer some of my questions."

"Hmm."

"Yeah, you hmm that." I slid out of the booth and grabbed my mug. "I'm switching this for iced coffee. It's two hundred degrees outside. Why would you order two-hundred-degree coffee?"

Reyes shrugged and waved me off. When I returned with a glass of cold, black coffee Reyes had a notebook and a pen out on the table.

"I'll answer your questions, but I also reserve the right to not answer."

"That's vague." I scooted back into the booth.

"Just don't ask me something compromising," he said

That was still vague. "Fine."

Another kid screamed at a pitch I didn't know was possible. Reyes and I both jumped and looked. The little darling was standing three feet from our table. He was wearing damp swim trunks and a fedora. Apparently, he had discovered the neon-ringed clock on the wall. It was delightful. Just like him.

Reyes shook himself. "You were saying something."

"Oh, yeah. Questions. You go first."

"Fentanyl. What do you know about it?" he asked.

"Synthetic opioid. Potent, but volatile as hell. You want to narrow that question down?"

"Do you deal it?"

"Detective Reyes, I don't deal any drugs." I fought the urge to grin at him.

He grunted. "Have you ever sold fentanyl?"

"No."

"Why?"

"I like my customers alive. They buy more product that way."

His mouth set into a hard, straight line. "Who does deal it?"

I shrugged. "Not sure. Jerome St. Maris might. He's been moving in on my customers. And he doesn't mind if people die."

"And that answer has nothing to do with the fact that he's your rival?"

"Jason Warren is a possibility. But he's sitting in County right now. Danny Cicero or Christi Jerod, but I'm guessing they already are on your list."

Reyes smirked. I had no compunction about giving these guys up. I knew the cops were already interested in them. Including their names didn't damage my compatriots at all. It did, however, make me look very cooperative.

"Can you give me something viable to look at?" Reyes sounded skeptical. It seemed he had realized that my compliance wasn't quantifiable.

"Honestly, that's all I got." And it was. "Fentanyl isn't common enough to warrant a market. If someone is building a business around it, they're new. I'll ask Nate. He's up on trends more than I am."

He wrote some notes. "What about someone selling counterfeit pills?"

"Like placebos?"

"No, like claiming a pill is Oxy, but really it's a cocktail that mimics Oxy."

"Sounds like a short-term plan." There were plenty of dealers who used similar business models, but it was too unpredictable for me. And douchey. That too.

"How so?" He seemed less curious about the broad answer and more interested in my answer.

"You can't build a client list. Once someone takes your shit and realizes it isn't what they paid for, they won't buy from you again. If you make money going to raves and festivals, then you can get away with unreliable product. But if you want consistency, you need to provide consistency."

"But if someone wanted to make a quick buck…"

"Yeah, they could probably do it that way."

"Okay. Thanks." He wrote that down, then carefully set his pen on the notepad. He made a face like he was preparing himself. "What do you want to ask me?"

I did my best not to laugh at him. "Do you have anything new on Jerome St. Maris?"

"Come on, Braddock. You know I can't answer that. And saying no makes me look like a jackass. Ask me something I can answer."

"He stole half my clients already."

"I thought you didn't deal drugs." He didn't bother to hide the smirk.

"Maybe I just want to see the asshole squirm. I'm hemorrhaging money and clients. I don't have a supply line or clients even if I wanted to keep my business afloat. And this dick is sitting pretty. Ease my inadequacy."

"I don't even have anything to tell you. I'm sorry." He seemed it. "Ask me something else."

"Where is Kallen right now? Why didn't she take this meeting?" That was not the question I had planned, but after last night's encounter, I couldn't help it. Was she avoiding me?

Reyes broke eye contact. "She's in meetings."

"This is a meeting."

He made eye contact again. "I was serious. Her schedule is a beast this week."

"Then why was she out till three last night?"

A flicker of confusion crossed his otherwise pretty features. "I don't know. Was she?"

I ignored his question in favor of my own. "Why are you being vague about her schedule?"

"A complaint was filed against her."

I wasn't sure if he got bored of being evasive or just had run out of non-answers, but at least we were making progress. "For what?"

"I don't know. She isn't allowed to tell me the details."

"Of course. So don't tell me the details that she didn't tell you." My tone suggested the exact opposite of what I was saying. "What is the complaint about?"

"You. Her involvement with you."

"But I didn't file a complaint."

"Interesting."

Super. So Reyes thought the complaint could have come from me? "What's in the complaint?"

"I knew I shouldn't have agreed to this." He straightened the already straight pen and pad of paper on the table.

"It's cool. I'll just tell Kallen that you wanted me to tell you everything I knew about fentanyl and asked me a bunch of very specific questions."

He sighed in a masculine way. "The complaint alleges that Kallen has an inappropriate relationship with you."

"Meaning what?"

"Favoritism, ignoring evidence of ongoing distribution, targeting your business rivals to aid you..." Reyes became very interested in the tabletop. "An ongoing sexual relationship."

I laughed because I kind of felt like vomiting. It was the worst sort of accusation. There was just enough truth to make the utter fiction damning. "Well, at least we know it didn't come from

I got in the car. Kallen's only acknowledgment of our presence was to pull away from the curb. After some muttering in the front seat, we made a detour and stopped outside a coffee shop. Reyes went in. Kallen and I waited in silence. It wasn't insanely uncomfortable or anything. Nope, it was fine.

Reyes came back and distributed massive coffee cups and scones. Kallen tossed her breakfast on the dash. Like she was above food. Everything about her was obnoxious. Where did she get off acting like we were inconveniencing her? The staccato of her fingertips on the steering wheel was the old brag of Esther's heart, rapid and constant and arrogant. The muscles in her bare forearm rolled with each tap. It was sensual and obscene.

Why did I have to be so fascinated by her?

We parked at the police station and I remembered why Laurel Kallen was so dangerous. I followed them upstairs and did my best to pretend I was there voluntarily. They stuck me in an interview room and promised they would return shortly. I stretched out on the sad, sterile couch and tried to go back to sleep. It didn't work. Twenty minutes passed. I finished my coffee and scone, moved to the conference table, put my feet up. Tossed the napkin from my scone at the trash can. Missed. Picked it up and tossed it again. Missed again. Threw it away and glanced around surreptitiously to confirm that there were no cameras to document my defeat. None visible.

When the door finally opened, it was a dude I didn't know. I'd seen him the handful of times I'd been at the station. He was tall and bulky. Not quite fat yet, but his muscle mass was clearly at war with the onset of middle age.

"Ms. Braddock, I'm Detective Gibson. I need to ask you some questions." He opened a file in front of me. It contained a mug shot of one of my former customers.

"Sure." I glanced at the photo, nodded. "But I need either Reyes or Kallen here."

"Excuse me?" Gibson didn't like that response.

"They are my handlers. It's their names on all my paperwork. I wouldn't want anyone to get in trouble for crossing a line. You understand." I didn't ask. It wasn't a question.

"I just need to know if you recognize this guy." He jabbed the photo with a modicum more force than necessary. "A few follow-up questions. Nothing earth-shattering." Despite his best efforts to sound casual, he was clearly on edge. My simple denial had kicked him right up to an abyss he didn't like staring at.

"Then it shouldn't be an issue to include one of my handlers."

"Damn, Kallen really does own your ass, doesn't she?" His tone was jocular, his statement was not.

"Excuse me?"

"Nothing. It's just strange that you won't answer a few simple questions. Are you looking for an obstruction of justice charge?"

"To be clear, you are just as much a pig as Kallen." I stood. "I will happily answer questions according to parameters of the agreement I have with the Sacramento Police Department and the Sacramento District Attorney's office. Detectives Kallen and Reyes, despite their inherently piggish nature, never seem to be confused about that. Feel free to direct any questions to Sergeant Ionescu, either of my handlers, or my lawyer." I let myself out of the interview room.

As I pulled the door quietly shut behind me, I looked around the squad room for Kallen and Reyes. They shared a desk that was situated midway down the row. They were seated across from each other, both typing and glaring at computer screens that were easily a decade old. I made my way to them. Kallen saw me first. Then Reyes realized that she had stopped typing and followed her gaze.

"What's up?" Reyes asked.

"Yeah, didn't we tell you it would be a few?" Kallen had tamped down her earlier anger. It was still present, but time had seemingly exhausted it.

"So neither of you sent in a detective to question me?" I asked.

They seemed confused by that question.

"No, we're waiting for an agent from the Sac field office to join us," Reyes finally said. "Did someone question you?"

I shook my head. Not in response to his question. Today was complete suckage. I looked around until I spotted Ionescu's office. It was the only office with a closed door.

"That Ionescu's office?" I asked.

"Yeah, but..." Kallen's eyes locked onto something behind my shoulder. "Motherfucker."

Reyes spun and added his curses to hers. I gave in and looked. The door to the interview room was open and Detective Gibson was stalking toward us.

"Have fun." I made a beeline for Ionescu's office. They could sort out the territory on their own. Ionescu was behind his desk looking much fresher than any of his detectives. He still appeared to be here at an ungodly hour. Voluntarily. On a Sunday. That probably should have tipped me off that something sketchy was happening.

"Can I help you?" He didn't sound super eager to help me. Or maybe that was his scary voice.

"Yeah, you mind if I close this?" I pointed at the door. He gave a short nod. "Your detectives showed up at my home at an absurd hour this morning." I sat across from him. If that was too forward for him, he could toss my ass out.

"If they could have avoided that, they would have." His tone suggested that they would have gleefully shown up earlier if possible. My convenience was clearly not a factor for this guy.

"They said I was here for an interview and left me in an interview room for twenty minutes."

"I believe we are waiting for Agent Michelson before interviewing you." Ionescu was rapidly getting bored of this conversation.

"And I get that. All of it. I'm at your beck and call." I settled into my uncomfortable chair, my narrative. I hadn't planned this, but if I was going to fuck with Sac PD, I was going to do it well. "But Kallen and Reyes are generally respectful of the lines of professionalism. As far as I'm aware, they don't lie to me or ask me to violate the rule of law, or my agreement with your department, or any sort of moral code."

Ionescu's eyebrows, which were barely distinct from each other as it was, moved steadily closer together as he tried to follow my line of reasoning. "Are you here for a specific reason, Ms. Braddock?"

"Yes. While I was waiting to be interviewed, Detective Gibson decided to take advantage of my expertise."

"How so?"

"He wanted to know if I recognized someone. Showed me their mug shot." I had no intention of actually identifying the kid to anyone other than Kallen or Reyes. "He refused to include my handlers in the discussion. Then he implied some unsavory things about my relationship to my handlers. Finally, he threatened me. It was disconcerting and inappropriate."

"I agree. That does sound inappropriate." Ionescu was a wall. I couldn't read anything off the guy. "I can see a few ways to move forward, but what would you like to see happen?"

"I'd like a written record of the incident including Gibson's implications and threats in order to establish a pattern in the event that we see similar behavior in the future," I said. Ionescu started taking notes. "Ideally, I'd like an apology for his attempt to bully me. I'd also like him to apologize to Kallen and Reyes for suggesting that the relationship we have built is anything other than professional."

Ionescu smiled, just barely. "Those are not unreasonable terms. Would you mind writing up a report of the incident for me?"

"No problem."

Ionescu stood and came around the desk. He shook my hand. "Thank you for bringing this to my attention."

I followed him to the door. As soon as he opened it, I could hear Kallen, Reyes, and Gibson arguing. They weren't shouting, but they might as well have been. Ionescu's brows went right back together. We stepped into the main room.

"Gibson, my office." Ionescu didn't need to shout. His voice undercut every conversation in the room. "Kallen, Reyes, a moment."

The three detectives filed toward us. Gibson slid into Ionescu's office without meeting anyone's eyes. He looked pissed. Kallen and Reyes stood at casual attention. Reyes looked like he wanted to say something, but Kallen carefully cleared her throat. He took a deep breath and waited.

"Sir?" Kallen asked.

"Ms. Braddock needs to write up a report. Preferably without interference. Will you set her up at a computer?" Ionescu asked.

"Of course." Laurel led me back to her desk. She cleared space on the desk, minimized what she was working on. "Let us know if you need anything."

"Thanks." I sat at the desk. It smelled faintly of her. Soap and cedar. I allowed myself to enjoy it without judgment. It was just scent. It didn't matter that it calmed me or made my chest tight. I opened a blank document.

CHAPTER FIVE

L aurel had pulled a chair up to Reyes's side of the desk. They were reviewing some report. The only other detective working left the room. I stopped typing my careful retelling of my aborted interview with Gibson.

"Can they hear us in his office?" I asked without looking up from the computer.

"No," Laurel said.

"Gibson suggested some inappropriate things about our relationship. If you're looking for whoever filed a complaint about you, I'd start there."

"Braddock," Reyes said. But it was too late for his warning.

"You told her?" Laurel was fighting to pretend to focus on the report she was no longer studying.

"It's not his fault. We can talk about it later. I just wanted to give you a heads up."

The tension emanating from Reyes's side of the desk was stifling, but I didn't expand. They eventually returned to their files. I was doing a second proofread when Agent Michelson finally arrived. That is, I guessed he was Agent Michelson. I'd seen him before when we were staking out Laurel's apartment. He was about the same age as Reyes, but his hair was completely gray. The guy had been intended for federal law enforcement. He just had that look. Tall and slim, but muscled. No identifying features, but vaguely attractive. Average in every possible way. The last time I'd seen him, he was in jeans and a T-shirt. Today, he was wearing a dark suit and white shirt. His proportions were so common he'd probably bought everything off the rack and it just fit.

"Agent," Kallen said. She shook his hand and he grinned at her.

"Detective, good to see you again." Michelson turned to Reyes and shook his hand too. "You still owe me a run."

Reyes laughed. "Good luck with that." They all laughed. Well, wasn't this just fun?

"Michelson, this is Cash Braddock. Braddock, Agent Daniel Michelson," Kallen said.

I stood and offered my hand. He shook it. "Good to meet you," I lied admirably.

"You too. I understand you're going to help us out. Thank you. We need all the help we can get." He smiled.

Everything about him screamed good, sincere American boy. I'd had my fill of good boys. My instinct was to leave. That wasn't an option. My other instinct was to say something with a delicate balance of condescension and curse words. Also probably not a great option. Instead I nodded and went back to my proofreading.

Reyes escorted Michelson to the interview room. Their voices carried enough to catch the tone, but not the words. They were buddies.

"What was that?" Kallen asked after the door closed. She kept her voice low.

"What?"

"That. You totally blew him off."

"No, I didn't," I said.

"You said like two words and went back to typing."

"Sorry, Detective. You know how us drug dealers are. No manners."

"What is your problem?" she asked.

"You have to ask?"

"I'm at a loss. I can't imagine what he did in those ninety seconds to piss you off. Unless it's your usual sunny disposition."

As if I conjured a poor disposition to inconvenience her. "The man followed me for a month. Photographed me. Recorded me. Watched me with my friends and family. And he just came in here all smiles like, 'oh, it's great to meet you.' When, in reality, he's like, 'hey, I think the blue boxer briefs really brought out your eyes more.'"

She rolled her eyes, which felt super legitimizing. "I did the same thing. You talk to me."

I shrugged. "You at least bought me dinner before violating me." I went back to the computer. This was all information she already knew. I didn't see a need to rehash the whole thing.

"That's grossly unfair."

"I'm glad you can admit it," I said.

"No." She grabbed her chair and brought it around to sit next to me. I ignored her. She gently spun my office chair so I was facing her. "Your analysis is unfair. We were doing our jobs." Her tone was a fascinating mix between pleading and anger.

"So what?" My tone had no plea. "Take out the fact that you guys are law enforcement. That dude stalked me. You led me on, manipulated and used me. Which is more abhorrent? Can you quantify violating someone?"

"You're glossing over a pretty crucial detail. We are law enforcement. We did those things because we are law enforcement. Stalkers have completely different motivations."

"Tell that to a stalking victim. I'm guessing they don't really give a fuck about the perpetrator's motivations." I tried to spin back to the computer, but Laurel gripped the armrest and kept me in place.

"Stop."

"I'm trying to stop this conversation. You're the one dragging it out."

"No, I mean you need to stop talking about us like that. Your language is cultivated to make us—to make me sound like a rapist. I'm tired of it." Her voice caught. She was right. That was exactly what I'd been doing. "Do you—I'm sorry, okay?" She took a few deep breaths, swallowed convulsively. She was trying not to cry. "Did—"

I'd pushed it too far. I put my hand on her thigh to stop her. "You're right. I was trying to make you feel shitty."

"I didn't—Did I—Cash?" She couldn't bring herself to ask. Maybe that was cowardice. Maybe that was human.

I was suddenly very aware that we were in an empty squad room that could become not empty at any moment. This was not the place to have this conversation. "It was consensual. You lied and I'm pissed, but it was consensual."

"But could you consent?" Her voice was so low I could barely understand her.

"Yes. With Laurel Collins." There was a longer answer. A much longer answer. We couldn't get into it though. So I finally admitted what I knew was the truth. "You were going to tell me who you are beforehand. That's why you were so hesitant, right?"

Laurel nodded but still refused to meet my eyes. I really didn't want to feel this. Any of it. I didn't want to feel guilty for making her feel guilty. I didn't want to make her feel better. I didn't want to want to kiss her. But denying it didn't seem to be making it less real.

"Listen, we obviously need to work some shit out or this is never going to work. And then you won't be the Sac PD golden boy and I'll be in jail and you won't be able to get me out 'cause you won't be the golden boy anymore. It will all be super tragic."

She smiled a little and finally looked at me. "That does sound tragic."

"So we will talk or whatever."

"Or take up bare knuckle boxing," Laurel said.

"I actually prefer that idea."

"But not here, right?"

"Definitely not here. Later," I said. "So get your shit together."

"Okay."

I watched her put herself back together. It was captivating. She rolled her neck, arched her shoulders. She popped her collar and refolded it. After vigorously rubbing her eyes, she stood. Whatever vulnerability had been present was gone. But I knew it was there. She was just better at burying it than most people. Not exactly shocking.

"I'm almost done here. If you want to go wait with Reyes and your boyfriend." I nodded at the interview room.

Kallen rolled her eyes, but this time it felt like I was in on the joke. "You're an ass."

"Yep." I smiled.

"That hat makes you look like a twelve-year-old boy."

"If I'd known we were having important meetings with FBI agents, maybe I would have dressed appropriately."

She laughed. "No, you wouldn't."

That was true.

She left and I was finally able to finish proofreading. I'd nailed my report. It was perfectly self-deprecating in that my memory for exact words was imperfect, but my memory for feelings was impeccable. Ionescu and Gibson emerged as the report was printing. Ionescu looked surprised when I handed one of the copies to him. The other, I folded and tucked into my pocket.

"You're finished?" Ionescu asked.

"Yeah." I was surprised that he was surprised.

He slid it into a folder and tucked it under his arm. "Where are Kallen and Reyes?"

"Interview room with Michelson." I pointed at the closed door.

Ionescu nodded once. "Let's try this again." He led the way to the interview room. I followed him. Silent Gibson surprised me by following as well. Was he included in this circle jerk? Ionescu opened the door and ushered both of us in.

Michelson and Kallen were intently studying a piece of paper. Reyes hovered behind them, pointing at a highlighted line on said paper. It looked riveting.

"Agent, thank you for joining us." Ionescu shook Michelson's hand. "This is Detective Gibson. He will be sitting in today."

"Good to meet you." Michelson shook Gibson's hand.

The detectives fanned out around the conference table. Ionescu sat at the head of the table, but in an unobtrusive way. Like he was trying to be the farthest from the action. Reyes made it a point to sit next to me. It felt protective rather than intimidating, which was nice.

"Ms. Braddock, we have an unusual case that crosses some jurisdictional and departmental lines. We're hoping you can point us in a better direction. Any direction, really," Michelson said. I hated how appropriate and polite he was. It gave me nothing legitimate to dislike.

Kallen laid two mug shots on the table. One was Gibson's perp. She added a glossy picture that looked like a senior photo. The last two photos were candids. Gibson's perp, the senior photo, and one of the candids were former customers of mine. I wasn't digging that connection.

"Do you recognize any of these men?" Kallen asked. Men was a generous term. All of them were teenagers or early twenties.

"Yes." I pulled the three photos toward me. I almost identified them, listed their drugs of choice, the intricacies of their vices, but then I remembered Reyes's advice that morning. Don't elaborate. "I recognize these three."

"Can you identify them?" Kallen asked.

"Yes." I was tempted to leave it there since she only asked if I could, not if I would. But the silence stretched and I only wanted to make them irritated, not angry. "Freddie Bauhaus." I pointed at the mug shot. "Josh Erickson." The senior photo. "Miles Yang." The candid.

"And how do you know them?"

"I used to deal drugs to them."

"Can you expand on that?" Kallen asked.

I glanced at Reyes for guidance, but he couldn't give me any. So I tried to keep it simple. "Freddie is smart as hell and uses his brains to be as lazy as possible. He used to buy recreational amounts of Oxy from me." The detectives all wrote that down. "Then he started using five times that amount overnight. I figured out pretty fast that he was selling it. I was never a wholesaler so I cut him off. He got mad. I blocked his number. Haven't seen him in…" That was the summer Nickels got fleas and drove me insane. I remembered seeing Freddie when I was buying her a flea collar. "Two years." More note taking.

"He was reselling Oxy? He would need to charge quite a bit to make a profit," Reyes said.

"Yep." This wasn't the time for speculation.

"What about the other two?" Kallen asked.

"College students. Both of them. Josh is probably in grad school by now. Miles is younger. He's an undergrad. Should be in his final year."

"What kind of substances did they purchase?"

"Josh was strictly an Adderall guy. He ran cross-country or something for the school and was deep into academics. I don't think he slept all that often." They wrote that down.

"So Erickson didn't use any recreational drugs?" Michelson asked.

"No. He did briefly buy Oxy. He had an injury and didn't want to stop training. He burned through it pretty fast. I told him I was out."

Michelson consulted his notes. "And when was the last time you sold him Adderall?"

"Just before winter break." I counted back the months. "About nine months ago."

"Why did you stop selling to him? Or why did he stop buying?" Kallen asked.

"He wanted steroids. I didn't have steroids and I didn't plan on seeking them out. Josh was upset. He stopped calling."

"And Yang?" Kallen asked.

"He's a raver, likes recreational drugs. He came to me for codeine, Ambien, Oxy, whatever he needed to manage his high. Miles is the type of kid to cultivate different experiences for different occasions," I said.

"So did he buy other drugs elsewhere? You said recreational drugs," Kallen said.

"Yeah. I wouldn't sell him acid or Molly. I don't know who he bought from." The detectives didn't like that answer.

"Any information about his other dealer would help."

I shrugged. "Sorry."

"Are you still in contact?" Kallen asked.

"Haven't heard from him in a while."

"How long?"

"A year in August. It was the beginning of fall semester. He transferred schools."

Kallen nodded without looking at me. "Where does he go to school now?"

"Davis." My attempt at circumspect failed.

Her head snapped up, then back down. Real casual. "So that means he's Nate's customer now?"

"Presumably. I can't confirm either way." Fuck.

"So you haven't seen any of the victims in over six months?" Michelson asked.

"Victims?" I realized my fundamental error. I hadn't asked the connection between any of the boys. Not that I could have answered the questions differently.

"Yes. All of them overdosed in the last month." Michelson watched my reaction very carefully. "Two of them in the last forty-eight hours."

"Have you asked them where they bought the drugs?" The detectives didn't answer. Again, it was the wrong question. "They're dead, aren't they?"

"Yes." Michelson waited, studied. "With the exception of one." He tapped the remaining mug shot. "He's in a coma."

"What did they overdose on?" I tried to maintain my facade, but it was a challenge. Freddie, Josh, Miles, those boys had made poor decisions, but poor decisions didn't mean they deserved to die. It wasn't even their lost potential that bothered me. Plenty of people had potential to squander in their twenties. I realized that it was simply a loss. Dead boys didn't sit well with me.

"Fentanyl," Kallen said.

I stared at her hard. I really wanted to look at Reyes, but he would lose it if I did. Or I would. Either way, it would look bad.

"Does that hold any significance for you?" Michelson asked.

"Not particularly. I've never sold fentanyl. It's not as common as other substances. And definitely less demand for it," I said.

"Do you know anyone who does sell it?"

"No."

"What about Mr. Xiao?" Michelson asked.

"No. Nate and I always shared inventory," I said.

Gibson shook his head and smirked. Which pissed me off.

"You claim you never sold fentanyl? But you sold other opiates?" Michelson shuffled his notes like it was an offhand question. It didn't feel offhand.

"The opiates I sold were commonplace. My main supplier was a cop." There was uncomfortable shuffling around the room. "He had better access to the more prevalent drugs."

"So you haven't started selling fentanyl since your operation was shuttered?" Michelson asked.

I watched my hands start to shake. This wasn't an interview to help an investigation. It was an interrogation. "No."

"You briefly sold MDMA tablets this summer. Is it possible that they contained fentanyl?" Michelson asked. Reyes shifted uncomfortably next to me. Gibson grinned again. Kallen studied her notes. Her eyes weren't moving so she wasn't reading. Just staring.

"I don't know. Henry brought the tablets to me. I refused to sell them. We had words. I accepted the pills, but I never distributed any." Nate had, but I wasn't going to tell them that.

"And what did you do with them?" Michelson shuffled his notes again. "I don't see anything about MDMA tablets collected from either your residence or Mr. Xiao's."

"We sold them to Jerome St. Maris." I enjoyed giving that answer.

"Was it common for Henry to bring you mystery pills?" Kallen asked. The question felt like a betrayal all over again. Either she believed I was dealing pills that killed people or she was treating me as collateral damage to resolve this case.

"No."

"You allegedly—" I stood and Kallen aborted her question. "Do we need to take a break?"

"I've cooperated with your questioning, but it's clear this is no longer an interview. It's an interrogation. If you want to continue, I need to have my lawyer present. If you want to charge me in the death of any of those boys, go ahead. Good luck. I'll let you discuss." I carefully navigated around Reyes's chair. Ionescu stood to let me pass. I studiously didn't look at Laurel.

The squad room was still quiet. Two detectives were working at their computers, but they didn't seem to register my presence. I paced the length of the room to burn off the adrenaline that continued to make my hands shake. Pacing didn't help. It made me feel like I looked weak so I sat in one of the chairs lining the wall. I shoved my hands in my pockets and focused on deep, careful breathing.

The interview room opened. Kallen came out. She looked around, then walked over to me.

"Can I sit?"

I shrugged. She sat.

"Do you think I killed those boys?" My voice was shockingly steady.

She shook her head. "You're not exactly a killer."

"But do you think I killed them? Do you think I sold them drugs that resulted in their deaths?"

Laurel stared at my face. I didn't turn to look at her. "No."

"Does Reyes?"

"No."

"Then what the fuck was that?" I asked.

"We were just doing our jobs."

"Your job is to try to incriminate someone you don't think is guilty?"

"No. We have to look at every possible angle to find the truth."

"I'm your CI. Doesn't that suggest some level of reciprocity? You think I broke a law, fine. But respect me enough to be up-front." I pointed at the interview room. "That was an ambush."

Laurel nodded. "You're not wrong."

"So what do we do from here?"

"I'm supposed to be getting you back in there."

"Are they trying to exploit your favoritism?"

Laurel laughed bitterly. "No, you've got it backward. Allegedly, I'm giving you special treatment. But Ionescu knows you loathe me."

"I don't loathe you."

She shrugged. "Whatever."

"Why would he send you out if he thinks I hate you? Wouldn't Reyes have better luck?"

She grinned. "He doesn't entirely believe the complaint against me. But he's absolutely convinced that you and Reyes are too close."

I laughed. "Why?"

"Lucas tends to insulate you. A lot."

"At least someone is." I arched an eyebrow at her.

"Fuck off." She shook her head. "Actually, no. You're right. Give me five minutes and I'll drive you home."

"Seriously?"

Laurel stood. "Yeah."

CHAPTER SIX

It was only two minutes. Laurel came out of the interview room, went to her desk, and pulled her briefcase from under it. She hit a couple keys on the computer and turned off the monitor.

I stood, stretched. "Ready?"

"Let's go." She led me down to the parking lot. Her truck was already outlined by a thin wave of heat. We climbed in. Laurel tossed the briefcase behind her seat, then proceeded to unbutton her shirt and toss that too. The center of her white V-neck was slightly damp. She started the engine and the dull rumble woke me from my haze of watching her. I took off my own long sleeve. Doing so knocked my cap off. I picked it up from the floor and settled it back on my head. Laurel smiled and shook her head at me. We rolled down the windows once we turned on Freeport Boulevard. Breeze whipped through the car. The air movement and engine noise made talking impossible. I stretched my legs out and enjoyed the warmth against my AC cooled skin.

I knew a part of my seeming trance was due to lack of sleep. Robin and I had been out late. Three hours of sleep wasn't the same as it was when I was twenty. But part of it was the comfort of driving in Laurel's truck with a tentative peace. I knew I needed to be wary. I still couldn't trust her. I couldn't trust me. Other humans were entirely off the table.

By the time we pulled up at my place, I was half asleep. I rolled up the window and climbed out. Laurel was blinking at her dashboard.

"Come inside. I'll make coffee." She nodded and reached for the handle without looking. I led the way to my front door. She stumbled on the stairs. Twice. "Reyes said you were up all night."

"Yeah. Miles Yang was brought in yesterday afternoon. He died." She wasn't enunciating. She wasn't even trying.

"Couch." I pointed. "Sit while I start coffee."

Laurel aimed for the couch. She sat down and leaned her head back. The woman needed sleep. I knew she wouldn't willingly take a nap, but hopefully she would crash if I left her unattended. It was that or let her drive home. Driving wasn't a good option. Whatever adrenaline she'd been operating on had run its course.

I went into the kitchen and finished putting together my abandoned coffee machine. I stuck my head around the corner again. Laurel was asleep. Thank God. If she slept, I could sleep.

Laurel didn't notice when I untied her oxfords and slid them off. She didn't even react when I lifted her feet onto the couch. She just turned onto her side and settled in.

In my room, I stripped off my jeans, tossed my hat, and fell into bed. My head was pounding. The sheet next to me moved, then meowed. Nickels wiggled out from under the sheet.

"Did I disturb you?" I asked.

She meowed and jumped off the bed. I closed my eyes. When I opened them again, the room was warm and the sun had shifted. I could hear water running in the bathroom. The clock read mid afternoon. I'd been asleep for five hours. I got out of bed and went down the hallway. The bathroom door was open. Laurel was washing her face at the sink.

"You just wake up?" I leaned against the doorframe.

"Yeah." She straightened. Water dripped off her chin. I handed her a clean towel. "I haven't slept that much in a week."

"You should work on that." I leaned around her and opened a drawer. There was a stack of new toothbrushes somewhere. I dug around until I found one. "Here. I'm going to start that coffee for real now. If you want, T-shirts are in the second drawer of my dresser. Take your time."

"Thanks."

I nodded and left her to it. I didn't know why I was being kind. Not one of my usual instincts. Maybe I was going soft in my old age. I hit the button on the coffee machine, then went in search of sustenance. Sadly, it was my kitchen so there was no sustenance. Plenty of beer. Andy had left one lone bottle of trendy soda and half a case of sparkling water in my fridge. I heard footsteps in the hallway.

"Is it weird to order pizza for breakfast if it's after noon?" I asked.

"Depends." Laurel rounded the corner. "If we drink all the coffee before it gets here, can we have beer?" She had chosen a vintage Little League T-shirt. The sponsor was a video rental place. Half the number on the back had worn off. It was one of my favorite shirts.

"I think it's probably a requirement. Coffee and pizza would be blasphemy."

"Sounds like solid logic to me," she said.

I poured coffee and handed her a mug. She took it to the couch and checked her phone. I called in the pizza, then joined her.

"We've got forty-five."

"This is odd. Right?" she asked.

"What?"

"This. Us. Here. I don't know if I'm a cop or a guest or your ex or what. Like am I supposed to pretend I don't know where you keep the coffee mugs?"

"I don't know." I shrugged. "I'm pretty sure there are no rules about the proper conduct in this situation. Our circumstances are slightly unique."

"Just slightly?" She grinned.

"And pretending that you don't know where the coffee mugs are probably won't solve our problems."

"I suppose not."

"So we'll figure it out. And it will probably be fucking weird sometimes."

"Super fucking weird."

"I'm not ready to forgive you."

"And I'm still mad that you're mad," she said.

"Hey, look, we agree," I said brightly. "We're both pissed. And it may or may not be rational."

"We also both think the other's job is bullshit."

"And we both think the other lies to themselves about the morality of the job," I said.

Laurel started laughing. "Christ, we're broken, aren't we?"

"But broken in very similar ways. So that's cool." Sarcasm was a perfectly functional coping mechanism. There was no need to weigh down honesty with sincerity. "More coffee?"

"Please." She handed me her empty mug.

We were so polite.

There was a knock when I was getting coffee. Back door, not front. I handed Laurel her mug on the way to the door. Andy. Dammit.

"Hey, tiger."

"Isn't it too hot for coffee?" Andy walked past me and got her own mug of coffee from the kitchen. She came back and leaned against the doorway to the kitchen. "Hey, Laurel."

"Hey, bud."

"So what's up? Mom said you guys broke up. Isn't it too soon for the whole lesbian exes becoming best friends thing?" Andy asked.

Laurel looked at me. It was the first time I'd seen genuine panic from her. Insane dirty cop shoots her, she's like shrugging and glaring at me. Angry uniform kicks her ass while fake arresting her, no big. But a fifteen-year-old wants a relationship update and she's having a silent meltdown?

"It's complicated," I said. Too late, I realized how vapid it sounded.

Andy started laughing. "That's insulting to literally everyone in this room. Are you together or not?"

"Not," I said.

"Are you screwing?"

"Anderson Ward," I said. Laurel was still rocking a paralyzed thing.

Andy did a teenage sigh-eye roll-huff combo. "Sorry. Are you romantically involved?"

"None of your business. You can ask us questions, but don't be a dick. That's not cool."

"Fine. Are you friends?"

I didn't want to lie. But I also didn't know the answer to that question. Honesty would have been easier without Laurel sitting there holding me accountable.

"We're working on that," Laurel said.

"Like working on becoming friends?"

"Yeah."

"Why did you break up?"

"Take it down a notch, kid. You don't get to interrogate us." It felt strange to put up boundaries. I'd rarely done so with Andy.

"Is it 'cause of your job?" Andy asked me. "And that whole thing?"

I took a moment to breathe. Maybe I didn't owe her an explanation. But maybe I did. She was still a kid, but she was on the cusp of adulthood. I absolutely owed her respect. "Yes. And you can speak freely. Laurel knows everything."

The panic was back in Laurel's eyes.

"So she knows you're a drug dealer? And she's not cool with it?" Andy asked.

"I was totally cool," Laurel said. She sounded upset. As if suggesting she wasn't cool with drug dealers impugned her honor. Not the hill I would have died on, but that was her call.

"Then why did you break up with Cash?" Aww, it was nice to have Andy fighting for me. Even if it was based on erroneous assumptions.

"I didn't," Laurel said. "I mean, technically, she broke up with me."

I groaned. And then I realized I'd groaned out loud. "Seriously?"

"I'm just trying to be honest here." Laurel made it sound like I was the asshole.

"Okay, will someone tell me what's going on? Mom was all weird and vague. You two are awkward as hell," Andy said.

I looked at Laurel. I knew damn well I wasn't supposed to tell people that she was a cop and I was a CI. She knew damn well too. We had an intense staring contest. I wasn't sure which of us won.

"Have a seat, Anderson," Laurel said in cop voice.

Andy straightened. It looked involuntary. She tilted her head to the side, waited a beat, then sat rigidly next to Laurel on the couch.

"Laurel," I said. My warning was token. We both knew it.

"You already told Robin, right?" Laurel asked me.

"Yeah."

"Andy will find out eventually. This way we can control the flow of information and explain the importance of keeping silent."

"Your call," I said. Andy was watching our exchange, but she was mildly cowed. This was the most silence I'd ever gotten from her.

Laurel caught Andy's eyes and held just long enough to guarantee she had her attention. "I'm going to share some information with you, but I need you to promise that you won't share it. Not with your friends. Not with your teachers. Not with the cute girl at the record store. This is not something you can brag with or use to win an argument or threaten someone. It doesn't matter how much you trust someone or how cool they are."

"Okay."

"If you do tell someone, it could put Cash in danger. It could also endanger me or Nate."

"I got it. I promise." Andy's hands were wrapped tight around her coffee cup. Her skin was turning streaks of white and rose.

"I'm a detective with the Sacramento Police Department. I was investigating Cash."

A minute passed in silence. Two minutes. Andy set her mug on the table. She stood and shoved her hands in her pockets. She looked caged.

"Andy," I said.

She shook her head at me. "So you dated Cash to investigate her?"

"Yes."

"How did you get the case? Why was it assigned to you?" Andy asked.

Laurel hadn't been expecting that question. "I sometimes work with an FBI task force in conjunction with my Sac PD detective unit. The lead agent asked for my help. My sergeant agreed."

"They asked you 'cause you're gay?" Andy leaned forward. She was towering over Laurel.

Laurel held steady. "I think that was part of it."

"Why else?"

"I'm experienced at undercover work. I have a background in narcotics investigations, as does my partner. I fit the physical description they were looking for." Laurel ticked off points. Andy nodded along. She seemed to relax as Laurel lulled her out of her anger with rote facts.

"I saw you kissing Cash. That day we were barbecuing." It was both a statement and an accusation.

"Yes."

"Did they tell you to do that?" Andy asked.

"No."

"Why did you?"

"I don't know," Laurel said.

"That's not good enough." Andy wasn't quite shouting, but she wasn't using her inside voice either.

"All right, back off a little, tiger," I said.

Andy spun to face me. "No, that's not fair."

"That's not the point."

"It is the point. You guys like each other. But they ruined it. They used you. They made Laurel a whore. And they made you a—What do you call someone who hires a whore?"

"A John?" Laurel was so fucking helpful.

"Yeah. A John. They made you a John."

Laurel and I were silent. I wasn't sure how to respond to that. It wasn't a kind assessment. It wasn't entirely wrong either.

The doorbell rang. I answered it in a daze. Pizza. I signed the receipt, tipped the guy. Laurel and Andy hadn't moved. I put the pizza on the table.

Laurel dropped her gaze to her lap. Her hands were clenched together. "I have a set of rules for undercover work. Every detective does. What you're willing to do, what you're not willing to do. The drugs you'll use to prove yourself to a perp. The lies you'll tell. But romantic entanglements are so rare. Most detectives never have to add that to the list." She looked up at me. "I knew going in exactly what my rules were."

I looked away. I still couldn't hear this.

"What changed?" Andy asked.

"I became invested."

"Is that why you're still hanging around? 'Cause it's probably not cool to try to date someone you just took down."

"No, I wouldn't."

"Then why are you here?" Andy didn't even try to make that sound polite.

"Continuing to date is a cover. Cash is my informant," Laurel said.

"Why?" Andy asked me.

"I was offered a plea deal. I help Laurel and her partner. They don't put me in jail."

"You've got to be fucking kidding me. So the cops make her investigate you by dating you." Andy was angry pointing. It felt confrontational as hell. "You guys—like idiots—fall for each other. And now you have to pretend to date someone you're legit in love with. But it's probably totally illegal or against the rules for you to actually be together."

"Umm," Laurel said. I fully supported that umm.

"Jesus Christ. And you're both totally cool with it." Andy stomped to the door. "This is fucked. I'm a kid and I can see that. You guys need to think about your life choices or something."

She left Laurel and I staring at each other.

"Well, that was…" she said.

"Yep."

"You said there's beer?"

"Yep."

Laurel went to the kitchen and returned with beer and plates. "I know where the plates are."

I took a long pull from my beer. "I can see that."

We ate half the pizza. Finished our beer. I got up and brought back another beer for each of us.

"So you want to just bury everything Andy said and pretend it never happened?" Laurel asked.

I laughed. It was only a little forced. "Yeah. Let's do that."

She reached out her bottle. I tapped the neck of mine against hers. "We're healthy."

"You're not a whore," I said. We could gloss over all that unpleasantness. For now. But she needed to know that.

"You're not a John."

"Thanks."

"One thing," Laurel said.

"What's that?"

"I know you don't trust me. I get that. But I need you to trust me professionally. Trust that I'm working for your best interests."

Sure she was. Cops always worked for the best interests of drug dealers-turned CIs. "I will as long as you actually work for my best interests."

"I will." There was something desperate in her tone. I looked up. She was staring intently at me. Something in her eyes made the words a covenant. I desperately wanted to believe her, and I hated myself for that trust.

"It goes both ways though." I gathered our plates and bottles and took them into the kitchen.

"What do you mean?"

I came back and leaned against the doorway to the kitchen. "The complaint that was filed against you. Assholes like Gibson. It affects me too. I don't want to be collateral damage when some dick is trying to ruin your career."

Laurel grinned. "Gee, thanks."

"You know what I mean."

"I do. I just don't think you can do much about that stuff. I can't even do anything about it," she said.

"I can't if I don't know about it. You have to trust me professionally too."

Laurel nodded. "Yeah, okay."

I didn't know if either of us meant it. We could have been exchanging empty words. It felt better than silence though.

CHAPTER SEVEN

The closer I got to Braddock Farm, the more numb I became. Last time I'd been to the farm, it made me sick. I had expected the same this time. Instead it was underwhelming emptiness.

Today, I wasn't fighting Clive. He and I had never been good at it. Not when I was the unruly kid he was raising, not once I'd grown and we were equals. It helped that we rarely disagreed. But now we disagreed.

It didn't matter. Today, I'd bury my disbelief. He would hide his distrust.

I didn't know if I should be disappointed in myself for giving up on Clive so quickly. It didn't feel like giving up though. It felt like waiting. At some point he would get his comeuppance. He would admit how wrong he'd been. Hopefully, Henry wouldn't need to actually kill someone for that moment to come to fruition.

Until then, I would wait. Every day that passed in stasis felt like it degraded my bond with Clive. But that was on him. I'd done everything I could.

I parked behind the house. Shelby's car was there. Not surprising. She did work at the farm, after all. But I hadn't been expecting her. Maybe she could be a buffer. I didn't know if wanting a buffer was a good or bad thing. I let myself in. Clive and

Shelby were at the dining room table with every piece of paper in the house spread before them. Dining room meant serious.

"There's my little felon." Shelby jumped up and hugged me. "I'm getting more tea. You want some?"

"Sure, thanks." I didn't want tea, but I knew better than to tell her that.

"Hey, Cash." Clive leaned back and wrapped his arm around my waist. I hugged him back briefly. I knew I was stiff, but I didn't try to hide it.

Shelby came back with a glass of iced tea for me. She topped off her and Clive's glasses. I sat across from Clive. An upside-down look at the documents on the table suggested they were in the middle of a financial review.

"This looks fun."

"It's worse than it looks. We've been doing this for hours," Clive said.

Shelby gave him a sympathetic look. "You know how he feels about numbers."

I smiled at her. "I remember."

"They aren't natural. I like soil. That's real. This isn't real." He sounded petulant.

"That's silly and untrue," Shelby said.

"So why are you guys torturing yourselves?" I knew we needed to review our finances. The farm needed to be indisputably separate from my business. But we had already done the bulk of that work. This was overkill.

"I want the farm to be sustainable on its own," Clive said. That wasn't new information. Our goal had always been independence. "Our last projections put that date roughly five years away. We clearly need to move that timetable up."

"We talked about all of this. If you minimize the next few seasons, stop maintaining the east fields entirely, then you'll be self-supporting in a year or two." That had been the least painful of our conversations. And it hadn't been fun.

"And I'm willing if that's what we need to do, of course. But I went over it with Shelby and she had some thoughts."

Shelby smiled at us. Shelby always had thoughts. "Take a look at this." She handed me a stack of spreadsheets stapled together. "These projections are based on The Old Firehouse and Fifty-Three Cafeteria. Fifty-Three projections are very rough because we've only been in the restaurant two weeks."

I read the lines of numbers. They looked idealistic, even for Shelby. "I think you're overestimating here. I don't want to be a downer, but this doesn't seem realistic."

"No, no." Shelby came around my side of the table. "The first sheet is hard numbers. That's last month at Firehouse. The next is Cafeteria Fifty-Three's first two weeks." She turned the page and pointed out the relevant numbers. "These will shift once they settle into what they need from us."

"Seriously?" I reread the numbers. We didn't pay Shelby enough. "You're not going to suggest we expand this though, right? We barely have enough produce to fill these orders." I glanced through what I assumed were supply sheets.

"Hear me out. You guys want to leave the east fields because the summer veggies are on their way out. So, in another month, we won't lose any resources. Empty fields don't lose money, but they don't make money." Shelby reached over me to turn the page again. "I've got two more restaurants interested. Here are my projections. Fifty-Three Cafeteria has a sister location down the hill." Another page flip. "And Flight, the brewery on Main, is introducing a small plates menu. I hesitated to meet with them because they are requesting produce we don't have. But the east fields will be available soon."

"And planting those fields requires bodies to maintain them. Your summer help is back in school. We can't afford to hire new people," I said.

Clive shook his head and grinned. "That's what I said."

"Okay, Shelby. Rock my world." I waved a hand.

"One of the teachers in 4-H runs a work experience program. She thinks Braddock Farm would be a good fit for their needs." She pulled a stack of applications in front of us. "It means more work for us. Paperwork, monitoring, managing. If it were just that, I still probably wouldn't do it. But there's a fair amount of overlap of students in each program, which means some of the kids have already been working here for two or three years." She handed me a smaller packet clipped together at the top of the stack. "These three students are seniors. They worked at the stand the last two summers. They know how the farm runs."

"That sounds great, but it doesn't negate the paperwork," I said.

"True, but it increases the quality of the work we get from the students. Which means a few hours of my time equals five part-time employees who are paid by the school, not us. The more experienced ones can guide the younger ones," Clive said.

"Which means that next year the younger ones will be the older ones. It's a self-sustaining cycle." Shelby moved her hands in a circle. To demonstrate what a cycle was, I guess.

"Impressive. I take it you're both in agreement on this?" I asked.

They nodded. "But your opinion matters. It's your farm, not mine," Shelby said.

"I say go for it. And if you need a warm body, let me know. I can follow directions."

They seemed to find that amusing.

"Hey, Shelby, you mind giving us a minute?" Clive asked.

"Sure. I need to check the drip system in the greenhouse annex anyway." Shelby danced off.

Without discussing it, Clive and I stood to go outside. There was no need to be inside on a day like this.

We sat on the patio. I stared into the seemingly infinite distance. I knew a few degrees and a hint of elevation would reveal civilization, but in that spot, that moment, there were only trees and rolling hills.

"I want to give Shelby part ownership in Braddock Farm," Clive said.

I looked away from the view. He seemed nervous. "No," I said. He took a deep breath before responding. I continued before he could start in. "Not for the reason you're thinking. She absolutely deserves it. And, frankly, we can't afford the raise we were planning. So we can do it, but not for a few months, at least. Ideally, a year."

"Why?" he asked. Then he answered his own question. "You're still afraid we'll be shut down."

"That, and it just looks suspicious to add a partial owner this soon."

"I'll give you that. But you need to stop blaming yourself for this mess," he said.

"Who else am I going to blame?"

"No one. It just happened. Now we need to deal with the reality."

"You know, I know that intellectually. But I'm having trouble using logic to dismiss the emotional piece."

"So you're still mad at Laurel?"

I shrugged. "Not really. I know she was doing her job. I'm also pretty sure she and her partner have sacrificed a fair amount professionally to insulate me."

"Even though she—Even with what she did to you?"

No one ever knew what to call it. I knew. She had made love to me. I was terrified to tell anyone, but that was the truth of it. It was so much better to tell the version that everyone else knew. That we had dated. And she lied. But I realized that she hadn't lied. She had loved me. That part was honest.

"What she did was fucked up. But it's not that simple. All of the reasons I'm mad at her are just extensions of being mad at me."

"So then you're not angry about all this?"

"No, I'm still angry. At the system. The police, the Feds, the DA's office. I'm pissed as fuck at Henry."

"Henry? How so?" Clive asked.

"He's just such a fucking asshole. I know the result would be the same if he hadn't gone rogue, but he made that night so much worse than it needed to be. If not for him, Nate and I probably wouldn't have spent the weekend in jail. He made all of us look like arrogant, misogynistic psychos by association." I was pissed about the whole tying me up and punching me in the face thing, but that paled next to the whole trying to kill someone thing.

"That's a bit extreme, don't you think?"

"Which part?"

"Misogynistic psycho? Come on, Cash. You've known the guy since you were nine years old. He's a good boy."

"No. There's nothing debatable here. Henry has treated women as inferior his entire life. The only reason he had a modicum of respect for me was because my gender presentation isn't feminine."

"Henry isn't anti-gay," Clive said.

"I didn't say anything about being gay."

"He's not hateful. He's not violent." His protestations made me wonder what exactly his definition of violence was.

"Not all violence is physical. Violent language is just a precursor to violent behavior."

"He's not like that."

I didn't want to hear his excuses. "He is exactly that. And until someone locks him up, I'm just waiting for him to come back and finish the job."

"That's not fair. He wouldn't hurt you," Clive said.

Except I had described Henry hurting me. I had described that exact instance on too many occasions. "Clive, I need you to hear me. Henry tried to kill someone because it was the easiest solution to his problems."

"But—"

"No. There are no extenuating circumstances here. He shot someone. I don't know who he was aiming for, but he pointed a gun at a person and pulled the trigger. He could have killed her or me."

"But he wasn't trying to kill you."

"But he was trying to kill her," I shouted.

"Calm down. I'm still trying to understand this." He spread his hands against his thighs like he was suppressing something. Himself or me, I didn't know. "I think you're being too judgmental. Try to see where he was coming from."

"I know where he was coming from. He's entitled. He thinks he deserves more than other people. He didn't want to lose his lifestyle, his reputation. The price he was willing to pay was someone else's life, my freedom, your farm. And clearly he way overshot the mark because despite all of that, you still think he is a good guy."

"Cash—"

I stood. I couldn't have this conversation again. "I need to go. Send me whatever paperwork and I'll sign it." I walked to my SUV. Every joint felt too loose, too hot. At the same time, I was stiff. Like my anger and frustration had seized every muscle. I climbed in my car. Shelby waved at me from the door of the greenhouse. She titled her head and mouthed a question. I rolled down my window and she jogged up.

"Where are you going? I thought you were staying for lunch."

My phone vibrated. I glanced at the screen. It was Nate.

Need to talk. U available?

"Can't. Nate needs me." I held up the phone. It was a sorry lie.

Shelby made a face. "Sad. Maybe later this week? I'd love for us to all go to Cafeteria Fifty-Three. See what they are doing with our lovely vegetables."

"I can't. Sorry."

"Are you okay? You seem off."

I forced a grin. "I gotta go."

She backed away and nodded. She was looking at me with far too much kindness. I wanted to call her back. Ask if Clive casually defended good guys to her. Hey, Shelby, remember that guy who terrorized you in high school? Can't you try to see things from his perspective? When he assaulted you, he probably just really liked you, right? His behavior was bad according to every standard of decency, but maybe you were too harsh on him.

But I couldn't. It wasn't fair to invoke her past to assuage my anger. It wasn't fair to draw the connection my psyche insisted on compulsively tracing.

"Bye, Cash." She seemed to realize I wasn't going to be back for a while.

"Later, Shelby."

CHAPTER EIGHT

Nate was on the porch when I got home. He stood and straightened his short-sleeved button up. He slid his hands into his pockets, which pulled the shorts tight across his thighs.

"Rough day, buddy?" he asked when I was in earshot.

"Can we not?"

"Aww, but I like talking about your feelings."

I unlocked the door. He followed me inside and flopped on the couch. I leaned against the doorframe and waited.

"Mateo checked the pills. You want good or bad?"

"I don't care."

"Okay." Nate drew the word out. I was glad he was having a super fun day. Really. I just wasn't there with him. "The Oxy is Oxy."

"But?"

"But the potency is inconsistent between pills. Mateo did a small sample and the results varied so widely he had to test a larger sample."

"That's fucking great. How much did you pay for this shit?"

Nate sat up. "Hey. I don't know what made your day so shitty, but I'm pretty sure it wasn't me so back the fuck off. Take a deep breath. Take up yoga. I don't care. Just don't treat me like your punching bag."

I nodded and went to the kitchen. I took a deep breath because I wanted to, not because he told me to. I grabbed a couple of Andy's sparkling waters and went back out in the living room. Nate took the can I handed him. He drank half of it and waited.

"Can we sell the pills? Is there any way to sort out the different dosages?" I asked.

"No. Sorting would be impossible. He would need to test each pill, which would degrade each pill." He shook his head.

"So we're out a couple hundred bucks?" It wasn't the end of the world. It just felt like everything was an obstacle and I was tired. I needed something to go right.

"Not necessarily. We have two options. One, sell it as a grab bag. Parties, raves, festivals we can get away with that sort of thing."

"And what? Just say, hey, this is Oxy, but we don't know how strong?"

"Basically, yeah."

"I don't like that idea." It seemed like asking for trouble.

"Neither do I. But there's an anonymity at raves that will protect us both from dissatisfied customers and any industrious police detectives."

"I'd rather not shield myself from the results of selling questionable product. I'd rather just not sell questionable product."

"I feel you. That's why there's an option two," he said. I waved my hand for him to continue. "Mateo can blend the pills and press them into new pills with consistent dosage."

There was plenty that could go wrong with that idea. But it held more promise than the other. "We can do that?"

"It's relatively simple from what I understand. He can customize them however we want. You want orange pills in the shape of bunny rabbits? He can do it."

"We're not selling Molly. I just want the Oxy to look like Oxy," I said.

"That's doable. Should I tell him to go ahead?"

I didn't see that we had much of a choice. Our options all sucked. This option sucked less. "How much do you trust him?"

"As much as you can. We've known each other for a few years. He's got a similar world view to mine. He's discreet."

"Would he rip us off? Would he put something other than Oxy in the pills for any reason?" I asked.

"I wouldn't consider this if I thought he would," Nate said.

"That's fair."

"There is..." He stopped. Hesitated. "There is the issue of Kallen."

"Yeah, we're not supposed to deal." I really wasn't concerned about that. "But I wasn't planning on telling her."

"Right. I'm sure that's what they had in mind. It's fine to deal as long as you don't tell any cops about it."

"Shut up. They know we're going to keep dealing. Hell, I think they want us to. How else are we supposed to maintain the contacts they need?" I asked.

"Yeah, I get it. But I think pressing pills—in light of the whole counterfeit, adulterated pills thing—might be pushing their willingness to look the other way."

"Well, hopefully, they never find out."

"Solid plan," he said.

"So if we do this, how long will the whole process take?"

Nate grimaced. "Not long, but right now we can't afford a couple days."

"Same. How bad is it with your customers?"

"I've promised drugs I don't have in the next two days."

"Wait here." I went back to my bedroom and grabbed the duffel bag Robin had dropped off the other day. Nate and I had shoved every bit of paraphernalia in my house in there, but I had no clue what that encompassed. Packing was a blurred memory.

Nate watched me dig around for a couple minutes before he grabbed the bag and upended it on the coffee table. He started plucking bags of pills out from the pile. I sorted out the various plastic baggies of money.

"Hey, Cash?"

"Yeah?"

"I thought we were broke." Nate stared pointedly at the growing pile of cash.

"Can you pay rent with cash?"

"No."

"Me neither." I dumped the load on one of the couch cushions. Our mound of crap was getting smaller. "Do you have an operational system to launder money through?"

"No." He dragged it out. Apparently, he was tired of my shit.

"We are effectively broke."

"Can I pay Mateo with this though?"

"Yes." I opened a bag and counted out a stack of cash for him. "Buy some Visa gift cards too. I'm low so you must be." He double-checked it before folding it and shoving the wad into his pocket.

We sorted pills into colors. Nate counted out conservative amounts. I noted them in my register. It was just like old times.

"This should hold me over."

"Do you know who you're losing customers to?"

Nate shook his head. "Not sure in Davis. Sac, especially around the college, it's Jerome and his boys."

I sighed. "I'm not even mad, really. He's filling a void."

"Same here. We're going to need to be creative to get our customers back though," he said. I nodded. I wasn't ready to think that far ahead. "I'll keep you updated about the whole Mateo thing."

"Thanks." I walked him to the door.

"Hey, you know if you actually want to talk about whatever you're so pissed about, I'm here," he said.

"Yeah. I know."

He hesitated to see if I would pour out my heart. When I didn't, he shook my hand, tapped my shoulder with a closed fist, and let himself out.

I appreciated the gesture. But I didn't want to talk. People were too disappointing when you talked to them.

Nickels was in the living room when I returned. She was staring at the strange lump of plastic and cash on the couch. I scooped up the pills from the coffee table before she could investigate it. I stashed the drugs and cash in fun, new places. Nickels watched me open drawers and cabinets. She harshly judged the amount of noise I was making. By the time I was finished, she had fallen into a disapproving sleep.

I drove to Kyra's. The afternoon heat made everything shimmer. Nothing felt real. Kyra opened the door and stood there watching me. I didn't speak or explain myself. I didn't know how. She linked her fingers through mine and led me inside. She opened a beer, pressed the cold bottle into my hand, and sat me on the edge of the bed.

"Five minutes," she said. I nodded.

Kyra moved around the painting in the center of the loft. She wrapped oil-soaked brushes in plastic. Covered her palette. Stowed away tubes of paint. I took a long pull from my beer. Kyra poured soap and olive oil into her palms and scrubbed at the bright drops of purple on her fingertips. She was only partially successful. She roughly dried her hands and tossed the towel at the counter. I drank more beer and tried not to think or feel. Hot breeze from the open window battled with the AC running full blast. The air movement helped diminish the smell of solvents, but it was still pervasive.

She carefully stripped off her shirt and turned it inside out to trap the smears of paint. Her curls shifted direction when the cotton pulled at them and she pushed them out of her eyes. She stopped in front of me. I looked up at her and found that I didn't mind the hint of pity.

"I'm okay," I said.

"No, you're not."

She pulled my T-shirt up. It got stuck at the bottle I was still clutching. Kyra took the beer and drank from it as I freed myself from the shirt. She set the bottle on the dresser behind her. I toed off my shoes. Kyra kicked them aside. She pushed me back and unbuttoned my jeans. I lifted my hips so she could strip them down.

Kyra's breath was warm on my skin. I studied the ceiling, tried to find patterns in the stucco where there weren't any. I concentrated on the sensation of her tongue against me. My breathing went ragged when she sucked my clit into her mouth. She pushed me hard and fast and I came quickly. She didn't stop. I came again. My chest rose and fell rapidly. I rubbed my hands across my face and they came away wet. I was crying?

Kyra didn't lie to me, tell me it was okay. She just crawled up and gathered me into her arms. At first, I was just silently weeping. Then I thought about Laurel and Clive and Andy and Nate. And myself. I started sobbing. Gasping, ugly sobs. Kyra traced her fingertips over the lines of muscle and bone in my back. She ran her hands over my hair. Tears pooled and gathered in the hollows of her chest. It took me a long time to stop crying.

I stayed there against her, waiting for my body to calm. I took in deep—at times gasping—lungfuls of air. I marveled at the unfamiliar feeling of moisture in my eyes. I never cried like that. It felt like drowning. Kyra smelled like sweet soap and soft skin and caustic chemicals. The turpentine fumes were comforting. It reminded me of the miniature studio she had in college. Half of the windows were painted shut. Kyra was careless in cleaning and storing her supplies. It reeked, but it never bothered her. She was better at ventilation now, but the smell was still familiar.

Eventually, I fell back against the sheets. Kyra reached over and spread her hand across my chest. The gentle pressure of her palm was comforting. Her fingertips dug into my flesh. I felt the tension in my chest start to abate.

"Talk."

"I don't know what to say," I said.

"Try. You did the not talking thing. It's not working."

"I'm not avoiding. I truly don't know what to say."

"Tell me what brought you here today then," Kyra said.

I didn't think it would help. But she was right. Whatever I was doing wasn't working. I told her about the farm and Clive that morning. I told her about Nate's plan. She asked questions. None of them were out of curiosity. She wanted me talking. I told her about Laurel. How everyone else was more invested in me hating her than I was.

"Okay, you want my opinion?" Kyra asked.

"Sure." I was mildly concerned that she was going to tell me some bullshit about forgiveness or love or whatever, but this was Kyra. She didn't do bullshit.

"You're probably not going to figure this shit out. Don't try. You need to stop punishing yourself. When's the last time you ate a meal for pleasure? Drank a beer because you wanted it, not because you needed it?" she asked. I didn't tell her that my pizza and beer with Laurel had almost fit that criteria. "When was the last time you got a haircut?"

I counted back. "About a month and a half ago."

"And how often do you normally go?"

"Once a month."

"You need a haircut."

I ran my fingers through my hair. "Is it that bad?"

"No. But you like getting your hair cut. It calms you. Plus, it's routine. You need normal right now."

"Okay."

"Okay? I love how easy you are." Kyra grinned at me.

"Fuck off." I grinned back. "You're right. Whatever the hell I'm doing isn't working."

"I am an artist. It makes me naturally intuitive."

I groaned. "You were doing so well."

"I'm still doing well." She poked me in the ribs.

"So I get a haircut and eat indulgently and everything will be fine?" That was a plan I could get behind.

CHAPTER NINE

It wasn't late, just late enough that no one should have been pounding on my door. I lifted Nickels off my chest, much to her chagrin. Judging by the volume and seeming impatience of the knocking, the list of people it could be was short. Which was good because I was wearing cutoffs with so many holes you could see the dancing penguins on my underwear. I opened the door. Laurel marched in. She slapped a file against my chest as she passed me. I caught it when it started to fall.

Laurel went into the kitchen and grabbed a beer. As she walked, she pocketed her tie clip and pulled out the knot of her tie. She set the beer on the coffee table and started unbuttoning her shirt.

"You never heard of air-conditioning?"

I didn't bother answering her. She shrugged out of her stiff shirt and tossed it—the tie still tucked under the collar—at the back of the couch. Her familiarity seemed more bred out of anger than comfort. She sat down hard on the couch. She spread her legs and planted her elbows on her knees.

I opened the file. He was one of my customers. Pedro Morrison. Twenty-year-old Sacramento State student. He lived with a bunch of other undergrads in a house just off campus. Most of his roommates were common idiots, but Pedro was a sweet kid.

Sensitive. Had a strangely deep voice. He was one of those rare, genuine people. When you spoke he listened with his whole body.

Pedro was smaller than all the other guys in his house. Height, that is. He was a rower or soccer player or something. His thighs were massive. The last time I'd seen him was a house party they'd invited me to. I'd left early when I met Laurel. Nate finished the party for me. Laurel and I had shut down The Depot.

I grabbed my own beer from the fridge, leaned against the living room wall, and waited.

"He's dead," Laurel said.

I drank my beer to disguise my compulsive swallowing. Grief suddenly seemed like a physical object. Pedro couldn't be dead. But I knew that wasn't true. Of course he could be dead.

"When?"

"An hour ago. Overdose like the others." She drank her beer. Stared straight ahead. "He was one of yours?"

"Are you asking?"

"Yes."

"You know the answer," I said.

That broke her staring contest with the wall. "Why would I know? Just because he bought drugs doesn't mean he bought them from you."

I tried to wrap my head around what she was saying. It seemed like a vote of confidence. Maybe. "He was at the party where we met. He lives with six other guys. They throw a lot of parties like that."

"No." She crossed the room to take the file from me. "That party was in the Fifties. That's not where he lives." Laurel pointed out his address in the file.

"Then, he moved." I took back the file and flipped to the next page. "There."

Laurel read the paper, her eyes flicking back and forth. After confirming, she resumed her spot on the couch. After two long, silent minutes she spoke. "So I'm culpable too."

The statement didn't make sense. "How?"

"Because I made a decision that night. I could have just arrested you and Nate. I had ample evidence from that one party. I could have shut it down right then."

"But we didn't sell him the drugs that killed him."

"You'll forgive me if that technicality isn't easing my guilt."

It took me a moment to process what she had said. And then I did. And I got angry. "I won't forgive you. That's bullshit."

"No, it isn't. Three months ago, I could have broken the cycle this kid was in. I didn't. I chose to play the long game. It worked out fucking beautifully, didn't it?" She spread her arms wide to indicate my home, me, her, I didn't know. "And the collateral damage was a dead undergrad. He was going to start an internship in the fall. Did you know that? The Kings' marketing department picked Pedro Morrison out of seventy-five qualified candidates."

"Hey," I said harshly. Laurel finally met my eyes. "Pedro made his own choices. Were they different than his peers? No, probably not. I guess he just got lucky. One out of seventy-five, maybe. But that's on him."

"Do you realize what you sound like?" Her voice caught. "A fucking drug dealer."

"I am a drug dealer." In that moment, I couldn't think about Andy's recriminations. I could only see myself. The kid who had been told too many times that they couldn't be what they wanted.

She dropped her head. "You were supposed to be better than that."

"That's a fucked up thing to say."

"Is it?"

"Yeah, and it's no less insulting than last time you said it."

"You're really going to keep this going? You're going to keep pretending there's nothing about being a drug dealer that is beneath you?" She was incredulous. "I know you're stubborn, but I never took you for a liar."

"A liar?" I didn't understand.

"I see you, Cash," she said. That statement hung between us. I didn't know what she meant or where she was going, but it felt heavy. "You can't sell this idea to yourself anymore. But you can't seem to admit that you were wrong either. Why is that?"

I took a long drink of my beer. Then I remembered what Kyra had said about enjoying beer. So I set the bottle down. Kyra had told me to take care of myself. I realized belatedly that she hadn't just meant physically.

Andy hadn't quite been judging me, but she wasn't forgiving either. I couldn't carry it anymore. I couldn't posture and claim that other people made their own decisions. This game was systemic. I'd been a willing cog for too long. But I didn't know how to say that. Just like with Andy. How could I just admit that I was wrong?

Or maybe it was that simple.

"It's so much worse than you know," I whispered.

Laurel took a deep breath. Like it was a relief. "Tell me."

"We sold to Sophie's sister's boyfriend." I said it fast.

"Who is Sophie?"

"One of Andy's best friends," I said. Laurel nodded, but she didn't get it. "Sophie's sister is a baby too. Seventeen. The only difference between Andy and those kids is two years. Same location, socio-economic status, school, neighborhood. The only difference is two years." It didn't matter that she didn't understand. Not yet anyway. Once I started, I had to purge it all.

"Which part of this is throwing you?"

I laughed, but it was a painful gasp. "All of it? I sell drugs to children. How is a fifteen-year-old different from a seventeen-year-old? How is a twenty-year-old different from a forty-year-old? Why are pills any better than fucking heroin? Because more people use them recreationally? Addicts use pills too. Pills still kill people. Ask Pedro Morrison."

Laurel nodded and launched in. "I'm not going to justify any of that because you're not wrong and I don't think you want me to." I laughed roughly again. "But you survived in a gray area for years. It's gray because there aren't absolutes in morals. Which you are damn well aware of." This was her version of kid gloves. It was somehow exactly what I needed.

I nodded because I didn't know what else to do. "So what do I do now?"

"What do you want to do?"

Did I want out? Did I want to light the world on fire? Only one clear thought came to mind. Everything else was convoluted. "I want to nail the bastard killing these guys."

Laurel smiled. "Good. Because I need you."

I crossed the room and sat with her on the couch, relieved she was willing to drop the rest for a moment. "How do we get them?"

"Find out who it is. Get evidence. Arrest them. My job description is simple most of the time." Her tone was an odd blend of self-deprecation and confidence.

"What do you do when it's not?"

"I used to talk it out with Reyes or my brother until I understood my boundaries. You should probably do the same. Figure out your new boundaries."

"You said used to. What do you do now?"

"Apparently, I just sleep with the person I'm investigating." She smiled and heat flooded my chest. "I can't say I recommend it though."

"Ouch."

Laurel laughed. "No, I mean, you're already wrestling with your morals. I just lit mine on fire and tossed them out a window. Fun, but a bitch in the morning. It would probably fuck you up extra good."

"Sounds tragic," I said. But it was forced. I was suddenly very aware of her proximity. Heat poured from her body. The few inches between her thigh and mine seemed to shimmer. My bare toes were just close enough to brush the hard leather of her oxfords. And then she did the unthinkable. She put her hand above my bare knee and squeezed. Whatever air was in my lungs evaporated.

"I know this won't be easy. But if we have to do anything the hard way, I'm glad I'm doing it with you."

I managed to breathe and smile at her. Which I thought was impressive. "Yeah, same."

She stopped squeezing. Her palm was just resting warmly on my thigh. The white scar on her hand was stark against her deepening summer tan. Her gaze flicked over my mouth so fast I thought I imagined it. She stared at her hand, my leg. Her eyes raked over my mouth again. It was unmistakable. Her chest rose and fell in deep, measured breaths. I listened to the sound of my breathing and realized it matched hers. Somehow the knowledge that she was thinking the same thing I was made it impossible to think of anything else. Like we were locked in some loop where the only escape was to stop thinking about the loop itself. Laurel leaned forward. Just a little. I froze. Then she pushed herself back, back. She stood with effort.

"We should come up with a plan or something. You know, for this case."

I nodded. Nodding seemed like a solid move. "Can we do it over food?"

"Sure." Laurel looked around the room. The walls were closing in. She could feel it too. "Maybe we should go out."

"Yeah. Is Burgers and Brew still open?"

"Probably."

"You look up what time they close. I need to change into pants."

Laurel pulled out her phone, careful to look at it, not me. I escaped down the hallway. My life felt entirely too complicated to be dealing with this too. So I decided to not acknowledge it. That had worked for the better part of my life.

I pulled on a pair of jeans that were more acceptable for going out in public. When I was tugging on my shoes, Laurel called down the hallway.

"They are open for another two hours."

I rejoined her in the living room. "Should we drive?"

"Sure. I will."

"Is that like a cop thing? Driving all the time?" I asked.

Laurel went stiff and then she grinned halfway. "Umm, yes? But not the way you're thinking."

"That was a normal response."

"My truck is rigged with GPS, video cameras, and an audio transmitter." She looked both nervous and amused.

"Your truck is bugged?"

"Yeah, I can trip it to record and transmit from under the dash. It also automatically engages if the lock opens without my key."

It took me another second and then I figured it out. "You watched me break in."

"Yeah, that was why we left the field office. We didn't realize Henry had broken in until we were driving back. One of the cameras caught him coming down the staircase." Laurel's hands were balled and shoved in her pockets. I couldn't read what her feelings were.

"I'm sorry."

"It's not like he was sorting through my panty drawer." She shrugged. "As far as I could tell, he looked through my desk and files. But that was it."

I knew I had to tell her. It sucked. But we were doing a trust thing. "Yeah, but I went through your panty drawer. No, wait. I searched your bedroom. I mean, I was just looking around to help Henry, but then I totally lost it and left him there." I wasn't explaining the reasoning behind me breaking in very well. Then again, that wasn't something you could really explain.

Laurel stared at me. "Why did you lose it?"

"Because it smelled like you and looked like you." Cedar and boot oil. Mid century vintage. Worn books arranged on dark wood shelves. "The entire apartment screamed Laurel. And then I found your uniforms. Everything I knew about you was real, but the truth was hollowed out." We stared at each other.

"I'm sorry," she said.

"Yeah, me too." We both nodded. I was tired of apologies. I was sure she was too. "Let's stop apologizing."

"I can get behind that."

I bumped her shoulder with mine and led the way outside. A shoulder bump was safe. I liked the contact. And it had almost no chance of ending with us making out.

CHAPTER TEN

Once we were in the truck, Laurel pointed out the button installed under the dash to activate the tracking equipment. She pointed out the bolts that weren't bolts. The microphones were in the headliner.

"These are fancy ass cameras. I didn't know city cops were given this stuff."

"Sometimes for specific jobs, we get the good stuff. But mine came from the FBI. I paid to have their equipment installed." She cranked the engine and turned toward 19th Street.

"Why?"

"My mom had a case years ago. I was like eleven. There was this undercover cop whose cover was blown when he was caught wearing a wire. He was executed. It was a pretty unremarkable case except for the fact that my mom presided over it. But there was one detail that came out during the trial. The officer could have been wearing a different type of wire, something harder to detect, but funding was delayed. Usual bureaucracy. The family ended up suing the department." She waved her hand like it was irrelevant. "Mom has been fixated ever since. When I started undercover work, she totally lost it."

"Isn't that a relatively normal parenting reaction?"

"Yeah, except my mom can call my sergeant. Or my FBI supervisor. Once, Lance—my brother, he's a cop—was reassigned and she didn't like the posting. So she cornered the chief of police at a cocktail party."

"The chief of police? Like the guy who is everyone's boss?"

"Yeah. He's about fifty pay grades above Ionescu."

"So he probably wasn't responsible for the move?"

She shook her head and grinned. "Hell no. But that didn't stop my mother. She demanded he reassign Lance. It was a fucking nightmare."

I started laughing. "Did he reassign him?"

"No." She laughed too. "In his mind, Lance Kallen was the five-year-old who peed on the mayor's azaleas during a garden party. He had only the vaguest idea that Janice and Randy's boy had grown up and joined the force."

"Your mom sounds super fun."

"She's a blast. You know, unless you reassign her kids. Or actually are one of her kids."

"So how does this relate to the upgrade?" I pointed at the camera lenses. "Did your mommy call the FBI and ask nice?"

"No, she tried to get me pulled from undercover work entirely."

"What the fuck?"

"I know, right? Thanks for the vote of confidence, Mom." Laurel turned onto R Street and paralleled her massive, rumbling truck. I was far more impressed than I should have been at her ability to do so. We climbed out. She came around and leaned against the hood on the passenger side. "Thankfully, Ionescu isn't easy to bully. He shut her down. Michelson and I landed on this solution. I'm extra safe. My poor truck is permanently disfigured, even though I'm the only one who knows the extent of it." She rubbed her finger over a rust spot on the door. Baby blue paint flaked away. "And any sucker who gets stuck talking to my mother at a social function can point out that I have equipment no one else has."

"I'm starting to get an idea of why your parents are terrible."

"I love them, but sometimes it's really hard to like them." She smiled and grabbed my hand to drag me toward the restaurant. We took a few easy steps before remembering that we weren't dating, we were reluctant colleagues who sometimes pretended to date. She let go and I shoved my hands in my pockets.

It was early enough in the week that Burgers and Brew was relatively empty. We waited two minutes for a table. They even sat us in an isolated back corner of the patio after Laurel pointed out the table we wanted. I'd never even been seated in under an hour. This was unprecedented.

"So weeknights after ten are the best time to hit the restaurant scene."

"Weekends are overrated," she said. I realized Laurel didn't really get weekends. She was constantly working in some capacity.

The waitress interrupted to take our orders. It wasn't until after she left that I realized we had ordered for each other. Laurel picked out beer. I chose our appetizers. We ordered the same burgers. Maybe this would work. Maybe we could just be buddies. Buddies who wanted to fuck each other. And couldn't fuck each other. Maybe not.

"Okay. Plan for nailing asshole to wall," Laurel said.

"Yes, I'd like one of those."

"Lucas and I think they are selling at raves and festivals. There's also clearly some individual business as well."

That wasn't unreasonable. "Based on what?"

"There are only superficial connections between the vics. All male. All under thirty. Most of them were college students. Bauhaus is the only outlier there. But most of them were into the rave scene."

"Miles and Pedro," I said. Those were the only two I knew who went to raves.

"Pedro Morrison was a raver too?"

I nodded. "I don't know about the rest though."

"Bauhaus also. And one of the guys you couldn't identify. Blake Welter. He's the one in the coma."

"Josh Erickson definitely suggests a personalized sale."

"Why is that?" Laurel asked.

The waitress approached us. I raised my hand a couple inches off the table to warn Laurel to stop talking. The waitress deposited glasses and curly fries and melted away. At least she could read our vibe.

When she was out of earshot, I continued. "Josh was paranoid as hell that someone would report him to the school. That he would lose his scholarship or his spot on the team. There's no way he would go to a rave. Too risky."

"Not even an organized one?" Laurel asked.

"Come on, Detective." I smiled so she knew I wasn't using it as a pejorative anymore. "Organized raves might have working bathrooms and proper permits and running water, but the drug use is the exact same."

She grinned. "Yeah, okay. So Erickson takes out party angle."

"No, I think it's still highly probable. I think he just adds in an intimate angle. This dealer would have met him in person and not in public."

"William Seldin also wouldn't have gone to a party. He was weirdly antisocial," she said.

"Tell me about him. How was his being antisocial weird?"

"He was our first victim. Freshman at Davis. His roommate said he only left their dorm for classes. Didn't even leave for meals. Just ordered groceries on Amazon."

"Okay, that's pretty weird."

"So not only did his dealer not sell to him at a party, he basically delivered. Either during class or to his dorm room," she said.

"Did the roommate offer anything else up? What kind of drugs was he into?"

Laurel took a handful of fries. "I think I just want to eat curly fries for the rest of my life."

The change in subject threw me. "Any other food? Or just curly fries?"

"Beer too. Is beer food?"

"Do you want it to be?" I asked. She nodded. Her mouth was full of fries. "Then, yes."

She sipped her beer. "Fries and beer. So you support this?"

"Seems like a solid plan." I took my own handful of fries.

She laughed. "You were asking about Seldin."

"Drugs of choice."

"Right. Roommate wasn't sure. Seldin apparently watched nature documentaries and porn constantly. He spent most of his time jerking off, not to the documentaries. And he frequently stayed up all night playing video games." Laurel grimaced. It wasn't a pretty description. Not abnormal, but being common didn't make it any more pleasant.

"So his roommate kind of hated him?"

She shrugged. "Yeah. I guess when he was interviewed by the detective, he was scraping blackout plastic off all the windows. Wouldn't stop and sit for ten minutes. The detective said the kid had already boxed up all of Seldin's belongings. Even the mattress was stacked up against the wall."

"And that wasn't suspicious?"

"It was. But he had basically moved into his girlfriend's dorm room three weeks prior. The girlfriend's roommate was less than pleased about that. Between both women and his class schedule, the roommate had an alibi for a couple weeks straight. He also cooperated fully. It was a dead end. Davis PD got nowhere with the case."

"How did you guys end up with it?"

"Josh Erickson was the next victim. Then Freddie Bauhaus. So both were in Sac County. It wasn't until Bauhaus that we realized the cases were all connected. Blake Welter made us look at the colleges because he's a Sac State student. Miles Yang was next. He was enrolled at Davis, like you said. That was when Agent Michelson's team got involved."

It took me a second. I always forgot that Davis was in a different county. "Oh, two victims in Yolo County, three in Sac County."

"And, essentially, four police departments."

"Four?" Not unless Sac and Davis had multiple police departments. Maybe the County Sheriff's department got involved?

"Campus police at both universities completely impeded our investigations."

"Jesus Christ. Shouldn't dead kids kind of override reputation?"

"Welcome to police work."

The waitress returned with our food. We repeated the silent dance. She left. Laurel bit into her burger and grinned. I started in on my burger. I mentally ran through the list Laurel had provided.

"Wait. Seldin and Erickson were first?"

Laurel's eyes briefly flashed hope. "Yeah."

"Both of the non-ravers were first, then all of the club kids? So somewhere between the first two and the third, he started going to parties."

Laurel rolled her eyes. "Duh. Why do you think you and Nate were at the top of the list? College students, Davis and Sacramento, higher socio-economic status, private parties, pills." She ticked off points and my heart sank with each one.

"Oh."

"Yeah."

"And all the victims were douche-bros. That's kind of your signature."

"Hey, I sell to Land Park housewives too."

"Sold."

"Yeah, whatever."

Laurel set her burger down, drank some beer. "I think we need to start attending raves and parties. Find out who is selling fentanyl."

"Me and you, we?" I asked.

She nodded. "I can't send you alone. And Reyes won't fit in."

"If I'm going to ask questions, it will have to be a college party. And people will expect me to sell drugs."

"Yeah, that's a problem. Because I'm kind of supposed to arrest you for that."

"Is that one of your unbreakable rules?" I could get away with selling to a few visible people. That was gray area I could survive in for a while.

"I wouldn't say unbreakable."

"So if you didn't see the behavior, you wouldn't be inclined to arrest me?"

She shrugged exaggeratedly. "If I didn't see it, I wouldn't have any reason to."

"Okay. So we attend a party, ask questions. Find out who is selling fentanyl, then what?"

"Buy some, have the lab test it."

"Will the lab be able to match it to the fentanyl that killed our vics?" That would tie it up nicely.

She shook her head. "No. They can identify the fillers used, but that will only narrow it down. Apparently, everything used to make the pills is common."

"So how will that help?" I wasn't trying to be dense.

"If we buy from the same supplier multiple times and the dosage varies wildly, then we have our perp."

"And then you arrest them?"

"No. Then we gather enough evidence to nail the fucker to the wall."

"That's going to take forever."

Laurel shrugged. "Building a case takes time. We're early still."

"But more people will die."

"Yes, they will. We should work quickly."

"We also need to consider that the perp is selling batches wholesale. That would explain the shift in victims. And it would account for the twenty-mile radius."

"Yeah, Reyes pushed that idea for a while. But the problem would be more widespread. We haven't seen anything to support it. Yet," she said.

That was good. Small wins were still wins. "I assume you guys looked for other fentanyl related deaths in Northern California."

"We did, but the majority were heroin laced with fentanyl, not pills." That seemed to comfort her. "The only pill related cases were entirely different circumstances. There were two deaths in San Francisco. Both were Oxy laced with fentanyl. And there was a case in Chico. A kid tried to turn patches into pills. He failed spectacularly."

"How recent?"

"San Francisco was eighteen months ago. Chico was about a year."

"So chances are slim it's the same person?"

Laurel nodded. "Yeah. Most of the parameters are different. The only real similarity is the drug itself."

"All right. I guess you've got that covered."

"That's the advantage of the FBI. They have minions. We do our part, they will keep us updated."

"Cool. So you wanna party like twenty-year-olds this weekend?"

"Sounds super fun."

"Yeah, I know how to show a girl a good time." I winked. Laurel laughed. I didn't question the feeling in my gut. It felt deceptively like happiness.

CHAPTER ELEVEN

M y phone buzzed with a new text. Andy had sent me a screenshot. I opened it and found that Tower Theater was doing showings of *Top Gun* all day. I texted her back.

350 showing?

Bitchin. Dads after?

I wasn't entirely sure how Dad's sandwiches had become our tradition when we went to the movies, but I wasn't going to deny the kid. *Duh.*

My phone buzzed again. I assumed it was Andy until I realized it was ringing. Andy wasn't big on calling unless prompted. It was Nate. I swiped.

"What's up?"

"They are perfect," he said.

"Going to need an antecedent here."

"What's an antecedent?"

I rolled my eyes to myself. Then I judged me for having done so. "What is perfect?"

"The Oxy. I just met up with Mateo. The Oxy looks like Oxy."

"Badass. So we're back in business?" I walked into my bedroom to grab my wallet. Andy would be coming through the door any minute.

"Yep. Now we just need to find a way to launder money. Preferably before my tuition payment."

"And before my mortgage."

"And my rent."

"I've got till the beginning of September. So a couple weeks. You?" I asked.

"Same for rent. Tuition is due in the middle of September."

"So we're fine." We weren't fine.

"Totally." He knew we weren't fine.

"I miss the old days when every transaction wasn't recorded and monitored."

"You weren't alive then."

"That doesn't mean I don't miss it." There was a knock at the back door before Andy let herself in. "I gotta go. Andy's here. We're going to see *Top Gun*."

"You're better at adulthood than I am."

"I know," I said.

"Oh, the Adderall was delivered. I gave it to Mateo to check the dosage. I'll let you know what he says."

"Cool." We hung up. I turned to Andy. She had pulled my copy of *Top Gun* off the shelf and was reading it.

"I thought you said there was a hot lesbian chick in this." Andy held up the case to make sure I got the full heteronormative visual.

"Hot chick." I pointed at the cover.

"Why's she all up on dude if she's a lesbian?" Andy went back to reading the cover. "Is it one of your dumb subtext things? Like it's about pilots or the air force or whatever so everyone is secretly gay? Subtext is bullshit."

"They're in the navy."

"So it is a subtext thing?"

"No. The character is straight. The actor is a lesbian."

Andy flipped the case back over so fast she dropped it. Then she tried to catch it and sent it flying across the room. "Shit."

I laughed. "This is what happens when you doubt me."

Andy picked up the movie and put it back on the shelf. "Angry lesbian gods made me throw that movie because I doubted you? Yeah, that makes sense." She tripped on her way to the front door.

"Do not anger the lesbian gods."

She glared at me over her shoulder. "You're a jerk."

I shrugged and followed her out to the car.

❖

When the lights dimmed after the previews, Andy started getting antsy. Sometimes I forgot that she was just a tall child, but when she was supposed to sit still, I was reminded. She was the MVP of fidgeting. The thing was, she also had that childlike ability to become entranced when engaged. By the time "Danger Zone" started playing, her hands were clasped in her lap and her gaze was hyperfocused on the screen.

Tower was an old theater. It had been around for the better part of a century. Which meant that every jet engine roar, every guitar riff made the seats tremble a little bit. It was ideal for experiencing *Top Gun*.

I did my best to not watch Andy watching the movie, but it was difficult. She reacted in all the best ways. She scowled and scoffed whenever the dudes said unnecessarily masculine things. She lit up when Goose was lovable. When they were playing volleyball, she got bored and started to fidget again. When Charlie used big words, she relaxed. I'd never realized what a litmus test for queerness this movie was. Or maybe that was all movies made in the mid-eighties.

When we left the theater, Andy blinked at the bright, late afternoon sun. She rubbed her eyes vigorously and pulled her sunglasses out of her pocket. They were knockoff Wayfarers. She sighed at them and slid them on. I dug out my own sunglasses.

"I'm going to need a jumpsuit. And probably aviators. I mean, Kate McKinnon made the jumpsuit thing pretty clear, but like I thought I needed goggles. I was wrong. I need aviators," Andy said.

"I feel like a failure for not having provided said jumpsuit already."

"Same. You're totally a failure."

"So I take it you were into the movie? What did you think?" I asked.

"I think we need to reevaluate our high-fiving technique. And Charlie was hot. And she was an astrophysicist. I don't really know what that is, but I'm pretty sure it makes her hotter."

I clapped my hand on her shoulder and squeezed. "I'm so proud of you, tiger," I said in the most patronizing voice I could manage.

"'Cause I like a hot chick?"

"No, because you think her being an astrophysicist makes her hotter."

"I have standards." We climbed in the car. "Which is why I'm so upset about this high five business. How could you not tell me we were doing it wrong?"

"I think that's pretty obvious. I was afraid you would become cooler than me. The *Top Gun* high five is my Hail Mary."

Andy shook her head. "That hurts. I'm devastated that you would deceive me."

"I'm sorry it had to come to this, but I couldn't abide you surpassing me in coolness. One day your therapist will help you come to terms with it, I'm sure."

She laughed. "Gosh, I hope so. Otherwise, I might internalize it and never recover from my high five shame."

"We could just start high-fiving properly. It might mitigate the damage."

"Mitigate." She pulled out her phone. "Mitigate." She said it slow the second time, sounding it out as she typed. "'To make something less severe.' Yes, let's do that for my psychological damage."

I parked in front of Dad's. It was a tiny-ass building with an empty lot on one side and a large brick facade on the other. Both seemed to dwarf the small sandwich shop. The exterior was painted bright blue. Graffiti covered large swaths of it, but it was cultivated graffiti, commissioned graffiti.

Andy held the heavy, metal screen door for me. I'd never seen the inner, actual door closed. Didn't matter if it was dead of winter or middle of summer, that door was open. We got in line and Andy stared at the menu board scrawled across the entire wall. As if she wasn't going to order vegan meatloaf like she always did.

"Pick out a soda." I nodded at the cold case by the counter. Andy sauntered over to study her options. I ordered our food and a beer. After careful deliberation, Andy set a glass bottle filled with pink liquid on the counter.

"You guys sitting on the patio?" the guy taking our order asked. I nodded. He popped the cap off my Lagunitas and Andy's soda. "I'll meet you out there."

We had to cross the sidewalk to get to the patio built next to the curb. If I carried my beer from inside the restaurant to the gated patio, the world would likely end. Those teetotaling five feet of sidewalk were all that separated us from the animals.

Andy picked out a table. A minute later, our drinks were delivered. We discussed astrophysics and came to the conclusion that neither of us knew what astrophysics was. Also, we were bad at science. Andy had the math thing nailed. I did okay with words. Social sciences were fine. But science, science wasn't our thing. It was the physics part of astrophysics that was really throwing us off. We were cool with stars.

Our sandwiches were delivered. They were wrapped in butcher paper and taped shut. We opened the sandwiches, then traded. I disagreed with vegan meatloaf on principle.

"You sure you don't wanna try a bite?" Andy waved her abomination at me. Enticing.

I grimaced. "I'm good."

We started in on lunch. Andy got real quiet. Not just because she was eating, but because she was thinking. Finally, she set the sandwich down and took a long pull from her soda.

"Hey, Cash?" She spread her hands on the table and studied them.

"Yeah?" I drank some beer and leaned back. Whatever was going on was serious. Andy was rarely nervous like this.

"I'm sorry."

"For what?"

"For what I said to you and Laurel."

"Are you apologizing for what you said or how you said it?"

She looked up at me. "I don't know. What's the difference?"

"If you're apologizing for what you said, then you didn't mean it. You just wanted to hurt our feelings. If you're apologizing for how you said it, then you meant what you said, but you probably could have said it better." I did my best to keep my tone neutral. I wanted to know how she really felt. And I wanted her to figure out what she really meant, not just base her answer on my perceived approval or disapproval.

"Well, I guess I kinda meant what I said." Her gaze dropped again. She gathered whatever feelings were rolling around and readied herself. "I'm really mad at the whole system or whatever. You know, the police and the laws. But I'm more pissed that you guys are just going with it."

"You mean that we are complying?"

"Yeah. It's like you don't respect yourself at all." The kid had courage. I'd give her that.

"Okay. I can see why you'd think that. Why else are you angry?"

"I mean, you're a drug dealer. That's pretty dumb."

I fought a smile. She was right. It was dumb. "That's valid."

"It is?"

"Yeah. I'm realizing that maybe I've gotten too good at lying to myself." That was vague. She wasn't going to get it. "Lying about what I think is right and wrong and why. I had convinced myself pretty thoroughly that my dealing was harmless. I was wrong."

Andy nodded. Slowly. For a full minute. "Okay. So what are you going to do about it?"

"I don't know. Honestly. I need to figure it out. I think it's pretty clear that I can't continue. So there's that."

"That makes me happy. Is that weird?"

"Nope." I shook my head. "If you have any questions, I'll try to answer them."

"Actually—" Her eyes were back on her hands. "Do you think I could have Laurel's number?"

"Laurel's number?"

"Yeah. I want to talk to her. I mean, I need to say sorry for the way I talked to her." Andy met my eyes and grinned. "But also like other stuff."

"Other stuff?" I was nailing this parrot thing.

"Yeah."

"Umm, sure. Yes. Let me run it by your mom and Laurel first though," I said. Andy gave me a strange look. "Because she's a random adult. I want to make sure it's not weird that you're texting her."

"Yeah, I guess that makes sense." Andy picked up her sandwich again. "So where are we getting jumpsuits?"

"We?"

She blinked at me. "We."

Right. "Are we wearing them out? Like is this a regular clothes thing?"

She rolled her eyes. "We're cool. We're not ghost fighting slash jet plane flying cool."

"Okay, so where are we wearing them?"

"Why are you so concerned about where we're going to wear them?" she asked.

I sipped my beer. "I don't know. I guess *Ghostbuster* style jumpsuits are a lot harder to pull off when you're just walking around. Fighter pilot jumpsuits we can fold down and it's like wearing army cargos. But like better."

"I feel like you've thought about this too much."

"Are you seriously judging me? This was your idea."

"Was it?" Andy was total deadpan. And a little judgmental. The little shit.

"Whatever. When I get a jumpsuit, you're going to be jealous."

"Am I?" The look morphed from judgment into pity. This kid spent way too much time around me.

CHAPTER TWELVE

At the beginning of summer, the vapidities of college parties had annoyed me. I was astounded that said vapidity had grown so impossibly large in the intervening weeks. It didn't matter that I was the one who had changed. It was no less underwhelming to watch undergrads imbibe booze and attempt to fuck each other and regurgitate the lecture they'd attended three weeks before.

"I don't know how I used to do this," I whispered into Laurel's ear.

Laurel shook her head. "I don't know either. Come on." She dragged my arm around her shoulders and leaned into me. Heat poured off the bare skin of her arms. I felt greedy soaking it up. But if the only contact I'd get from her was residual summer heat, the possessive pull of her fingers wrapped around my wrist, statue-tight muscles pressed against my chest, then I would be gluttonous.

"Where are we going?"

"Outside. I can't think in here. There's a backyard, right?" She dragged me through the house. We stepped around a couple aggressively making out in the hallway. When we got to the back of the house, the hallway split and spread in both directions. Large windows showed the backyard, but I couldn't see a door out. White twinkle lights were strung over the patio and through the trees. It gave the yard an early aughts romance movie vibe. It was bad enough that suburban children went to college in the city. Bringing their suburban culture with them just seemed excessive.

"Oh, down there." I finally was able to see cement steps leading to one of the windows. When I looked closely, I realized the window was a sliding glass door. I pointed out the anomaly.

Laurel turned down the hallway. She flung the door open with her free hand. Her other was still gripping my wrist, keeping me close. The backyard was only marginally less crowded than the house, but the sky was clear. Stark white moonlight nearly drowned out the lights in the trees.

There was a small portable fire pit set up in the center of the lawn. Well, it was an attempt at a lawn. Summer heat and lack of water had destroyed whatever grass had once existed. A loose ring of white plastic chairs were set around the fire pit. Sacramento County and City had plenty of regulations about fires. These kids were violating all of them.

Opposite the illegal fire was a massive oak tree. Thick roots lounged on the ground, bragging about where the water for the lawn had gone. We posted up against the trunk. Laurel studied the people around us. She looked entirely casual. But every muscle was still tensed. After about five minutes, a boy came up and asked me for Oxy. Laurel ducked out from under my arm, muttered something about beer, and wandered in the direction of the cooler by the door. As soon as she was out of earshot, I named a price to the kid. He gave me a couple of damp bills, I gave him a baggie of drugs.

Laurel came back and handed me a sweating bottle. She leaned against the tree next to me. "Do you always feel this old at parties?"

"Perpetually." I took a swig from the bottle. The beer was light and cold and bitter. Offensive in its candid lack of flavor.

"Is it because we actually are old?"

"And not drunk. Or groping each other. Or screaming our inadequacies into the abyss. College students are a strange balance between ill-fated and infinite potential."

Laurel grinned and nodded. "I've never had issues blending, but this feels off. How do we fix it?"

"Aside from making out?" I smiled so she would know I was kidding, but her face reflected panic for a brief moment. It looked like my own panic. Could she possibly realize how much I wanted kissing her to be the answer? But, no. That was idiotic. Kissing her wouldn't change anything. Besides, we had cheapened that defense mechanism. It seemed like we spent every operation making out. The Sacramento PD probably had hours of us kissing on record.

No wonder someone accused us of a sexual relationship.

"Yeah, aside from that," she said.

"Loosen up. That's really all we can do." I draped my arm over her shoulders again. "Just do what feels natural, easy."

Laurel shrugged and slid her arm around my waist. "I guess you're supposed to stand out a little anyway, right?"

"It helps move product, yeah."

She leaned her head against my shoulder. "Don't look, but there's a kid to your left who keeps looking at you. I'll tell you when you can check him out."

"What's he look like?"

"Kinda tall, average weight. Dark blond hair. Hipster bro type." She was describing half the college students in East Sac.

"That narrows it down."

"Shut up."

"Can I look yet?" I asked.

"No, he's sitting and facing us. I'll let you know when he gets up."

I scanned the side of the yard I could see. Most of the kids were vaguely familiar. They cycled through every four to six years, but they didn't change a whole lot. Twenty-year-olds were far less imaginative than they thought they were.

A girl opened the door and stood on the steps, scanning the yard. She squinted at Laurel and me, then made her way down the steps. Damn kid wanted to buy drugs. What was this world coming to?

I tightened my arm around Laurel and pulled her to face me. She leaned back to look at me, which pressed her hips into mine.

"There's a girl coming this way. She wants to buy," I said.

"So you think if you're otherwise involved, she might go away?"

I shrugged. "Maybe."

Laurel's eyes locked on mine. She threaded her other arm around my waist. The beer she was gripping was cold and damp through my T-shirt. She was going to kiss me. I knew it. She knew it. The rational part of my brain pointed out that we were working undercover. We had to maintain that cover. It was for our safety. And upholding the law. Yeah, we needed to make out in order to uphold the law.

Laurel pressed her body even closer. Her warm curves and smooth plains of muscle felt exquisite against me. She pressed her fingertips into my jaw, shifted my chin down. My chest went tight. Even the muscles in my lungs seemed to have frozen in anticipation. A tantalizing ache grew between my shoulder blades and spread down my spine. I was wet and all we were doing was staring at each other.

I dipped my head and tried to capture her mouth. She tightened her grip against my jaw and held me still. When I stopped moving, she leaned forward and pressed her lips against mine. I groaned. Which was probably good for that whole cover thing, right?

Laurel opened her mouth. The inside of her lip was soft. She pulled back, kissed me again. Her tongue flicked over my lip. She tasted like cheap beer and warmth.

"Hey, uh, Cash?" The voice was deep and low and probably did not belong to the girl who had been approaching.

Laurel pulled back. I did my best to not look like I wanted to punch whoever had interrupted us. Laurel smiled, then shifted away from me. I looked up.

The guy was wearing denim cutoffs that were a size too small. His shirt was also too tight. It was buttoned all the way up. I hated that. It was suffocating to look at. But it was the hair that finally placed him. The top was foppishly long, but oiled into place. The sides were shaved almost to the skin.

"Dawson." I put out my hand. He shook it. "This is Laurel." He shook her hand too.

"Sorry to interrupt. I just..." He broke eye contact. This guy had always been obnoxiously confident. Even with things he had no business being confident about.

"Did you hear about Pedro?" I asked it gently. He had that look like he was going to break any second.

Dawson nodded. "That dumb fuck." He sniffled. "How could he be so stupid?"

"I don't know, man. I heard it was an OD."

Another wet sniffle. "Yeah. Idiot took some pills and..." He shrugged. "I don't know, bro. It was like what the fuck, you know?"

"Totally." I did not know.

"Is this that guy you were telling me about?" Laurel asked.

I nodded. "Yeah, awesome kid. Super smart and shit. Really genuine, you know?"

Dawson started actually crying. "He was so fucking smart. Like how was he so fucking dumb?" He leaned in toward me.

I let go of Laurel and held out an arm. Dawson launched himself at me. He was half a foot taller than me. So that was a bit awkward.

Laurel backed away. I put my other arm around Dawson and did my best to comfort him. His body felt wrong so close to mine. I wasn't a hugger. I wasn't really into touching other people. But I couldn't deny this man-sized boy his grief. A few uncomfortable minutes passed before he pulled away. I looked around and realized Laurel wasn't there.

"I'm sorry, bro. I didn't mean—" Dawson took a deep shaky breath.

"Hey, it's cool. This just blows."

"Yeah." He nodded. "Yeah, it really fucking blows."

Laurel returned. She had a stack of plastic chairs braced on her shoulder and a precarious handful of cheap beer. "Here." She held out the bottles. Dawson and I grabbed them. We unstacked the chairs and set them in a small circle. When we sat, our knees were nearly touching. "I'm really sorry about your friend," Laurel said to Dawson.

"Thanks."

"Tell me about him."

Dawson stared at his hands. "I don't know. He was my buddy." He shrugged. "He woke up at five a.m. every day. Naturally. Never used an alarm clock. Just woke up and went for a run. Used to drive me nuts, but like I was never late to class so that was cool."

"You guys lived together?" Laurel asked.

"Used to." Dawson drank a third of his beer. "We shared a house with five other guys. But we all moved out last month."

"What happened?"

"Two of the guys, James and Jimmy—Cash, you remember them?" Dawson asked. I nodded. "They started fucking, which was fine. Like it didn't mess with our dynamic or whatever. But then I guess they fell in love or some bullshit." He smiled like he wasn't going to admit that he was into the idea of love, but he secretly thought it was cool. "They got their own place and we couldn't find anyone who wanted to share a three-bedroom house with five dudes."

Laurel cocked her head. "There's so much to unpack there."

"Bunk beds," Dawson said with a measure of pride.

"I'm still stuck on James and Jimmy. So they're both named James?"

"Not the point, babe," I said.

"Right. So bunk beds?"

"Me and Pedro had the coolest one. We built it ourselves." Dawson looked quite pleased with himself. "Out of reclaimed pallets. Chicks were so into it."

"Chicks were into…" Laurel trailed off when she caught the look I was giving her. "Cool. Out of pallets?"

"Yeah." Dawson teared up again. "We were going to share custody of it. He took it when we moved out. I was supposed to take it back in six months. I guess it's just mine now though."

"Oh, so you guys moved to different places?"

"My girlfriend thought we should move in together. But we broke up and Pedro already had a roommate." He shrugged. "I should have stayed with him. Maybe then he wouldn't—"

"Hey, man. Don't do that. It's not your fault," I said.

"But like we were so careful. That's why we always wanted you and Nate around. 'Cause other people sell some sketchy shit."

"Do you know who else was selling to him?"

He shook his head. "No. You don't know either?"

I grimaced. "No. But I'd like to."

"Why?"

"Honestly?" I asked. He nodded. "I wanna fuck them up."

Dawson brightened. "Really? Can I come?"

Nothing says fun like a good ass kicking? "Totally. Can you find out who it is though?"

"Fuck yeah. I'll get all the guys on it."

I glanced at Laurel. She shrugged. I read it as acquiescence. "Awesome."

Dawson finished his beer. I offered to grab him another. We spent the rest of the evening listening to drunk college boy stories. They were all really into their genitals. So that was neat.

Laurel had a talent for listening. She saw people and coaxed intimate detail from them. I wasn't sure how I'd missed that before. She was also a master at making it look like she was drinking as heavily as everyone else, but staying absolutely sober.

The party broke up after three. We convinced Dawson to let us walk him home. It was a long four blocks. On the way back to her truck, Laurel yawned and veered into me.

"Sorry." She righted herself.

"Tired?"

"No, I just think it's fun to stumble around."

"I feel like that was unnecessarily sarcastic," I said.

"No one cares about your feelings."

"Is it weird that I think you're super hot right now?"

Laurel laughed. "Yes. You're fucking weird as hell."

The moonlight we had been walking in dimmed as we went under a massive tree. The roots were starting to crack the sidewalk. It reminded me of Scout and Jem being stalked. I wondered if the ground would feel cooler if I was barefoot. "So I've got a strange request for you."

"Cool. What is it?" Laurel veered the other direction. I dragged her closer to me and draped my arm over her shoulder. To help her walk. That was all. She put her arm around my waist. I liked the weight of it.

"I need you to tell me if you're not down. Or even if it seems uncool. No pressure. Okay?"

"Sure." There was a distinct lack of sincerity.

"You understand that it's no obligation?"

"Cash, tell me."

"Andy wants your number. So she can talk to you or something," I said.

"Andy? Little baby Andy with the big angry words wants to talk to me?" She stared pensively at her feet, which made her trip. The sidewalk and trees ended suddenly. I looked up and realized we were at the end of the block. We crossed the street. Laurel blinked at the single streetlight.

"Yeah, she got all weird when I asked why so I didn't push it. I think she wants to talk about me. I told her I would get back to her."

"But what about you? Like what does she want to talk about?"

"Probably the drug dealer thing," I said.

She nodded and made a noncommittal noise. The trees of the next block closed overhead. She rubbed the seam of my shirt between her fingertips. It was rhythmic and soothing. She seemed unaware that she was doing it.

We finally got back to the truck. Laurel let go of me. She crossed her arms and leaned against the bed. She misjudged the distance and a loud, metallic pop echoed down the street.

"You should give her my number," she said.

"Are you sure?"

"No, I just thought about it for five minutes to lend an air of legitimacy."

I laughed. "Fine, I won't ask dumb questions."

"Yeah, okay." Laurel nodded. She closed her eyes and leaned her head back. Her breathing got deep for a moment. I was pretty sure she had just fallen asleep standing up.

"Let's get out of here." I took advantage of her diminished reflexes and pulled the keys out of her pocket.

"Hey." Her eyes shot open.

"I'm driving. You apparently don't function well when you're tired. Everything you say is extra snarky and arrogant. And you forget how to walk."

"Nuh-uh. I'm a badass cop."

"Kinda proving my point."

"I'm not tired." She squinted at her watch. "It's barely after four."

"And you get up at disgusting times. So you've probably been awake for like twenty-four hours."

"Twenty-three." She rubbed her eyes. Which made me want to tuck her in and kiss her head. I didn't like that feeling. It was creepy. "Besides, if you drive, how will I get home?"

"You won't. You're crashing at my place. Or I'm crashing at yours. It doesn't matter. You can't drive." I opened the passenger door and hit her with a pointed look.

Laurel stared me down for a solid minute before she got bored. Or sleepy. So she climbed in. "You're overreacting. I hope you realize that." I closed the door.

The drive was fast. The streets were empty. Laurel crashed before I even got to a main road. She had slung her arm over the back of the seat. The crystal face of her watch caught the passing streetlights and shot glowing patterns across the dash. One of her feet was up on the seat, her legs spread wide like taking up space was so ingrained she did it in her sleep. Despite that arrogance, despite her oxfords and chinos, she still looked shockingly innocent. There was a purity in her that couldn't be stripped by the accoutrements she hid behind.

I knew it was unnecessary to tell her to sleep at my place. I could just as easily drop her off and take her truck. Or walk home. Or twenty other options. It was an excuse. I wasn't proud of myself. But when I looked over at her, slumped and curled between the bench seat and the door, I didn't really blame myself either. I felt an odd sense of honor. Not that I was protecting her, but that she allowed me to see this vulnerability. We both knew I didn't deserve such a measure of faith.

CHAPTER THIRTEEN

I was pouring coffee the next morning when Laurel stuck her head around the corner. I jumped and barely managed to avoid pouring coffee everywhere.

"Christ. I didn't even hear you get up."

"Sorry. I didn't mean..." She yawned. "Can I have some coffee?"

I handed her the mug I'd just filled and grabbed another from the cabinet for myself. "Sleep okay?"

She nodded. "But I'm becoming far too acquainted with your couches."

"You know, if you start sleeping like a normal person, you might have better success with the whole making it to your own bed thing."

"Yeah. Maybe."

"Or not. Porch?" I asked. Laurel nodded and followed me outside. "I kinda like you when you're sleepy. You say really dumb shit."

Laurel set her coffee down and stretched before lowering herself into her chair. "I do not. I'm always in control. That's why I'm so good at undercover." There was no arrogance in it. It was just a statement of fact.

"You know, that's similar to what you said last night."

"What do you mean?"

"You informed me that you were a badass cop."

She blinked at me. "Fuck. I did, didn't I?"

I just grinned. My phone started vibrating so I wrestled it out of my pocket. It was Nate telling me to let him in. I made a noise that was part curiosity and part panic. And then I decided to analyze the panicked guilt later. "So Nate is here."

"Hmm. Yeah. Okay."

And with that uncomfortable conversation firmly behind us, I went to answer the door. Laurel didn't follow me.

"Hey, I've been knocking for like five minutes." Nate walked in and closed the door behind him. "But I saw your car." He looked around pointedly. I felt the moment he zeroed in on Laurel's oxfords piled on the floor. He took a couple steps forward and glanced into the study. The pillows and blanket felt like a condemnation. "At least you're not fucking her. You're not fucking her, right?"

"I'm going to need you to not be an asshole right now."

"How am I being an asshole?"

"Because that's not how you talk about people. And that's not how you talk to me. I'm your friend," I said.

"Yeah, it's because I'm your friend that I say with the utmost respect: you're not fucking her, right?"

"Why would you think that?"

"Because she slept here and she's hiding on the porch right now like a goddamn shameful secret." He pointed out back.

"She's not hiding. She's having coffee. You want some?" I went into the kitchen and poured him a mug. He took it from me with a glare. "I'm not accountable to you, but you're obviously freaking out so I'll explain."

"You know, when you're guilty, you tend to tell the other person everything they're doing wrong." Nate set his coffee down and crossed his arms. "It's a defense mechanism that usually works in my favor, but right now I'm not digging it."

I didn't like that analysis so I ignored it. "We were working late at a party. We might have a lead on the douche selling fentanyl, by the way. But it was almost four by the time we were finished. She was tired, I told her to crash here. You really are blowing it out of proportion."

He relaxed infinitesimally. "If that's all it is, why are you acting so guilty?"

"I'm not. I just know it looks bad. I overreacted." I shrugged, which was a struggle because it felt like every muscle had seized the moment I started lying to him.

"Or you're not crossing any lines of propriety, but your judgment is still completely impaired because you're in love with her."

The door opened. "Hey, Nate." Laurel closed the door behind her.

"Kallen." Nate sat on the couch and picked up a book. "I need to speak with Cash. Are you going to be here long?" He didn't even glance at her. Laurel looked at me. I shrugged. I'd never seen cold Nate. I wasn't liking it. "I can come back if you guys are working."

"No, I was just leaving." Laurel went in the kitchen and rinsed her mug. She gathered up her wallet and keys, kicked into her shoes. Nate casually fake read some poetry. It wasn't awkward. On her way to the door, Laurel stopped in front of me. "Thanks for driving last night. I'll work on that normal sleep thing." We smiled at each other. She ran her palm down my arm. Heat flashed through me. I shoved my hands in my pockets to hide their shaking.

"I'll let you know if I hear anything," I said.

She hesitated and her eyes flicked to Nate. She decided against whatever she was going to say. When she left, I stayed still. Nate kept pretending to read. The door of her truck popped when she opened it. I didn't move until the rumble of her engine faded.

"What the fuck is wrong with you?" I asked.

Nate set the book down and shifted to face me. "What is wrong with me?" His eyes got wide. "Were you just here in this room?"

"I don't even know what that means, man."

"How can you still like her?"

I sighed. "We're going to be working with her for a while. We should probably aim for civility."

"Civility?"

"Yeah."

"Civility?" he shouted.

"Whoa. Take it down a notch."

"Civility is what I was just doing. I was polite. Not totally engaging, but polite. Which is straight up more than she deserves."

"Why is that?"

"Because she fucked over my buddy." He said it incredulously.

"Yeah, well, your buddy is telling you to back off."

"No. It's my right as your buddy to hate her on principle. You can—" He waved his hand as he cast about for something. "You can fucking marry her." He looked pleased with what he had landed on. "And I'll still hate her just a little bit. Not because she arrested me. Or you. Not because I resent her job. Not because I hate cops. But because she used you. It's irrational and childish, but this is how we are playing it."

"No. That's not how we are playing it."

"You can't hate her. Maybe you can't admit she hurt you. I can. I do."

I decided to refill my coffee. Mostly because I wanted to leave the room. When I returned, I wasn't any calmer. "What did you want to talk about?"

"I might have a lead."

"On what?" I could think of quite a few helpful leads. Steady supply line, money laundering, a way to nail Jerome.

"On the fentanyl thing."

"Seriously?" That got my curiosity. I sat on the couch.

"Mateo isn't the only one pressing fresh pills."

"Explain."

"Straight up, he told me someone else was using his lab equipment. He's pissed," Nate said.

"How do we know it's related to fentanyl?"

"We don't. But it's got enough commonalities to make it worth checking out. You said half the victims were Davis students. They were all pill users. Plus, we don't have anything to lose by looking into it. The cops don't have time for maybes. We have nothing but time."

I shrugged. He was right. "So is Mateo going to tell us who it is?"

"No."

Of course it wouldn't be that easy. "Well, that takes the fun out of it."

"He's skittish about the whole thing. Doesn't even want to process the Adderall I gave him—which is just as varied as the Oxy, by the way."

"So you're just an ambassador of good news, then."

He grinned in his devious Nate way. "I have thoughts. Your girlfriend won't like them."

I'd calmed down enough to let the girlfriend jab pass. He would become bored of that novelty soon enough. "Are they illegal thoughts?"

"How can thoughts be illegal?"

"Are they thoughts about plans that are illegal?" I asked.

"Probably. I'm unclear on a lot of the laws around surveillance. I'd like to stay that way. Ignorance is key."

"I can get behind that."

"We're meeting Mateo in his lab tomorrow evening. I told him you want to meet him."

"Why do I want to meet him?"

Nate studiously didn't look at me. "Because you need reassurance after offering to increase his fee to ease his fears."

"That was generous of me."

"I've always found you to be generous."

"And why am I so eager to meet him?"

Nate scooted closer on the couch and pulled out his cell phone. "Because I ordered two of these." He pulled up a photo and handed me the phone. It took me a moment to process that I was looking at a camera. The lens looked like a small glass teardrop. "And I'm going to distract Mateo while you install them in the ceiling."

"Ambitious." I handed the phone back. "But what if this other dude uses a different lab?"

"There's only one lab on campus with the right equipment."

"How will you distract him?"

"I'll accidentally lock myself out of the building."

"What if you're wrong and it's a dead end?"

"Then we wasted some time and money."

I tried, but I was out of questions. "Okay. Let's give it a shot." Nate didn't seem surprised that I agreed. If he was going to keep working autonomously, then I really needed to take him down a peg or two. Or not, since his arrogance tended to benefit me.

"Here's a list of supplies." He tapped his phone and mine lit up.

I glanced at the list. Drill, USB cables, tape, external battery pack, iPhone. "I don't know what to make of this list."

"Do you need to understand it?" He wasn't trying to be a dick. It was a valid point. He leaned over and looked at the list with me. "Oh, I got iPhones so don't worry about that."

"Plural?"

"Yeah. Get two of everything except the drill. And you should get cordless, but like super small so we can carry it in easily."

"What exactly are we building? Aren't the cameras self-contained?"

"Yeah, but we need a way to transfer the video. Unless you want to go in every twelve hours, wait for the room to empty, pull out the cameras, download the video, and reconstruct everything."

"I'm going to pass on that."

"Then we need the iPhones to transfer video to the laptop I'm going to set up outside the room. The external batteries will give us—"

I held up my hand. "You're right. I don't need to understand it." I went to the stash of petty cash in the hutch and pulled out some money for Nate. "This should cover it. And I know you need to eat."

"Yeah, I knew I shouldn't start that food thing. It's addictive." Nate grinned.

"I'm going to figure out a way to get money in our bank accounts soon."

"Yeah, I know." He tucked the cash into his wallet.

"Actually, I have a backup plan for tuition. You know, in case we don't figure it out."

"Oh, yeah?"

"Money orders."

Nate cocked his head. "Those things you get for security deposits?"

"No, that's a cashier's check. A money order is like cash, but not cash. I don't know. Crazy people who keep their money under the mattress use them. And drug dealers, I guess."

"Okay." He didn't bother hiding his skepticism.

"Drug dealers without the luxury of a money laundering business," I said.

"Why don't we just do that all the time?"

"It's inconvenient. And I'm pretty sure the max for a money order is a thousand bucks. So we have to go into a bunch of different 7-Elevens."

"Oh, so it will be less suspicious? Spread the love?" Nate asked.

"That too, but mostly I just want to show you the world. Take you to every 7-Eleven in Sacramento county," I said in my most dreamy voice.

"Aww, you spoil me."

"I know."

He stood. "So you're good with being the errand boy? You'll get it done today?"

"Yeah. I've got a customer in the Fab Forties who wants Xanax. I'll hit Home Depot when I'm out there." I loved living in an area so concentrated that five miles was a trek.

"Wow, there's a customer in the Fab Forties that Jerome hasn't poached?"

"She's skittish. I think her husband is a prosecutor or some shit. Jerome wouldn't even get in the door."

Nate laughed. "Who knew that you would be the respectable one?"

"I'm shocked too."

"I'll text later with details." He opened the door. "And be careful with Laurel. I don't know what's going on, but she's always going to be a cop first. Don't forget that."

I tamped down my anger. He was speaking out of love or whatever. "I know."

CHAPTER FOURTEEN

L aurel called an hour after Nate and I went our separate ways. I let it go to voice mail. Nate was right about her loyalties. I needed to be careful. But that didn't seem to alter my visceral reaction to seeing her name pop up on my phone screen.

I pocketed the phone and got out of my SUV. Heat enveloped me. I'd parked under the tangled limbs of a sycamore and a massive ash tree, but even that shade wasn't going to accomplish much. I went up the wide walkway and rang the bell. I could hear the faint rap of heels on the staircase. The heavy door swung in. Patricia Chadwell cocked a hip and smiled at me. She was wearing a simple shirtdress that came to her mid thigh. It moved gently when she leaned against the door.

"Cash, it's been too long." She tucked a soft, blond curl behind her ear.

"It has been. You never call me." I was aiming for admonishment, but fell short.

"I know. I'm terrible. Come in."

I stepped over the threshold. Patricia leaned close and kissed my cheek. It was a whisper of a kiss. Everything she did seemed that way. A suggestion of movement rather than something concrete. She spun and led me into the house. Air drifted through the hallway, cool and smelling of rosemary and cucumber.

"How have you been?"

She looked back over her shoulder and smiled enigmatically. "I take it you don't read the papers?"

"National, not local."

"I'm not surprised."

We entered the kitchen at the back of the house. Patricia's discerning tastes were most present here. The cabinets and sink were originals, painstakingly restored after a hundred years of abuse. The walls were covered in reclaimed tile. The only new items were the appliances, which were thirties retro. More environmentally friendly and functional than those they had replaced. There was also a single pane of glass that was new. Third down and one to the left on the French doors leading to the patio. It was the only pane that didn't waver slightly in the summer sunlight.

Patricia waved me into a seat at the bar. She started pulling ingredients out of the fridge. "You want a drink."

I smiled at being informed, not asked. "So what have I missed?"

"In skipping the *Sacramento Bee*?" She laughed. "Not much, I suppose. But my bastard husband left me for a twenty-two-year-old." As she spoke, she tore mint leaves and split them between two glasses. The scent filled the room.

I blinked at her in surprise. The woman was charming and brilliant. Gorgeous too. I knew she was approaching fifty, but she was too classic, sophisticated to have aged. The only time you could see she wasn't thirty was when you watched her eyes. "So he proved himself to be the idiot you always suspected he was?"

"It gets better." She poured an inch of cloudy lemonade into each glass. "The twenty-two-year-old hacked into half our bank accounts, stole my identity, did untold damage to Robert's stock portfolio." She muddled the contents of each glass with a small pestle. Her movements precise, yet flippant.

"You seem to be handling it well." I was aiming for neutral. What was the appropriate response to a woman's life being turned upside down by her husband's mistress? It was a conventional tragedy, but no less damaging for being plebeian.

"Oh, I'm absolutely tickled by the entire thing." She added roughly crushed ice to each glass.

"Tickled?"

"You see, if you read the *Bee*, you would know that my soon-to-be-ex-husband was arrested last month," she said. I laughed. "The twenty-two-year-old's brother is serving time in County. Robert was the prosecutor. In revenge, the girl posted the entire contents of his work computer online. Open cases, closed, briefs, what he really thinks of the judges in this county. It was a disaster." She topped off each glass with more lemonade. I took the glass she handed me. It was the most uselessly beautiful lemonade I'd ever seen.

"So how did he manage to get arrested?"

"Oh, the investigators were convinced that he was complicit in the whole thing. It's sorted out now." She sat next to me and carefully crossed her legs at the ankle. "Luckily, I filed for divorce a month before his little disaster struck. And my lawyer is far more competent than Robert—they were roommates in law school. It felt poetic to watch."

"I'm glad your divorce has been so fulfilling." I took a sip of the lemonade. It was exquisite.

"I told you I was tickled. You didn't believe me."

"I didn't believe you."

"Okay, your turn. Why are you a cash-only business now? I let it slide on the phone, but I want gritty details."

"I can't possibly compete with your husband's wandering passwords."

"Please, password. Passwords implies that he had more than one."

"I suppose that much was obvious from the story," I said.

"So titillate me."

I sighed heavily, but she was unswayed. "My distributor was this dirty sheriff from up the hill. Someone got wind of him raiding the evidence locker and tried to shut him down."

"Oh, I think the *Bee* did a story on that too. Didn't he kill a Sac PD officer?"

I wasn't sure what magic kept Laurel's name out of that story, but I suspected the FBI had something to do with it. "Tried to. Didn't succeed."

"What a fool. If you're going to kill a cop, finish the job. You're screwed either way," she said.

My vision went black for an instant. Not long ago, I would have agreed with that statement. Hell, I still did agree with that statement. But I realized in that instant that Laurel could have died that night. I'd known that all along. Henry had wanted to kill her. But before, it seemed so far from the realm of possibility. Laurel was invincible in so many ways that the concept was laughable. Yet it was real. That abstract idea of killing cops—something that never bothered me in the past—applied to someone I cared for. It didn't sit well.

Patricia was looking at me strangely. I forced a grin. "Apparently, my taste in business associates is bad."

"What about that other young man you work with? The tall Asian guy?" She raised a hand to indicate his height. In case I didn't know what tall meant, I suppose. "He's really handsome?"

"Nate." I tended to forget that Nate was good-looking until someone reminded me.

"Yes, Nate. He's smart, right?"

"Smarter than me," I said.

"Not possible."

"Smart enough to not go around assaulting people."

"Oh, I didn't realize the bar was so high," she said.

"Super high bar."

"So your former associate went ballistic?"

"Yeah. He's got a connection to the farm I launder money through, which means it's too hot for me right now." I wasn't lying, really. But I couldn't very well tell customers the actual story either.

"Can't you start a new small business to launder money through? When I opened the gallery, it only took about two minutes." Patricia owned one of those boutiques that refinished vintage furniture and sold it for a fuckload. It wasn't pretentious enough on its own so she called it a gallery to really push it over the edge.

"I would. Except the farm belongs to my uncle. I'd rather lie low and take the fiscal hit."

"Aww, but you came when I called? That's sweet."

"For you, anything." I winked exaggeratedly.

She threw back her head and laughed. "Does anyone not find you charming?"

"Plenty, I promise."

"Good, it wouldn't be fair otherwise."

I shook my head. My ego was big enough all on its own. "Okay. No more me. How's the store?"

"Oh, it's wonderful. *SN&R* did a piece on the nouveau vintage scene in Sacramento. It was indulgent and over-the-top, but we got a nice little boost from it."

"Nouveau vintage? What does that even mean?"

She lifted her shoulders artfully and let them drop. "It doesn't make a lick of sense to me. But the pictures were pretty."

I drained the last of my lemonade. Damn. That meant I had to go run stupid Nate's stupid errands. "On that note…"

Patricia sighed loudly. "All right. I suppose I'll let you go."

I pulled out a bag of white pills. They were long and slim and proudly proclaimed their brand. I wondered if Mateo was printing brand names on our repackaged pills. Patricia took the bag and tucked it into a drawer. She pulled a stack of bills, neatly folded and clipped, out of the drawer and handed them to me. "Always a pleasure."

"You spoil me," she said. We started walking toward the door. "Would it be crass to ask how you're paying the bills? I don't imagine you can pay them with cash."

There were plenty of people I would have minded that question from. Patricia wasn't one of them. "I'm still working on that. We've been getting by on cash, but tuition is coming up quick."

"Tuition? I thought you graduated years ago." She studied me like she might find some previously missed indication of age.

"Right. Sorry. Nate's tuition. He's a grad student."

"Got it." She nodded. "I'm sure you two will figure it out. You're both too good-looking to fail."

"I like that philosophy."

"It's been mine for years. I'll let you borrow it." Patricia opened the door. I leaned in and she kissed my cheek.

When I got back in the car, I checked my phone. Nothing more from Laurel. Kyra wanted to meet at a downtown brewery that evening. I sent her an affirmative. There was a series of messages from Nate. Two screenshots of an external battery and an ominous text.

They're out of stock everywhere except the Apple Store.

If he was suggesting what I thought he was suggesting, I was going to be pissed. *So we're getting a different battery?*

I made my way back to Folsom Boulevard. I was halfway to Home Depot when he wrote back.

Apple Store is holding two batteries in your name. K thanks.

He was sending me to the fucking mall? *Asshole.*

His response was entirely in emojis. It was too bad I didn't condone violence.

❖

Kyra was already sipping a beer on the patio when I arrived. The horizon was pink and orange behind the Capitol and deep blue toward the Sierra Nevadas. I sank into the chair next to Kyra and she slid a beer toward me.

"I love you," I said to the beer.

"Why thank you, Cash, dear."

"You too."

Kyra shoved me with her shoulder. "You're not very nice."

"Sorry. I had to go to the mall today. It was terrible. My filter is gone."

She looked appropriately shocked. "What possessed you to go to a mall?"

"Nate needed something from the Apple Store and he needed it right away. It was very serious," I said.

"Sounds like."

"But I got aviators for Andy. I saw Ray-Bans in one of those glasses shops and they had smaller sizes in stock and now I'm going to be her hero."

"Andy is next door, right? Robin's daughter?" she asked. I nodded. "I thought Ray-Bans were Wayfarers."

"They also make the best aviators. Duh."

"Of course. I feel shame."

"As well you should," I said. She ignored me. "I took her to see *Top Gun* so aviators are now a priority."

"I don't need to pretend to understand this, right?"

"Nope."

A waiter appeared at my elbow and deposited a large, paper-lined bowl on the table. He slid a piece of wood with cutouts for small condiment cups in front of Kyra. He pointed at each cup and named the dipping sauces. Two of the four were in French.

"Thanks." Kyra smiled at him.

"No problem. Do you ladies need anything else?"

"In about ten minutes, another beer for me." Kyra looked at me. "Same?"

"Yeah, that's perfect."

He nodded and went back inside.

"You've had fried pickles, right?" Kyra asked.

"Please. I think you know my pickle obsession." I studied the contents of the bowl. It was a pile of fried stuff. Pickles and onions were my guess. I snagged a pickle and tossed it in my mouth. It was glorious.

"This is why I picked this place."

"You're so good at food. And ordering."

"You're easy to impress." She wasn't wrong.

"I know."

"You seem better than last time."

I met her eyes and held for a minute so she would know I wasn't being flippant. "I am. I owe you, I think."

"No, just keep being happy. Or happier than you were."

"I can do that."

CHAPTER FIFTEEN

Nate led me across the UC Davis campus. It was a hike. Seriously, they took the whole agricultural, granola thing way too far. It was all trees and recycle bins and bicycle racks. I was all for a Mother Earth loving school, but this was absurd. Nate brought me to the building that housed Mateo's lab.

"Go through the main doors. There are classrooms on the ground floor, but the stairwell at the end of the hallway leads to research facilities and offices on the upper floors." Nate pointed at the mostly dark windows above our heads. "Mateo said he would prop the door to the stairs open because you need a keycard to get access at night."

"So I need to accidentally let it close behind me?"

"Yep. From there you need to go to the third floor. His lab is room 317. It's on the other side of the building. The door will be locked, but knock and he will let you in."

"Okay. I'll text you once I'm there." I sounded totally cool when I said it, but I was so not cool. Belatedly, I realized that I'd expected the plan to fall apart long before I was supposed to install cameras in a random lab at a university. At least when we had put trackers on our rivals' cars I'd had Nate with me. This solo thing was bullshit.

"You've got everything you need?" Nate's gaze flicked over my backpack as if he could see inside.

"Yeah, I'm good. Walk slow."

"You got it," Nate said.

I walked toward the door purposefully. Maybe if I looked confident it would make me confident? I let myself in. The hall was quiet, empty. Most of the classrooms I passed were dark, their doors pulled shut. At the end of the hallway I found the stairwell. A rock the size of my fist was stuck between the doorframe and door. I nudged it out of the way and let the door click shut behind me. My footsteps echoed as I climbed the stairs. It probably should have felt ominous, but I was pretty sure I was the bad guy in this scenario and I didn't generally frighten myself.

The third floor corridor was well lit, just like the main hallway on the first floor. I followed the room numbers until I found 317. A narrow strip of light shone from under the door. I knocked. The door opened.

"Hi, you must be Cash. I'm Mateo."

Whoever I was expecting Mateo to be, this kid wasn't it. He was strangely beautiful and ugly. His cheeks were rough with fresh acne and old scars. His golden-brown eyes were bright, lively, and framed by obscenely long eyelashes. Long, soft curls spilled onto his collar, his brow, his ears. The cut was awkward— nearly a mullet, but it looked more like he'd forgotten his last two haircuts rather than asked for that insanity. He smiled at me and tipped the scale to beautiful.

"Yeah, hi. It's good to meet you." I stuck out my hand. He shook it with both of his. "Did I beat Nate here?"

"You did, but it looks like he gave you good directions. Come on in." Mateo held the door and ushered me into his bright shiny lab.

Long tables divided the room into three distinct sections. Nate had sketched out the best places for our cameras. One above the door and one over the middle table where Mateo's equipment was.

I feigned a text message and dug out my phone. "Sorry." I held the phone up in apology.

Mateo waved me off. "No worries."

I typed out a message to Nate. *I'm in.*

Almost immediately Mateo pulled out his own phone. He frowned at the screen. I speed dialed Reyes because I knew he would pick up. It was the one advantage of being his CI.

"Hello?"

"Hey."

"Cash?" Reyes asked.

Mateo gave me a pained look. "Nate's locked out," he whispered.

"Sorry, just a sec," I said to Reyes. I moved my phone away from my mouth. "Oh, okay. I can wait," I said to Mateo. I brought the phone back down. "Sorry about that. What's up?"

Mateo hesitated. I'm sure he didn't want to leave me alone. Whether that was a trust issue or he didn't want to abandon his well-paying client, I didn't know.

"You called me," Reyes said.

"Well, yes. That's true. But I think that's irrelevant at the moment."

"How could it be irrelevant when you called me?" Reyes sounded annoyed.

"If that were true, I'd agree with you," I said.

"It is true. You called me."

"I'm going to let him in," Mateo whispered.

I nodded exaggeratedly so he would know I heard him. "Luke, I need you to stop focusing on minutiae and see the bigger picture," I said.

"Luke? No one calls me Luke. And you don't even call me Lucas...Oh, I'm your cover call," Reyes said.

Mateo took halting steps toward the door.

"It took you an embarrassing amount of time to figure that out," I said. Reyes laughed.

Finally, Mateo realized that I was ignoring him. He glanced at me once more, then let himself out.

"So what's up? Do you need help?" He stopped laughing suddenly. "Are you in danger?"

"No. I promise. But now I have to go. Thanks for picking up." I pulled the phone away from my ear, but Reyes started shouting so I lifted it again.

"Hey, Braddock. Wait. You need to tell me what's going on."

"I know, but I'm on a time crunch. I'm sorry. I'll call you in half an hour."

"Fine. But if you don't, I'm tracking your phone."

I hung up. And wondered about his ability to track me. I'd have to check that out. I shrugged off my backpack. I shoved the small electric screwdriver in my back pocket. It was adorable and had just enough power to drill. The roll of tape, I slid over my wrist for easy access. In the main compartment of my backpack were two shoebox-sized plastic bins. I opened one. A perfectly constructed camera and transmitting device was inside. Each piece of equipment and the cords were carefully taped to the bottom.

I dragged a stool to the door. We were lucky the ceilings were low, though I was sure Nate had considered that in his plan. I popped the rectangular ceiling tile up and angled it down. I jumped off the stool with my tile and set it over the trash can before drilling. White dust on the floor would have been a giveaway. I drilled, shoved the lens through the little hole, and carefully covered the entire contraption in fresh tape to keep it in place.

My phone buzzed. I glanced at the readout.

Coming up.

Plenty of time. Nate would ensure that ascent took longer than Mateo's descent. I shoved my phone back in my pocket and unlocked our transmitting iPhone. I checked to make sure the lens was unobstructed. It was. The phone was still recording and set to transmit. We had activated the whole thing in the car before walking over so the first twenty minutes of video would be the interior of my backpack.

I climbed the stool again, which was a bit tricky now because the camera and phone made the tile unbalanced. I got the tile settled and kicked the stool back in place. I hopped up on the middle counter and popped out the next tile. I repeated my setup and video check. I jumped up on the table, put the tile back, and jumped down. Voices echoed down the hallway. I shoved everything in my backpack. The zipper seemed unnecessarily loud. I pulled up my recent calls and redialed Reyes.

"So are you going to tell me what the hell is going on?" Reyes asked.

"Not right now. But I promise I'll fill you in soon. Right now I just need you to talk to me." I moved to the far side of the room and looked out the window. The streetlights were warming up as the sun went down.

"Okay. Let's see. Umm, no one has died of a fentanyl overdose in the last week. Kallen said you guys might have a lead from that party so that's cool. Thanks, by the way, for neglecting to tell me you were going to a party solo. I would have been backup, but that's fine. Safety is overrated."

"Avoid case stuff," I said.

The door opened. Nate and Mateo nodded at me. I held up my hand in apology.

"Sure thing. My ex-wife couldn't take our daughter to the pedicure appointment that they had so I got my first pedicure. I'm now a pedicure advocate."

"That's unexpected."

"You got a problem with men who like pedicures?"

"Yes, that's exactly what I was suggesting." I hit him with some heavy sarcasm.

"How long do we keep this going?"

"You know, Luke, I'd like to continue this conversation, but I need to cut it short." I smiled at Nate and Mateo and mouthed, "Sorry."

"Okay. You still need to call me back. Soon."

"Yes, of course." We hung up. "Sorry about that, guys."

"No worries," Mateo said.

Nate must have severely overpaid him if he was tolerating this much rude behavior. Allegedly, I had asked for this meeting, then spent the first ten minutes of it on my phone. And my associate had demanded that Mateo hustle down, then up three flights of stairs.

"Yeah, no big. I'm sorry I made you guys wait. I wonder if the cleaning crew knocked the door shut," Nate said.

"It happens all the time." Mateo waved a hand. "I get weekly emails from the department reminding us to keep the stairwell doors closed."

Nate and I nodded. "So I don't need anything from you, really. I just wanted to put a face to the name, make sure you're trustworthy. Allay any fears you might have," I said.

"Yeah, sure. That makes sense." Mateo shoved his hands in his pockets and leaned against one of the tables.

I realized that he was younger than I'd originally thought. And he was nervous. I wasn't sure if his nerves were due to me or the situation. "Do you have any questions? Is there anything you're concerned about?"

Mateo shrugged. "No. I mean, I think Nate has been good about talking me through everything."

"I'm glad we did this. So now you know that Cash has your back too." Nate clapped his hand on Mateo's shoulder. Mateo relaxed a bit.

"Totally." Mateo grinned.

"Exactly. You're a valuable resource. The work you do is fantastic," I said.

Mateo lit up. "Yeah? Thanks."

"All right. We will get out of your way." Nate stuck out his hand. Mateo shook it. Another two-handed shake.

"Thanks again." I held out my hand too and Mateo cupped it in both of his.

"It was good to meet you, Cash. Do you guys need me to walk you out?"

"No, we got it." Nate shook his head.

"Yeah, I think we can manage."

In the hallway, Nate asked, "We good?"

"Yep."

We went down one flight of stairs. Nate led me to the men's bathroom. It was the closest to Mateo's lab, which was good. Nate climbed on the counter and popped out the ceiling tile. I pulled the laptop out of my bag, checked to make sure it was connected to the iPhones upstairs. The signal was strong. This idiocy might actually work. I made sure the external battery for the laptop was firmly taped to the back of the screen.

"Everything operational?" Nate asked.

"Looks like." I handed the computer to him.

He tucked the laptop into the ceiling and replaced the tile. "Let's get out of here."

"Sure thing."

Nate braced himself on my shoulder and jumped off the counter. At the door, I waited for Nate to glance out and give the all clear. Chances were slim that Mateo would wander down to the second floor at the exact moment we were leaving, but it was better to err on the side of caution. Nate could just say he stopped to use the bathroom. Both of us would make it suspicious as fuck.

We hurried back to the stairwell. Nate stuck his head in, looked up and down, listened. He nodded me forward. I didn't take a full breath until we were outside.

"So that's done," Nate said.

"Hopefully, we get something from it."

"Hopefully, it's something we can bring to your girlfriend. The murky legality might be a problem."

I shrugged. "All the information we give them comes from sources outside the law. I mean, that's why they need us, right?"

"You're not wrong."

Nate probably should have realized how good I was at justifying practically anything. It was a questionable gift.

CHAPTER SIXTEEN

It was almost eleven on a Wednesday morning and Cafe Bernardo was packed. Why didn't these people have jobs?

The waitress brought Reyes out to my table on the patio. He thanked her and slid into the chair opposite me.

"Sorry I'm late. Did you get my message?" he asked.

"Yeah. It's no big. I just got seated."

"Thanks for meeting with me."

I opened my mouth to respond, but the waitress appeared with two mugs of coffee. "Have you had a chance to look at the menu? Or would you like me to come back?"

Reyes looked at me. "You know what you want?"

I nodded. "You?"

"Amaretto French toast, please. Does it still come with bananas?" Reyes asked.

"It does."

"Could I have strawberries as well?"

"Sure thing." She turned to me.

"Eggs Benedict. Extra hollandaise, please."

"All right. Anything else for you two?" she asked.

"We're good, thanks," I said.

She smiled and left us.

"You order breakfast like a chick," I said.

"You're kind of a misogynist, you know that? Between that and your judgment of my pedicures, I'm feeling pretty attacked."

"Hey, I didn't judge the pedicure."

"You didn't support the pedicure," he said.

"I'm neutral about the pedicure."

He huffed. "Neutral is a cop-out."

"Fine. I support your love of pedicures. Now why did you want to meet?"

"That support didn't feel very sincere."

"Reyes." I tried to use an authoritative voice, but Laurel was way better at that.

Reyes grinned at me, then sobered. "I need to apologize for taking you to the station. That's not how we are supposed to do things. I mean, it is. We treat CIs poorly all the time, but that doesn't make it okay. I didn't realize what was happening until far too late, but I should have stopped it and I didn't. So I'm sorry."

"Thanks," I said. His apology was simple. I liked that. "Can you fill in any details about what happened?"

"Not really, no. I can tell you that Gibson is on a warpath. He definitely is the one who filed the complaint against Kallen. That's not really relevant, but I thought you should know. I'll deny having said that, by the way."

"Any idea what he hopes to gain?"

"Honestly?" It seemed like he was actually asking.

"Yeah."

"He's just a jackass. Hates Kallen, hates me. Probably hates puppy dogs and sunshine. Definitely hates women, people of color, queers." Just those minor things. "We all got thrown on this case together and he's convinced we are blocking his access to the perp. I think he's shaking shit up to see what will happen."

"So just those two hundred reasons?"

"And I saw him throw out an ice cream cone once. Ate half and tossed it." He mimed throwing something away.

"No." I aimed for incredulous. "So he's a monster?"

"Yeah, that's the gist of it."

"So that's like extra motivation to figure out this case before him?"

"To spite him?" he asked. I nodded. "Damn right. Sometimes life is about winning."

"That's not petty at all," I said.

"I know. You have any updates?"

I was debating if I should tell him about Mateo when the waitress delivered our food. I spent the entire ninety seconds she was there deciding that I wouldn't mention it.

"How are those strawberries?" I asked.

"They are a goddamn delight." Reyes speared one and ate it. Like a man. So butch. "So updates on fentanyl?"

"Um, maybe?" Dammit. I dug into my eggs Benedict. Maybe if my mouth was full, he wouldn't follow up.

"What does that mean?"

Or not. I glanced around, but we were far enough away from the other diners. And the noise from the street drowned out their conversations so ours was likely indistinguishable. "If it involves, hypothetically, potentially illegal surveillance, do you want to know?"

Reyes studied me. He did his thing where he pressed his lips together and thought hard. "Hypothetically, what are we talking about?"

"For example, if we had a lead on someone possibly making their own pills in a lab at one of the universities, then maybe Nate and I would install security cameras in that lab to find out who that person was. Would you want to know that?"

"No. Absolutely not."

"Oh, okay. Then no updates."

"That's too bad," he said.

We nodded at each other. It was too bad.

"Maybe Kallen and I will get a hit from Pedro's friends," I said.

"She didn't give me much detail. What's the deal? These are Pedro Morrison's friends, right?"

"Yes. His BFF slash former roommate was at the party. I told him I wanted to jump the guy who sold to Pedro."

Reyes stifled a laugh, then lost spectacularly. "Jump?" More laughing. "You're going to jump him?"

"Oh, yeah. I'm big on violence. I like to punch people. With my fists." I kept a straight face. Like a champ.

"Of course. You're very frightening." He nodded, laughed, nodded again. "So, you're going to jump this fellow."

"But to jump him, I need to find him. Dawson and his boys are going to ask around and find out who the dealer is."

Reyes stopped laughing. "Okay, that doesn't seem terrible." He smiled. "Sorry, I'm still thinking about your punching of the people."

"With my fists."

"Yes, that's important. The fists."

I shook my head. "It's like you don't understand me at all."

"I'm sorry." He took a drink of coffee and composed himself. "All right. So Pedro's friends are going to ask around for you. That's good. It's separated from us. And it will mask our questioning because this group of kids will be asking the same questions."

"And there's at least six of them. All pill users. All college boys. Prime customer base. So they might actually find out who it is."

Reyes looked impressed. "Well done, Braddock."

❖

By the time I got home from brunch with Reyes, the temperature had hit triple digits. This summer was never ending. I turned on the air, got ignored by the cat, decided it was too hot for coffee, and officially hit boredom. I was a drug dealer with no drugs, no clients, and no clean money.

My phone rang and I practically lunged for it. Who knew I was so bad at nothingness?

"Hello?"

"Cash?" The voice was familiar.

I pulled the phone away from my face and glanced at the readout I had ignored. Patricia. Huh. "Patricia? Hey."

"Hi. I've missed you so."

I loved that she could be simultaneously sarcastic and sincere. "I'm sure."

"I think I might have a solution to your problem," she said.

"Which problem would that be? I've got many."

She laughed. "I told you. You're too pretty to have problems."

"Right. I forgot." I flopped on the couch. Nickels jumped up, perched on the arm of the couch, and watched me.

"I believe I have a solution to your money laundering issue."

"You do?" This was news.

"Since that article I told you about— the *SN&R* one—I've had people coming into the gallery trying to sell furniture and such. All old. Most of it is utter trash. A rare few vintage pieces. People are absolutely deluded about the value of the crap furniture they find in Grandma's attic."

"I'm not surprised. People are deluded about most things."

"Yesterday, a woman came in with this jewelry box. Most darling little wooden inlays. I bought it for the shop of course, but she also had jewelry in it. We don't sell jewelry. I would love to, but we can't. When I was younger, I worked in a store that bought vintage wedding bands. I generally know what I'm looking at."

"Why don't you buy and sell jewelry, then?"

"It's a different business model. The security alone is astronomical," she said.

"So you told this chick no?"

"Yes, sadly. But one brooch I just had to have. So I bought it privately, outright."

I tried to work through the implications. Nickels batted at my feet, which was helpful. "Did you pay her cash?" I knew the answer, but I needed to clarify.

"I did not. We agreed on seven thousand. I wasn't buying it for the store and I obviously didn't have seven thousand cash on hand. I wrote her a check."

"Have you ever done this before?" I asked.

"I have. When I first opened the shop, something similar happened. That was nearly a decade ago. Since then, I've privately purchased items on two occasions." She paused as if she were reviewing the last ten years. "No, three occasions. A silver and opal salt and pepper set, a pair of earrings, and a single pearl. The pearl was only a few months ago."

"So the pattern wouldn't be unusual."

"It would not."

"And you have cameras in the shop?"

"I do. They used to only store about a week's worth of footage, but now it's digital. If I forget, the files just pile up indefinitely."

There was the mild issue of exposing Patricia to scrutiny. I didn't love the idea of doing so. But she wouldn't have mentioned it if she minded. "This could make your life very uncomfortable."

She laughed quietly. "You know, I don't think it can."

"If someone decides to look into any of this, you'll be questioned. It's an unfortunate reality."

"No, you don't understand. Aside from whatever privilege I already carry, I'm also currently divorcing a Sacramento County prosecutor who has managed to thoroughly screw himself over. My lawyer is doing everything short of hiring bodyguards to keep anyone with a badge far away from me." She didn't even sound arrogant. She was simply reciting facts. This was the world according to Patricia Chadwell.

"Hmm."

"If a detective wanted to question me," she made it sound like the most absurd thing she could think of, "if they were that dedicated, they would ask approximately two questions, absolutely by the book, then politely ask for my security footage. I'm very kind so I would comply, despite their lack of a warrant."

"You are very kind." My tone bordered on sycophantic.

"I know."

"And your footage would show Nate offering to sell you a ring, or whatever. You would have a discussion, then write him a check."

"Basically, yes," she said.

"And you would be willing to do this?"

"It would be a thrilling little distraction. My life is too mundane."

"Your definition of mundane is interesting."

Patricia laughed. "I know. I think I'll have to imitate Robert and get myself a floozy. Can boys be floozies? I want a gorgeous twenty-two-year-old with muscles and a dazzling smile."

"I'm sure we can find you a boy floozy."

"Wonderful. You do that. I'll meditate on details of money laundering."

"I owe you," I said.

"No, that's silly. I'll figure out some concrete details and call you."

I acquiesced and we hung up. I stretched to set my phone on the coffee table. The movement made Nickels decide suddenly that my feet were made of deception and possibly catnip. She attacked. I froze. That seemed to confuse her. Her claws were on the cusp of full extension, her nails pressed into my bare feet. It was a perfect threat. We stared at each other, poised to react. She relaxed suddenly. Her claws retracted. She licked my big toe and started purring.

"It's not nice to threaten people like that," I said.

Nickels disagreed. The claws came out and she bit my toe. I froze again. This game wasn't fun. The front door next door closed loudly. Nickels jumped off the couch and sprinted for my room.

It was the middle of Robin's shift so Andy must have just walked in. I grabbed my phone and shot off a text. Two minutes later, there was a knock at the back door. Andy waited all of two seconds before letting herself in.

"Hey, what's up?" she asked.

I pushed myself upright. "I got you something." I went into the kitchen and grabbed the Ray-Bans box off the table. When I turned around, Andy was directly behind me. "Whoa."

"What is it?" She leaned into my space.

I handed the box over. Her eyes got big, but she didn't say anything. Guessing wrong would probably make the magical present disappear. She went back into the living room and sat on the couch. She wrestled the box open, shook the glasses case out. It wasn't until she popped open the case that she looked up. Her mouth was open in a little shocked O.

"What do you think?"

Her response was to put the aviators on and run to look in the bathroom mirror. I followed her.

"Dude, they are like totally bitchin'." She turned back and forth to get the full visual.

"They fit okay?"

"Yeah." Andy nodded. As if disagreeing would lose her the bright shiny present forever.

"Look at the floor. Make sure they don't slide down too much."

She complied. They stayed in place. Good.

"Alejandro is going to be so jealous. We watched *Top Gun* last night," she said.

I laughed. "So you kinda liked it, then?"

"Duh. I told you I did."

"Yeah, but seeing it once in a theater is different from showing it to your friends on repeat."

"Yeah. It's whatever."

Wow. All that. I backed out of the bathroom. Andy continued to pose. She could be enamored of herself for hours. Ah, to be young again.

CHAPTER SEVENTEEN

Y ou know I love art and you know I love you, but this is
pushing the limits of both."

Kyra tilted her head to the side. She took a deep breath. "I would really like to argue with you because I think art has inherent value."

"This doesn't have value."

The video looped again. It was two separate videos cut together. One was video of the Gulf War. The second, a naked dude painting himself with latex body paint. At the end of the video—which I had now seen three times—he removed the paint in a seemingly painful manner while the explosions from the war reached their crescendo.

"The more I watch it, the more I feel like I'm just being forced to look at this dude's penis," Kyra said.

"It's like the epitome of white male entitlement."

"Yes. War and dick pics, but under the guise of art."

"White. Male. Entitlement."

Kyra finally looked away from the screen. "I was told that it was inelegant, but the artist showed real promise. That's a direct quote, by the way. Inelegant, real promise."

"And who told you this lie?"

"A friend, an artist."

"Ten bucks it was a dude," I said.

Kyra huffed. "Yes."

"Your friend is blinded by his privilege."

"I'm aware, thanks." She tucked her hands around my arm and leaned into me. "He wanted me to tell him if the kid was worth giving a spot to in his artist collective."

"That's rough. I mean, not as rough as this, but still." We turned away from the wall of screens. It was bad enough that there were fifteen large televisions. The fact that they were high def just made the entire thing painful. Especially for the thirty-second close-up of the guy's scrotum.

The doorway to the rest of the gallery was across ten feet of whitewashed cement flooring. Projectors mounted on the ceiling played the video on the floor. To enter or leave the room, one was required to become a part of the image for a moment. As they hurried past, the viewers cast strange shadows on the floor.

Kyra and I left the room. The rest of the gallery suddenly seemed unappealing. The curator or owner—whoever had cast this space—clearly had questionable taste.

The warm evening breeze felt cleansing. Kyra convinced me to go to the Shady Lady. She slid her hand down my arm and threaded her fingers through mine. We walked a couple of blocks in comfortable silence.

"What are the chances the artist intended it as a criticism of white male entitlement?" Kyra asked.

"Was there some indication that it was meta or analytical?" I was asking myself as much as her.

We went another half a block.

"No. There wasn't. It felt more like he was asking to be reassured of his vulnerability and brilliance. As if stripping was worth something," Kyra said.

"Stripping could be worth something."

"If he were objectified. It was presented as though he expected to be objectified, but it wasn't actually objectifying."

I opened the door with my free hand. Kyra led me inside. It was busy, but nowhere near peak. We worked our way to the center of the room. The bar itself had three sides. The bartenders moved between sections depending on the ingredients they needed. The result was measured chaos. I used my scant height advantage to get Kyra to the bar. She used her pretty eyes to snag a bartender. He handed over my beer and Kyra's cocktail in record time. I looked up through the carefully stacked bottles to the other side of the bar. When I caught sight of Jerome St. Maris, it took me a moment to comprehend his presence. I needed to stop coming to this goddamn bar. Jerome seemingly hadn't noticed me. Maybe that meant he wasn't here to harass me.

Kyra and I grabbed our drinks. Halfway to the door, I realized she was talking to me.

"Huh?"

"What's up? You totally just checked out. That's not like you." Kyra squeezed my hand.

"Oh, sorry. Let's get out of here." I opened the door.

"Are you going to tell me what's going on?"

"Yes." I waited until we were on the patio and well out of Jerome's earshot. "There's a dude who's like my rival dealer. He's been picking off my client list. He was across the bar." I nodded at the now closed doors.

"I take it you didn't expect to see him here?"

I shook my head. "I never expect to see him. But I have run into him here before so I don't know why I'm surprised." I shrugged. "Maybe because he has a Victorian era bar built into his dining room." Shady Lady had a whole mid-nineteenth century vibe going. It was dumb. People loved it.

"He's your rival but you've been to his house?" Kyra asked.

"Oh, umm. I broke in once."

Kyra laughed. "You're interesting."

"Cash?" The question came from behind us. It was unmistakably Laurel's voice.

I turned, dreading the hell my night was about to turn into. Laurel was sitting with a guy who had to have at least a foot on her. He was skinny, but his arms and shoulders were ripped. He was good-looking in that boring straight guy way. I knew an hour after meeting him, I would struggle to describe his features. He looked familiar, but I was certain I'd never seen him.

"Laurel. Hey," I said. Kyra's grip on my hand tightened. I pulled her toward their table with me.

"What are you doing here?" Laurel looked at Kyra, then back at me. Her posture, her tone, everything about her was neutral.

"I was going to ask you the same." I attempted a smile, but it didn't go well.

"Just grabbing a drink." She didn't elaborate beyond that.

"And since my sister is being rude, I'll introduce myself. Lance." The guy held out his hand and I shook it.

"Cash. I'm—" I didn't really know how to explain my relationship to Laurel. Colleague seemed weak. Everything else seemed like a lie. Jerome made the decision for me when he emerged from the doorway behind the Kallens. "I'm Laurel's girlfriend." Laurel and Kyra both sucked in deep breaths, but neither of them said anything to contradict me. "Kyra, this is the guy I was telling you about. Meet Laurel's brother Lance."

Lance seemed confused at the sudden shift, but when Kyra smiled flirtatiously, he did too. Kyra dropped her hand from mine. I stepped into Laurel's space and kissed her cheek.

"What the hell?" Laurel whispered.

"Jerome St. Maris," I whispered back.

She groaned and pulled away. "I'm glad we were finally able to get you guys to meet," Laurel said to Lance and Kyra.

"Me too," Kyra said brightly. "How many times have we already tried?"

"Three at least." Laurel tried to match her tone and failed. "But now it's official. Lance Collins, Kyra Daneshmandan."

A lot happened when Laurel said those magic names. Lance seemed to realize that he was now participating in an undercover operation. He relaxed at finding his role. Kyra realized that Laurel had information. I saw the moment Kyra tucked away her anger. She was going to let me have it later. That wasn't going to be fun.

"Sit down," Lance said.

"Yeah, please do." Laurel shifted a seat to make room for us. I sat with my back to Jerome and hoped that would be enough. I was great at lying to me.

"Cash?" Jerome asked. Laurel and I turned. "And the bodyguard." He smiled at his joke.

"Hey, man. How's it going?" I was aiming for casual. I fell short.

"Living the dream." He shrugged as if living the dream was too much effort. Like he had so much chill he didn't even know what to do with it. He snagged a stool and dragged it to our table. The scraping of the heavy stool legs was grating and deafening. "So what are we up to tonight?"

Laurel looked at me. I looked back. I had no clue how we ended up here and I didn't know how to get away.

"Dancing," I said, inexplicably. I fucking hated to dance.

Jerome smiled. "I love dancing. Where are we going?"

"Badlands." Laurel upped the stakes with the gayest of the gay clubs.

"They have the best beats," Jerome said. "Plus, I always get hit on. Great for my ego. Even if they are just fags." I glared at him. He shoved my arm. "I'm just fucking with you."

"Good one."

"You know, I don't think that's very funny," Kyra said.

"Hey, girl. I'm just playing. Cash knows I love to fuck with her." Jerome smiled with the abandon of a guy who knew he could joke away anything. But he had never met Kyra.

"Be that as it may, jokes like that contribute to a culture of violence. When we aren't accountable for our language, then we lose accountability for our actions."

"Whoa. Someone went to college."

"I have to be educated to disagree with you? That's condescending as fuck." Kyra drained her drink and stood. "I think it's time to go dancing. Like I was promised. You're not invited," she said to Jerome.

Lance drained his tumbler and stood. "Everything she said." He grinned. It was good someone was enjoying this.

I took a drink of my beer. I hadn't even tried it yet. It was good. Laurel stood. I wasn't going to get to finish my beer. I was okay with that.

"Okay. I get it." Jerome put his hands up and backed away, still smiling. "You guys have fun dancing."

Kyra shook her head and led the way off the patio. She curled her hand into the crook of Lance's elbow. Laurel and I fell into step behind them. Laurel threaded her arm around my waist and I threw mine around her shoulders. It was for show. She was stiff. I was stiff. No one was happy. Actually, Kyra and Lance looked quite pleased with the direction their night had taken. They talked and flirted and laughed. We turned up Sixteenth, which finally removed us from Jerome's sightline. Laurel dropped her arm. I did too.

"That was a fucking disaster," Laurel said.

"You're goddamn right it was."

"What the fuck were you thinking?"

"What was I thinking?" I repeated. How was she mad at me?

"Yeah, you can't just bring the chick you're screwing to a bar where a known associate hangs out." She kept her voice low, but I was sure it still carried.

"That's bullshit. You can't regulate where I go. Also, I had no knowledge of him hanging out there."

"We ran into him there before."

"He followed me there before. That's an important distinction," I said.

Kyra and Lance cut through the park connecting Sixteenth and Fifteenth. We followed them, but I slowed my pace to let them get ahead of us.

"If you have to draw distinctions, you're not being careful enough. This isn't something you can participate in when it's convenient," Laurel said.

I was tired of being lectured. I stopped walking. "Fine, Detective. You have an issue, let the DA's office know. They can contact my lawyer."

Laurel stopped and glared at me. She crossed her arms over her chest. Her muscles were tight. I shoved my hands in my pockets and glared right back. This was never going to work if she wanted a puppet CI. That wasn't our deal.

Kyra and Lance must have realized that we weren't following them anymore because they looped back.

"Laur, I'm completely lost here, but we probably need to be a few more blocks away before we break up this party," Lance said.

"Yeah, okay." Laurel didn't acknowledge me. She just turned and kept walking. We were ten blocks from Badlands, but only two from Shady Lady. Lance was right.

We walked another five blocks. Kyra and Lance toned down the whole flirting and laughing thing, but not by much. Finally, we came across an alley and ducked into it. The four of us stood under a sickly orange streetlight and watched each other.

Laurel broke first. Which was probably fitting. "Cash is my CI," she said to Lance.

"I kinda figured." Lance shrugged and turned to me. "It's nice to meet you. When she's not being an asshole, which is rare because she's a total asshole, Laur speaks highly of you." He grinned. "But mostly she's just a jerk. So don't take it personal."

"Thanks?" I said.

"She's not even the biggest asshole. You should meet Logan. He's our younger brother. He didn't want to be a cop like the big kids so he became a lawyer." Lance shuddered.

I smiled despite myself. "At least one of you turned out charming."

Lance brightened. "Hey, that's me, right? I'm the charming one."

We laughed. Laurel scowled. Kyra fumed. This was going to get rough. Well, more rough.

"This has been super fun, but I think it's time for me to head home," Kyra said.

"Wait." Laurel put her hand out. "I should probably explain some things."

"Like what?" Kyra asked.

"Like how I knew who you were. It's not weird, I promise. You just came up as an associate of Cash. You're not in some file somewhere. According to Sac PD, you're a private citizen. That's it."

Kyra relaxed mildly. "But you know my name." She emphasized you. It felt loaded.

"And that's because I'm an asshole, like Lance said." Laurel attempted a smile. "You probably know that Cash and I had less than auspicious beginnings. I tracked her romantic involvements more closely than I should have. I was concerned about the validity of our cover. But that's about me, not you."

That was quite a speech. I wondered which of us Laurel was lying to.

Kyra nodded. "Thank you."

"I'll walk you home," I said.

"No. I'm good." Kyra started to walk away.

I rushed to catch up to her. "Kyra. Wait. I'm sorry."

"It's okay. Really. I'm just not feeling like being around people right now."

"You sure?"

"I'm pissed, but not at you necessarily." She shook her head. "I don't know what I am. But I'll let you know, all right?"

"Yeah, okay. Let me know that you got home safe though. Just text me," I said.

"I will."

I watched her walk away. We had been friends for years. This wouldn't change that. But it felt like a shift regardless. I didn't know what to make of it. I turned back to the Kallens. They both quickly shifted their gaze to the ground.

"So this has been an interesting night," Lance said. Laurel and I nodded. "I guess you two are used to this sort of thing. Since you're all up in the undercover business. But it was interesting for me. Oh, shit. Are you going to have to put this in a report?" He groaned. "My captain is not going to like this."

Apparently, Lance talked when he was uncomfortable.

"No. We don't need to report it," Laurel said.

"But that douche was an associate, right?"

"Yeah, but he's the subject of an ongoing investigation. That was barely a sneeze compared to the rest of his file. There wasn't much worth noting in that exchange."

"Fine, but if you get me in trouble, I'm calling my union rep."

"Yeah, okay." Laurel didn't seem overly concerned about that.

"You two have fun with your protocol debate. I'll catch you later." I backed away.

"Wait. We still need to talk. You were out of line," Laurel said.

"I wasn't, but you are. Right now."

Laurel started to respond, but I chose to walk away.

CHAPTER EIGHTEEN

Nate directed me down an alley and told me to park where there was no parking space. Apparently, we were barbarians. Having finished his job as navigator, he handed back my phone.

We went in the large, open door as per Patricia's directions. The hallway we entered was wide enough to drive a small truck down. It made sense. She moved furniture in and out of her space constantly. It would need to be big enough for large cargo. The building was an old warehouse split into smaller workshops. Presumably, the other mini warehouse units were occupied by similar businesses. Patricia's unit occupied the southwest corner of the bottom floor. We found it and knocked on the doorframe.

"Who's there?" Patricia called from the far end.

"It's Cash and Nate."

"Come in." She popped up from underneath a wide oak dining table. "Sorry about the smell. I should know better than to strip paint when it's too hot to open the doors."

"It's not bad. Just a bit stuffy."

"You should have been here an hour ago. I think I'm still intoxicated." Patricia came around the table. She was wearing lightweight coveralls, but had them unbuttoned far enough to show the flimsy cotton tank she was wearing underneath. "We've never officially met." She held out her hand to Nate. He shook it. "I'm Patricia."

"Nate. It's a pleasure."

"It certainly is." They smiled at each other, a mutual acknowledgment that they were both pretty. It wasn't sexual, necessarily. Just understanding.

"Cash said you have a plan to save us."

"I do. Come sit in my office." She led us to the outer corner of the space. Office was generous, but all of the furniture looked like it was both finished and used. Nate and I sat in spindly wooden chairs. Patricia went to the desk turned workbench and pulled a small gift bag out of the drawer. "Did Cash give you a rundown of everything we talked about?"

"Yeah. I'm a broke college student selling Grandma's jewelry," Nate said.

"Oh, nice detail." She nodded in approval at me. "Here." She handed him the bag.

Nate pulled out two sky blue jewelry boxes. They were worn. One's velvet had been rubbed off the corner, the other was slightly bleached from the sun. He opened the smaller box. It held a pair of ruby drop earrings. They looked art deco to me, but I knew more about architecture from the twenties than jewelry. A matching necklace was in the bigger box. The central ruby was cut to the same shape as the earrings, but larger.

"These are your pieces, I take it?" Nate asked.

"Yes, but I inherited them so there's no record of my possession." Patricia crossed her arms and leaned back against the workbench. The movement stretched her already slender form. I noticed that the coveralls were cuffed halfway up her calf. A partially healed pink scrape across her ankle suggested that she commonly wore them that way and maybe it wasn't a good idea.

"Aren't you and Robert cataloguing your assets?" I asked.

She grinned. "Ah, yes. Our declaration of disclosure. It's quite fun, I must say."

"Yeah. That. Isn't the jewelry listed there?"

She shook her head. "He has no idea what jewelry I own." She tucked back a wisp of blond hair that had escaped its knot.

"So I'm going to take the earrings into your shop?" Nate asked.

Patricia nodded. "The earrings are worth about eleven thousand. Well, the rubies are. The fact that they're vintage is worth more to some than others. Either way, you'll suggest twelve. I'll bargain you to nine."

"What about the necklace?" He snapped both boxes shut and put them back in their bag.

"I'll be so impressed with the earrings that you will tell me there's a matching necklace. I'll be dying to see it. We will arrange an afternoon meeting a few days later."

"And what am I asking for the necklace?"

"Fifteen. Which is unreasonable, you fiend."

Nate laughed and held up his hands. "I'm just a poor boy trying to make rent, miss."

"Oh, miss. Cash, he called me miss," she said wistfully. "Isn't that quaint? So much better than ma'am."

I smiled at the pair of them. They got on just as well as I imagined they would. Under different circumstances, they could have been friends. But this was our circumstance.

"So what will you bargain me down to?"

Patricia looked at him oddly. "Whatever is left over from the money you brought. Cash said it would be just under twenty thousand."

"Except I lied. I brought more." I attempted contrite. Failed contrite.

"Why?"

"Because I'm paying the transaction fee you refuse to acknowledge."

"Cash." Her tone was all warning, no substance.

"It's that or I don't charge you for merchandise. But it will take you a while to go through what I just sold you."

"Okay, I'll consider it."

"Thank you."

Nate tucked the gift bag into his backpack and pulled out a brown paper bag. He crossed to the desk Patricia was leaning against and cleared a small space. He stacked the cash we'd brought. It was a mix of smaller and larger bills.

"We both counted it, but you should check as well."

"I will." She stacked it back up and tucked it back in the bag. "But not now or here."

"But—" I started.

"If it's incorrect, I'll write you a smaller check," she said.

Nate looked at me and shrugged. I returned the gesture. "That's fair," he said.

"Good. Are you available tomorrow afternoon?"

Nate reclaimed his chair. "Sure. Is there a specific time?"

"Between noon and four, preferably. Natalie will be working here in the warehouse in the morning, but she will definitely be back in the gallery by noon."

"And is Natalie aware of what's happening?" he asked.

Patricia chuckled. "You think I'm going to tell my only employee that I'm laundering money?"

"No, I suppose not. So we will be meeting for the first time? And Natalie will be our guaranteed witness? Seems simple enough," Nate said. Patricia nodded. Nate and I stood.

"You're an absolute peach," I said.

"I know." Patricia kissed my cheek, then Nate graduated to a kiss as well. "I'll see you tomorrow."

Nate smiled. "Looking forward to it."

❖

I'd thought a beer would break up the monotony, but it just made me sleepy. We had four different screens playing footage from a week's worth of video of the lab. Our laptops were set on either side of my TV. Nate's TV was sitting on the floor. There was a mess of cords piled on the hardwood taunting Nickels, but she had managed to resist thus far. All of the videos were equally boring. I hit pause four times.

"What's up?" Nate asked. He sounded as sleepy as I felt.

"I'm making some coffee. This is too boring."

"Is there a threshold of boring? Like an acceptable amount of boring?"

"You're annoying," I said.

He didn't seem too upset about that.

I was halfway through making coffee when the doorbell rang. I stuck my head back out in the living room. No Nate. The faint sound of water running came from the bathroom. I glanced that direction. Yep, door was closed. I answered the door.

Shelby.

"Look, I don't know what's going on." She walked in without being invited and shoved a bag of produce into my arms. A sheaf of papers stuck out of the top. "But I don't like seeing him like this. And I haven't seen you, but I'm guessing you're just as pouty as he is."

"I'm not pouty," I said.

"That was childish. I'm supposed to be the charmingly youthful one. You're supposed to be serious and cynical. And Clive is supposed to be like the cool dad who isn't quite like a dad, maybe an uncle. Okay, I guess that's accurate because he's your uncle. But whatever. You guys are all fucked up and it's making me backward. And now I'm blaming you for my state of mind and you know I hate blaming people."

Shelby walked to the couch and flopped. I closed the door she had left open. She huffed at the ceiling. Nate came down the hallway. The shock of hair that fell onto his forehead was damp like he'd dunked his head in the sink.

"Did the doorbell ring? I thought I heard voices." Nate emerged from the hallway. "Shelby."

"Nate," she half exclaimed, half whined. She was able to accomplish a lot of strange, high pitches with her voice. Few were enjoyable. She jumped up and threw herself at him.

"What are you doing here?" He picked her up and spun in a circle.

She squealed. "Put me down," she said in a voice that suggested she did not want to be put down. Nate put her down. "I'm making Cash sign some dumb papers because she and Clive are having the most silent war ever." She flopped back on the couch.

"They are?" Nate shot me a look.

My eyes rolled entirely of their own accord. I set the bag of produce on the kitchen table and pulled out the folder. It was a document gifting a percentage of the farm to Shelby. Clive had done the exact opposite of what I suggested. Whatever. It was his mess now. I grabbed a pen and signed all of the pages with little neon sticky notes.

Nate and Shelby seemed perfectly content to speak with each other so I went into the study. I scanned a copy of the document, then shoved the papers back in the folder they had come in.

"Here." I handed the folder to Shelby.

She took it. "Thanks."

There was no way she knew what she was holding.

"We aren't at war. We just disagree about a fundamental value," I said.

"Okay." She drew it out. "What fundamental value?"

"The inherent worth of human beings."

"So nothing major?" Shelby turned to Nate and whispered, "silent war."

I wanted to shout. I wanted to shake her. I wanted to tell her that friendly Uncle Clive had a chink in his armor and it was going to kill us all. But I didn't. I went to the kitchen and finished putting together the coffee machine. Shelby followed me. She stood in the doorway and watched me move around the kitchen.

"Door is over there." I nodded at it.

"You know, I was going to tease you and leave, but now you're being a dick. Whatever is going on doesn't involve me. I've done nothing to warrant your anger. So don't take it out on me."

I took a deep breath and sat at the table. "What do you want me to say?"

Shelby loomed in front of me. Behind her, Nate sunk into the couch and tried to make himself invisible.

"I don't know." Shelby shrugged. "Tell me you want to fix whatever is wrong. Tell me you miss him. Tell me this sucks."

"Fine. Yes. All of that."

"Whatever, Cash. Screw you too." She turned to go.

"I was being sincere."

She spun back. "You could have fooled me."

"It does suck and I do miss you and the farm. I even miss him. But it's not Clive I miss. It's Uncle Clive and he's a lie. He's a memory from childhood that I just grew out of."

Tears started to gather in Shelby's eyes. "How can you say something so cruel?"

I sighed. "Because he doesn't trust me. It's complicated and messy, but that's the crux of it. He doesn't respect me enough to trust me."

"That can't be true."

"It is. I'm sorry." For a moment, I wondered why I was sorry. I'd done nothing wrong. Sure, I'd violated that unspoken rule of polite society that you always forgive your parents unless their crime is so egregious it cannot be spoken. Even then, they're your parents. You love them, but don't visit. That wasn't the line I was drawing. I hadn't cut Clive off. I was just waiting for him to understand something I'd known for years. It was amorphous and subtle, yet concrete. The kind of knowledge that Shelby possessed, but Clive—in his white masculinity—couldn't.

Shelby brushed at her cheeks. "Well, I hope you forgive him."

"It's not about forgiveness."

She shook her head, swiped at her eyes again. Then she leaned down and hugged me for a long time. Her hair tickled my face. It smelled like sunshine and strawberries. Her fingertips dug into my rib cage. Her arms tightened, squeezed, then she let me go. Nate stood. Shelby went up on her toes to kiss his cheek. She left.

I walked into the living room and sat on the couch. The screens in front of me showed the same two images. The lab, in darkness, from two different angles. Nate moved into my sightline. He held out a mug of coffee. I wrapped my hands around it.

"Tell me what happened," he said.

I didn't really think about not telling him. There was no reason to. I just hadn't yet. Last time I'd seen Clive, I'd been too raw. But that pain had dulled.

"It's not as dramatic as all that." I waved my hand at the kitchen as if it could contain the energy of my argument with Shelby. "Clive thinks I'm being too hard on Henry."

Nate made a strangled noise. He dropped to sit next to me. "Too hard on Henry."

"Yep."

"The guy who beat you up and tied you in a car and tried to kill Kallen and shot at all of us?"

"Yep."

"How are you being too hard on him?"

"Hmm. Well, last time we spoke, I think I called him a psycho. And misogynistic," I said.

"What am I missing here?" Nate asked.

I shrugged. "I've known Henry since I was nine. So like, I guess that gives him the benefit of the doubt? Oh, and he's a nice guy."

Nate stood and stalked to the other end of the room. "A nice guy." He spun and started a full on angry pace. "A nice guy," he said again.

I let him pace. A headache was starting to pound behind my right eye. My jaw hurt. I'd been clenching it without realizing it. I took a sip of coffee. The warmth spread out through my body. The AC had felt pleasantly cool, but now I felt stuck between extremes.

Nate completed another lap across the room. His righteous anger made me feel a hell of a lot better. It was validating.

"Nate?"

He paused long enough to make eye contact. "Yeah?" He continued walking.

"Thanks."

"For what?"

I shrugged. "Being my friend."

He huffed and sat down. "That's dumb. Shut up."

I squeezed his shoulder. "Serious."

"You want me to talk to him? I was there. I fucking hate Henry. Fucking crazy-ass douche bag."

"If Clive needs to hear it from a guy who was there to believe it, he doesn't deserve to know. I told him. In detail. On multiple occasions."

"So really there are two issues. He doesn't respect you enough to believe you at face value." Nate ticked off one finger. "And he defaults to trusting the piety of the white dude." He ticked off a second finger. "Which I guess is the same issue."

I shrugged and nodded. "If he doesn't see that by now, at his age." I shrugged again. With enough time and effort, I could probably convince Clive of my narrative. I loved him enough to try. But I didn't respect him enough to try. That had been thrown out the moment I realized he needed convincing.

"So why didn't you tell Shelby that? She will get it even though your dumbass uncle doesn't."

"She needs to lose Atticus on her own. I can't do that for her. I can't do that to her."

"But isn't there a danger in that? I mean, it's better she hear the lesson from you, right?"

"Maybe. I don't know." I took another sip of coffee. It felt like salvation. "It just feels petty. Like I'm upset with him so she needs to be too."

Nate nodded. "I get that. But, hey, now I'm mad at him too. Does that help?" He grinned.

I smiled back. "Immensely."

"You want to get back to the security footage?" he asked.

"Not in the least. Let's do it."

CHAPTER NINETEEN

All the videos were set to fast forward. For the night shots, any movement looked bizarrely out of place. We had footage of Mateo working until one in the morning after we'd left him. But that was it.

The videos all shifted to natural light. A minute later, a small class rushed in for their lab work. Nate stood and hit a button on the laptops to make them go faster. I did the same on the TVs. We had already discovered that watching the classes do lab work was pointless. No one was going to be pressing pills in the middle of a class. And no one worked in the labs solo during school hours.

I finished my coffee. A glance at Nate's mug showed that he had finished as well. I carefully lifted the mug out of his grasp. He looked away from the screens briefly.

"Oh, thanks," he said.

"Yep." I crossed behind the couch so I wouldn't block his view. I filled our cups and came back. I handed the mug to him.

We went through over fifty hours of video before we found something. The time stamp said it was four in the morning. Somehow that seemed even smarter than going in late at night. Plenty of college students stayed up late. Maintenance crews worked in the evenings. Surely someone would notice a light on at midnight. But there was little chance anyone would notice one at four a.m.

The guy was white. Like Nordic levels of whiteness. He had white blond hair and was pale. We couldn't see eye color yet, but I was betting on watery blue. He was lean and muscled, which emphasized how tall he was. His clothes were dark and slim fitting. Not much to go on there. Basically, he looked like an early Bond villain.

He spent an hour grinding and mixing and pressing pills. Partway through, Nate pointed at the laptop showing video above the workstation.

"Did you see that?"

"What?" I asked. Neither of us made a move to stop the video. We had noted time and date to review the entirety of the incident later.

"I think he just added color to the pills."

"What does that tell us?"

"Depending on the color, he's probably imitating a different pill. That could narrow our search a lot," he said.

"Oh, so we might be looking for a hydrocodone dealer, not a fentanyl dealer or something, right?" We'd known that was a possibility, but the field was relatively broad. Fentanyl was close enough to be used as a replacement for a number of opiates. It could also be used as filler. It was so potent that it could double or triple a batch of existing painkillers—or heroin. If we knew what he was cutting or imitating, we would have something to go on.

"Exactly."

Sunlight started to filter into the lab as the guy finished up. He cleaned the station and tucked his supplies into the leather satchel he was carrying.

We spent a few more hours finishing out the videos, but he didn't return. Nothing else that was worth noting happened. Nate set his long-empty coffee mug on the table.

"You order food. I'll queue up that video on the big screens so we can watch it a thousand times and crack this baby wide open," he said.

"Why do I feel like you don't think we are going to crack this baby wide open?"

"Because we're not. But I thought I'd try out optimism. People fucking love that shit. Maybe we are doing it wrong."

"Solid. Got it. What kind of food?"

"Thai. Do you have more beer?"

"Nathan Xiao, you wound me."

"Huh?"

"I may not remember to buy frivolities like food, but I always have beer and coffee."

Nate rolled his eyes. He pushed up off the couch and started rearranging cords. Nickels finally took the invitation. She shot out from the kitchen and landed, claws out, in Nate's lap.

"Jesus Christ."

I laughed. "Good job, Nickels." She meowed.

"She's a hellion."

"She's perfect in every way."

"A perfect hellion." Nate held out his arm and wiggled his fingers. Nickels jumped for his hand, freeing the wires on the floor. Nate scooped up the cords and dumped them on the shelf next to the TV. Nickels spun back and lunged for the pile.

"Nickels. Hey, sweetheart." I grabbed a mouse toy and tossed it in the air a couple of times. Nickels tracked the movement up and down. I launched it down the hallway. She meowed and gave chase.

"Will you order extra scallops in mine? And no shrimp. I'm over shrimp," he said.

"You're over shrimp?"

"Yeah. It's whatever." He started unplugging and wrapping up cords.

"People don't get over shrimp. Everybody likes shrimp."

"I don't. I'm over it. You know what I like?" He stacked the laptops on the coffee table. "Scallops."

"You're strange." I grabbed my phone and punched in our order. Nate was still fucking around with the TV. It had taken me months to dial in my system. If he screwed it up, I was going to be pissed.

I went into the kitchen and grabbed two beers. When I brought them back, Nate had the video paused on one TV. It showed a dark table. The TV on the ground had the camera above the door. Less detail, but hopefully we would get a face from it. Nate was skipping through video at a rapid pace.

"You want me to pause this one so we can watch them one at a time?" he asked.

"Yeah. There's no point rushing it now." I handed him a beer.

"Thanks." He paused the second video and switched remotes.

We started watching at normal speed. Which was riveting. The food was delivered before we even finished our first run-through. The pills he was making were round, which was common enough. This time I caught the moment he added color to the compound. We leaned forward and studied his movements. Nate paused, ran the video back, and started the segment again.

"Black?" I finally said.

"That can't be." Nate ran through it again.

We watched until he left. Nate ate his scallops. We finished our beer. Grabbed another. The video didn't change.

"Can you think of any pills that are black?" I asked.

"Technically, I think they were more charcoal than black."

"Fine. Can you think of any pills that are charcoal?"

"No. Never heard of charcoal pills. Or black. This is weird," Nate said.

"Okay." I pulled my feet up on the couch and turned to face him. "What if he isn't imitating a pill? What if he's creating his own color?"

"Like branding himself?" He imitated my stance. His feet were bare and his toes were weirdly long. Boy bodies are strange. Or maybe just tall bodies.

"Yeah. Similar to dealers at raves."

"Okay. So we are looking for a fentanyl dealer with black pills? That's abnormal. Kallen and Reyes better fucking love us," Nate said.

"Technically, they are charcoal."

He laughed. "Whatever. So what's our game plan?"

"Call the detectives. Give them a description of the pills."

"And Aryan Nations."

I busted up. "Yes."

"Right?" Nate started laughing too. "'Cause he's Aryan Nations personified."

"Gee, thanks for explaining the joke."

He shrugged. "I know you're a little slow."

"Okay, so we call the detectives. And we're basically the golden boys of CIs, right?"

"Totally," he said.

So why didn't I feel like that was enough?

I looked at the screen. All we could see was the top of Aryan Brotherhood's head. His pale blond hair was parted severely. The stark white line of his scalp shone in the fluorescent light. This was the guy who had killed Pedro. Because he snuck into a lab and played at scientist long enough to make a cocktail that killed people. He hadn't paid enough attention in class to figure out proper dosage, but he had taken notes on how to make pills look cool. It made me want to do more than tattle.

"I still kinda want to nail this fucker."

Nate studied me. "Why?"

"We're drug dealers. So we're bad guys. Whatever. I get that. But this asshole is just selling shit. He doesn't care if he kills someone."

"You're still upset about that kid."

"Yeah. Aren't you?"

"We've spent the majority of my grad school career cultivating a reputation around safe, responsible pill usage. That's not normal, man."

"Yeah. So?"

"Of course I'm fucking pissed about a bunch of dead kids. Like, yeah, my reputation is at stake, but my reputation is built on being the antithesis of this asshole." Nate pointed at the screen.

He made a good point.

"So you want to take him down?" I asked.

"Hell yes."

"I like your enthusiasm."

"So what's the plan?" Nate leaned over and grabbed his beer off the table.

"We need to find out if he follows a schedule or just makes pills when he runs out. Tell Kallen and Reyes to arrest him. Preferably when he's making pills."

"What if he's not the right guy?"

Shit. "That did not occur to me."

"What if we buy pills from him? If we make contact, we can confirm that he's selling fentanyl. And you should still tip off your girl about the black pills."

I nodded. "She and Reyes might be able to confirm some of the details with people who knew the victims."

"So how do we buy from him?" Nate asked.

"Follow him. Make contact. What's the best way to watch the building?"

Nate grabbed his phone and tapped the screen. "There's a parking lot right next to it, but it's staff only. We'll get a ticket if we park there." He showed me the screen. It was a map of the school.

"Can you see the entrance from the lot?" I hadn't bothered to look at my surroundings when we were there. Which was probably a bad thing in life or whatever.

"Yeah." He pointed at the necessary spot on the map.

"Are there any other entrances to the building?" I studied the outline of the building.

"On the other side, but I'm pretty sure they lock it at night."

"Don't they lock both entrances? How's Aryan Nations getting in?" I asked.

"His keycard to get to the upper levels. It unlocks the front entrance." Nate closed out the photo and dropped his phone in his lap.

"Okay, I have a plan."

"Okay?" Nate waited.

"We're going to buy a van."

"While I'm sure that's good for surveillance, it's still going to get ticketed in the staff lot."

"We aren't going to park it until three a.m. Then we'll leave at seven. I doubt the campus police will ticket us. Besides, if they do, I'll just pay the ticket," I said.

"Oh."

"As long as they don't tow us, it will be fine."

"All right." He unlocked the phone and pulled up Craigslist. "Van."

"Work van, not mini."

"Got it." He typed.

"Preferably white."

"So you don't want one with a mural? Because I've always appreciated a good van mural."

"Of course I want a fucking mural. But only if it lights up." I grabbed my phone and typed in Craigslist too.

He chuckled but didn't look up from his phone. "Built in lights. That sounds classy."

"We are classy motherfuckers."

"You're goddamn right."

"Where are you looking?" I asked.

"Yolo County. You should look in Sac."

We started combing through ads. Nate switched to Placer County and I switched to El Dorado. After thirty minutes, we'd sent five emails and just as many text messages. I got a response as I was sending my last email.

"I got a text back," I said.

"Cool, which one?"

"White, ten years old, two hundred thousand miles. Looks mildly sad, but in a nondescript way." I pulled the ad back up and handed Nate the phone.

He scrolled through the ad. "Looks boring as hell. Set it up."

I texted the owner and told them I was available. They didn't judge me for van shopping at six o'clock on a Friday. Then again, I didn't judge them for responding so quickly on a Friday evening either. We both clearly made poor life choices.

"We have an hour. The van is in Orangevale."

Nate scoffed. "There is nothing sad about what you just said."

"Huh?"

"Isn't Orangevale that depressing little town that's not as charming as Fair Oaks and not as shiny and new as Folsom? It's just cheap smog checks, cheap tires, and cheap car stereos."

He was right. Orangevale was bookended by suburban towns that were better at being suburban. Which was a pretty sad race to win at, but an even sadder race to lose.

CHAPTER TWENTY

Nate smacked my arm and I jerked awake.
"Hell no. I am not doing this alone," he said.

"I wasn't asleep. I'm fine."

"Sit up. Eat this." He handed me a bag of Lemonheads.

I pushed myself into a more upright position. "I don't want to eat that."

"It will keep you awake." He shook the bag.

"My teeth already hurt from the amount of candy I've consumed. I told you to get stakeout food." I rummaged in the grocery bag between our seats. "All of this is candy."

"I don't understand the problem." Nate ripped into a bag of Red Vines. "Sugar is the perfect food for a stakeout. It's not filling. It keeps you awake. And it's tasty." He punctuated each point with a whip of his Red Vine.

"Candy makes your teeth feel disgusting and it serves no purpose."

"What would you have gotten?"

"Grapes," I said.

"Grapes?"

"Yeah. They are hydrating, but don't make you have to pee. You can eat a million without feeling like crap."

"When have you ever seen a movie where they are getting ready for a stakeout and one badass looks at the other badass and says 'okay, I'll get the grapes'?"

"I haven't. But I have seen them bring jars on stakeouts. To pee in. So I'll pass on that."

"You are so boring," he said.

I stared at the time until it clicked to 4:17 from 4:16. I was pretty sure this stakeout was boring and it had nothing to do with me. The building we were watching opened into a quad ringed by other buildings. All of them were dark, including the one we were watching. In the video, Aryan had showed up at exactly four. But since we only had one incidence to go off, we had no clue if that was his norm. When we had parked, Nate walked around the building to see if any lights were on. None were.

The clock turned to 4:18. Still no sign of Aryan.

"Did you tell your girl about the black pills?"

I shook my head. "Not yet. I'll call Reyes today. After I sleep."

"Why Reyes? Isn't that the advantage of screwing the detective you're working for? You can send her messages at all hours?"

"I'm not sleeping with Kallen."

"Okay." He drew it out like he didn't believe me.

"Plus, we had a run-in a couple nights ago."

Nate turned and stared at me. Even in the low ambient light, I could see that his eyes were comically big. "A run-in? What happened?"

I shrugged. "Kyra dragged me to a gallery. It was crap so we went for drinks at the Shady Lady. We ran into Jerome."

"What?" His tone got real.

"And then we ran into Kallen and her cop brother."

"Are you fucking serious right now?" he asked.

"Yeah. Why?"

"You didn't think to mention this before?"

"It wasn't a big deal. But she's kinda mad at me so I don't want to push it by texting ambiguous shit that I can't explain the origin of."

"You need to make her un-mad at you."

It was my turn to stare wide-eyed. "I thought you were totally against any sort of relationship between her and me."

"No, I said I have a right to hate her. But we need you to have a relationship with her."

"Why?" I asked.

"Because her guilt works in our favor."

"That's wildly unfair."

"Oh, right. As if you just hate getting cozy with her." His sarcasm wasn't cute at four a.m. Maybe at three it would have been fine, but this close to dawn when I hadn't seen my bed, I wasn't having it.

"Not that. You want me to have a relationship with her, but if it gets too intimate, that's not okay. So either I'm lying to her or I'm lying to myself. Thanks for the wealth of options."

"You know, Braddock, there's this thing called friendship where you can have an intimate, honest relationship and you just don't make out. In fact, that's what we have. We talk. We have fun. We share our feelings. And we have never exchanged bodily fluids. You see how that works?" His level of condescension was just obnoxious.

"I'm pretty sure our dynamic is a little different. Mostly because Kallen and I have already exchanged bodily fluids. It's weird to suddenly stop and pretend that you're just colleagues."

"So you admit that you exchanged bodily fluids?"

"You saw us kiss on multiple occasions."

"I'm not talking about kissing and you know it."

This was not a conversation to have at four in the morning. Which was why I said, "Why are you so eager to know that we slept together?"

"I knew it." Nate leaned back against the door of the van and stared at me.

"Why does it matter?"

"Because it compromises the entire case they have against us."

"Does it?" It was rhetorical. I had spent plenty of time getting busy with that question. If Nate wanted to unpack it for a while, that was fine by me.

"She fucked someone she was investigating. We are the someone she was investigating."

"Are we? Or were we collateral damage?"

Nate looked at me like I was crazy. "Huh?"

"Everyone they've asked us to help investigate, what do they have in common?"

I watched the exact moment he understood. "The supplier. Henry," he said.

"We're just the path to the distributors."

"When they catch him, I'm going to punch him in his goddamn entitled face."

"Get in line, pal."

"So how is this relevant to the whole Kallen fucking you thing?"

"She didn't sleep with me to get information or gain my trust. Hell, she had enough to arrest us the night she first made contact. She waited to see if she could snag a distributor or two. The entire shit show would have turned out the exact same way even if we hadn't slept together."

Nate took a long, deep breath. "You would be less heartbroken."

"That's true."

"So I can still hate her as your best friend."

I scrunched up my face at him. "Are you my best friend?"

"I better be your goddamn best friend."

"I don't know. I like Robin an awful lot."

"Whatever, man. I'm your bro. She can be your chick best friend," he said.

It was good we cleared that up. Otherwise, things would have been confusing.

"Should we circle the building again?" I asked.

Nate shrugged and tossed his bag of Junior Mints on the dash. "Yeah, okay." He grabbed his phone and hopped out. We had disabled the overhead lights in the van and taped over the lights built into the door so they wouldn't broadcast our existence to anyone watching.

I alternated between watching the quad where we expected Aryan to show, the side of the building Nate would be approaching from, and all the mirrors to make sure we didn't have company. Five minutes later, there was movement at the edge of the building. I could only make out that they were tall and wearing dark clothes. Then I saw the flash of white rubber from Nate's Vans. He hustled back to the parking lot and climbed in the van.

"Nothing?" I asked.

"Nothing."

We gave it until half past six before giving up. Aryan never showed. I didn't know what to be more excited about: the fact that we would be back in twenty-one hours or that we would be continuing this stakeout until we actually found the asshole. Once we managed that, we still had to figure out a way to buy drugs from him.

I dropped Nate at his apartment and drove the van back to my place. When I got home, I called Reyes before falling into bed. It was before seven a.m. on a Saturday so I got his voice mail like I'd hoped.

"The perp might be a white dude with short, white-blond hair. He's about six feet tall, slim build. Probably a UC Davis student. The pills he's making are round and dyed black or deep charcoal."

I hung up. I had a feeling that was going to lead to a lot of uncomfortable questions. But Reyes knew where I'd gotten the info. Or he did if he wanted to know. Maybe he wouldn't ask. Either way, I was going to get some sleep before I had to engage.

❖

When I woke up, my phone screen was a wealth of missed calls and texts. I saw one from Laurel that demanded I call her. In all caps. So I opted for making coffee and ignoring the phone. In the five minutes that took, I heard two more messages arrive.

I tried to psych myself up, but it didn't catch. I sighed and picked up the phone. Reyes left a voice mail. I looked at the transcript. He wanted to know my source. And he wanted to meet. At eleven. Missed that appointment. After eleven, I had a handful of calls and texts asking where I was.

At noon, Laurel started in. Reyes clearly hadn't called her until after he knew I wasn't going to show. That was nice?

I'd missed a call from Kyra, which I was reasonably certain had nothing to do with the case. Just my poor life decisions.

Buried between all that bullshit was a text from Dawson.

Found him

That was it. The entire message. I hit Dawson's name. It rang and rang and went to voice mail. Great. I hung up. Thirty seconds later, I got a text.

What's up?

I should have expected that. I knew better than to call a twenty-year-old.

U found him? I asked.

Yeah Ps roommate gave me his number told him I wanted to buy tonight you in

Punctuation was so overrated. *Yeah.*

Dawson responded with the address of a party. At least I had something solid to report. Maybe that would distract Laurel. I thought about calling Reyes before Kallen, but he couldn't protect me. And it would piss her off more if she knew I'd called him first. So I texted both of them.

3 at Zebra Club. It was the only place I could think of that wouldn't be packed on a Saturday. It was a sad little bar that proudly opened at six in the morning. But no one would bother us. And the onion rings were good.

Reyes responded first. *Cool.*

Kallen was more conservative. *K.*

I had a luxurious two hours to drink my coffee and take a shower and figure out how I was going to lie about Aryan Nations.

Nate had already isolated screenshots from the video for me. I turned on my laptop. While that was starting up, I dialed Kyra.

"Hi," she answered.

"Hey. How are you?"

She sighed. "Fine. I think I'm still mad at you."

So she was mad at me? At least she was admitting it now. "That's not unfair. I'm sorry you got dragged into my bullshit." I really was. Nate and I had made decisions that led us to where we were. Kyra's only crime was being dumb enough to hang out with me.

"I'm not really upset about the jerk dealer boy." She laughed a little. "Actually, I'm not upset about that at all. It was fun."

"Fun doesn't cover it. Watching you eviscerate Jerome was highly entertaining. It was one of the highlights of my life thus far."

"I'm pleased I could entertain you."

"So what are you mad at me about?" My laptop finished starting. I opened the images I wanted to print. The little rainbow circle started spinning. Maybe it was time for a new laptop. This was taking longer than it needed to.

"You let me flirt with a goddamn cop."

"Oh, yeah." I started laughing. "I know how much you hate cops. I should have given you a heads up."

"That's all I'm asking." She sighed. "So how are things otherwise? Did you and hot girl cop make up?"

"No. I think she's still mad." I hit print. My printer purred to life. Nickels jumped out from under my desk and ran out of the study. The printer obviously had tried to kill her on multiple occasions.

"Hmm." There was a lot of disbelief in that hmm. "I'm sure you guys will figure it out."

Sure we would. Right.

CHAPTER TWENTY-ONE

I beat the detectives to the bar, which gave me a modicum of pleasure. I snagged a table in the back where I could watch the entrance and everyone in the bar. Kallen and Reyes would need to turn their backs to someone. I drew lines in the condensation on my pint glass and waited.

Three old dudes were at the bar proper. They didn't appear to be together, but they knew each other. They had probably been coming to this place since 1983 and hadn't ever considered going somewhere new. That was fitting considering the bar had been outfitted in 1983 and nothing aside from the taps had been updated since. The chairs were heavy vinyl and metal rejects from a conference room. Their angular backs were a shade of pink between dusty rose and maroon. The tinted windows kept it relatively cool, if a little too dark. Then again, it was an old sports bar with thirty beers on tap. They didn't need more than that and a Giants game playing on ten screens. Clearly, it was a business plan that was working out for them.

Two minutes after I'd gotten my beer, the detectives walked in. The waitress saw them sit at my table and brought over the 805 and Blue Moon I'd ordered for Kallen and Reyes, respectively. Reyes grinned at the orange slice and slid his beer over so it was directly in front of him. I'd guessed that one correctly. Why was it that the butchest men liked literal fruit in everything?

"You want to tell us what the hell is going on?" Kallen asked.

"No, I just really like the ambiance of this place. Something about that neon sign that says 'open six am' inspires me," I said.

She almost got up, but Reyes shot her a look. I wondered what had given him the magical talent to calm her the fuck down when she was ready to check out. I wondered if it went both ways. Reyes had never gotten well and truly pissed off in front of me. Did the dynamic reverse?

"Come on, Braddock," Reyes said.

The waitress returned with a basket of onion rings. At least the service was good.

"I've got two avenues for you to explore. First, we are going to a party tonight," I told Kallen. "Dawson set up a buy with someone who sold pills to Pedro. They are meeting at some house party."

Her eyes got wide. "What do we know about the dealer? Or the party?"

"That's all I got." I pulled out my phone and scrolled to my conversation with Dawson. I set it between the detectives.

She scowled. He silently mouthed the sentence.

"Why does he type like that?" Reyes asked.

"Your kid is young, right? She doesn't have a phone yet?" I asked.

"No." He dragged it out as if he was afraid of what I was going to tell him.

"When she gets one, she will text the exact same way," I said.

Laurel nodded. "My sister does it too."

Reyes graduated to a groan.

"So, obviously, I don't have much information. It doesn't feel like a setup, but that doesn't mean anything. I was hoping you could be backup," I said to Reyes. He smiled. My instincts were killing it today.

"Is Dawson expecting you and Nate to kick this guy's ass?" Laurel asked.

I shrugged. "Probably. Oh, I should tell Nate he's coming too." I grabbed my phone and shot off a text.

"I'd much rather we get contact info and make a simple buy," Laurel said.

"Same. Ideas?"

Laurel and Reyes looked at each other. There was a shrug and some facial movements and a noise from Laurel. She picked up her glass and drank her beer. This was Reyes's show now.

"We can bring in someone else undercover," Reyes said.

"Once we ID the perp, you and Nate and I will distract Dawson and his buddies. The other cop will make a buy, use Pedro's name to fish for information, Reyes will arrest as necessary," Laurel said.

Seemed like a solid plan to me. "Why are you so reluctant?" I asked.

"I'm not. It's the best way to handle it." Laurel was lying.

"Okay. Cool."

"So what's the other lead?" Reyes asked.

"Huh?" It took me a moment to switch gears. "Oh, that."

"Yeah, that. You can't call me at an ungodly hour and leave a detailed description of a potential perp who allegedly has killed five boys and put another in a coma and then not answer my calls." Reyes was displeased.

"I'm sorry. I was asleep. I didn't go to bed until...late." I realized at the last moment that I shouldn't give them more information than necessary.

"So what the hell was that?" Reyes plucked the orange slice off his beer and ate half of it.

"Well, hypothetically—"

Reyes groaned. "Seriously?"

"Do you want to hear or not?" I asked. He waved for me to continue. "Hypothetically, we got a lead and we need to do a lot of follow-up before it's worth passing on."

Reyes shook his head and ate the other half of his orange.

"I think we can decide that," Laurel said.

I looked her in the eye and held until she was fully engaged. "I need you to trust me on this one." She took a deep breath, then nodded.

"Okay, so no background." I slid a small stack of photos across the table. They were stills from the video, which meant they weren't great. "It's possible that this is your perp." I flicked a couple of photos aside until I got to a shot of the pills. "These might be the pills he makes. We think the color might be some sort of branding."

"Is there any way for us to help you confirm the validity? Because we can't sit on this for long," Reyes said.

"Can you just stick with the anonymous source thing? These pills are distinctive. Someone has seen them." There was no way Aryan was just wandering around with black pills. That shit built reputations.

"Yeah, but anonymous source only buys a few days. Ionescu and Michelson are going to want our source," Laurel said.

She was right. And I wouldn't be able to disclose much. Ever. "In the spirit of honesty, I'll tell you that I'm probably never going to give you the full story. And the source of this photo probably violates a number of laws. So, you know, heads up."

Reyes leaned back. He played with the damp napkin in front of him. "You know that's going to be a problem, right?"

"Yeah."

"What are you going to do about it?"

"Theoretically, I'm going to confirm the information with evidence outside of my current source. So we need time to make contact and make a buy. Give us a week."

They were seemingly not happy with that idea, but they both nodded.

"I'm getting so good at teamwork," I said.

Both of them grimaced, but neither outright disagreed. Still killing it.

❖

Laurel was early. Nate was late. That was apparently an invitation to review one million intricacies of protocol. She pulled up various maps and images of the house throwing the party. Last time, we'd clearly been off the books. This time, we were going to be covered in about fifty more ways than we needed to be. Reyes was in a van stationed a block behind the house. His range allowed for distance, but that wasn't good for backup. There were two units patrolling the neighborhood. Their response time would likely be faster than Reyes's.

We had been over this information three times already and I was getting bored. Really bored.

"I get it. All of it. Really. You've done your due diligence," I said.

Laurel opened her mouth, then closed it. She sighed. "I just want you to know what we are getting into. Last time we orchestrated a bust, the sector sergeant sent in an officer who was wildly unqualified." She started closing out the images and maps on her laptop. "Not in any obvious way, but he had just failed his detective exam. Again. He was warned about hitting his girlfriend twice in the past year. Not arrested of course, because that would look bad. And eighteen months ago, he beat the fuck out of a drug dealer because he didn't have enough cause to arrest the guy."

"So a perfect storm for mishandling a female undercover detective working with a drug dealer?"

Laurel looked surprised. "Yeah."

"Oakley, right? The guy who took a shot at you while he was fake arresting you? Yeah, I remember." I tried not to recall the image of Laurel bleeding, being guided by two burly uniforms, but it wasn't easy to forget.

"I didn't realize you had seen."

"Reyes and I watched most of it," I said.

She stared at me. I stared back. I was pretty sure we were still mad at each other about our run-in at the Shady Lady, but I couldn't quite nail down why.

"So you see why we need to constantly be aware. Other people might fuck up, but we don't have that luxury."

"Right. Yeah. I get it."

"And there are a lot of moving parts here." She closed the laptop and set it aside.

"You know, if we brought fewer people, there would be fewer moving parts. Just saying." I turned to face her on the couch.

She mirrored my movements. "This is the first suggestion of a lead we've had on this case. We can't treat it lightly."

"And what if this isn't the right dealer?"

Laurel shrugged. "It's been two weeks without a death. It's making everyone antsy."

"Isn't that a good thing?"

"Of course, but our chances of catching this guy are reduced every day." She started to trace the scar on her left hand. She was nervous.

"So you want me wired for this?"

Laurel swallowed and nodded. "Ionescu does. In case we get separated. Do you want me to have Reyes wire you before we get there?"

I didn't understand. "Don't you have the wire?" She nodded. "Then let's just do it here."

"Yeah, okay." Laurel stood abruptly. She bent over and grabbed one of the bags she'd dropped by the door. I took the opportunity to stare at her ass. "Bedroom or bathroom?"

"Umm, why?"

"Because I need you to take off your shirt."

"Right." I realized why she was nervous. Mostly because I was suddenly nervous. "Bedroom, I guess. More room."

She nodded and awkwardly waved me ahead of her. I led the way down the hall. I wondered how bad my room was. I'd sort of made the bed. I knew that much. Laurel paused at the threshold and took a deep breath. There were shoes piled by the closet, but no clothes on the floor. Nickels was asleep in the middle of the bed, which made it look like the messy blanket was her fault. Thanks, Nickels.

"Go ahead and take off your shirt." Laurel set her bag on the end of my bed. When she opened it, Nickels sat up.

I took a deep breath and pulled my shirt over my head. I was wearing a sports bra. With plenty of coverage. This was fine. Laurel carefully didn't look at me. I tossed the shirt on the bed. Nickels was highly offended so she jumped off the bed and took off down the hallway. No chaperone for us.

Laurel and I were alone in my bedroom and I wasn't wearing my shirt. We were totally okay.

"Where is the wire going to go?" I was trying to fill the silence.

"Turn around," she said. I did. "Okay turn back." I spun the rest of the way. She was staring intently at my jeans.

"Verdict?"

"You're going to have to wear it like me."

"What's that mean?"

"You're a T-shirt, tank top type. And it's warm, so layers will look odd. Basically, we can put the wire on your torso, but the transmitter is going to have to go in your pants."

"In the movies, they just strap it to your chest."

Laurel almost grinned. "Even if you put on a baggy shirt, do you think the outline might be visible?"

"Maybe." Definitely. "So in my pants?"

"Yep."

"How big is the transmitter?"

"It's up to you actually." She held up two slim black boxes. One was noticeably smaller, the size of a matchbox. "These are transmitters. The bigger one transmits farther, better, which makes the operation safer. But it's more difficult to hide because of its size, which makes the operation less safe."

"The bigger one is fine. You wear tighter pants than I do. If I'm wearing that, we both will have better coverage, right?"

"Yeah. I mean, my transmitter still has decent range, but not as good as this. Of course, I have more training than you. If I'm separated or stranded, I'll be able to handle myself better." She shrugged. "That said, Nate will be wired. Duarte—he's the undercover kid helping us out. He will be wired. We don't need to worry."

"That's not quite true." It wasn't. We always needed to worry, but mostly I was remembering when she got shot and told her colleagues not to intervene. She had plenty of training, sure. But that didn't mean she was indestructible. "It makes sense for me to wear a larger transmitter, since I can."

"Okay." She looked at the two inches of mint green boxers above the waistline of my pants. "Some of the guys wear it outside their underwear, but I think it's too easily visible that way."

"So inside my underwear? That won't be weird."

"If it helps, I wear it the same way." She raised her arms. Her shirt lifted enough to reveal the wide band of elastic above her chinos.

"It's fine."

Laurel nodded and laid the transmitter on the bed. "This will just take a sec." She started unpacking the magic bag. A tightly wrapped wire with a small microphone at one end joined the transmitter. Next was a roll of tape. Then a tube of adhesive. This shit was complicated.

"Do I need to do anything?" I asked.

"Umm, I need you to lose the bra too." She carefully lined up her supplies.

I looked down. The bra was practically a tank top. The base stretched halfway down my rib cage. It was cut high too. Almost to my collar bones. Which was, of course, why I'd bought it. It worked well under baggy tank tops.

But Laurel wanted me to take it off.

At least Nate wasn't present for this.

I stripped and tossed the bra on top of my shirt. It wasn't a big deal. We had slept together. Half naked was not a big deal.

"So umm, microphone first?"

"Yeah." Laurel carefully unwrapped the wire. The coil slowly dropped to the hardwood floor. She picked up the tube of adhesive and seemed to weigh the two items. "This only takes a moment to set. You just have to be still for a sec."

I nodded. Speaking wasn't currently in my list of talents because Laurel had just stepped tentatively into my space. I shoved my hands in my pockets because I didn't know what to do with them. She dabbed glue about halfway down my sternum. The backs of her fingers brushed against my skin. She made the mistake of looking at me. She stopped moving. I knew because my breathing sped up. With each deep inhale, her knuckles grazed me. And then we were kissing.

Her lips pressed hard against mine. She shifted and opened her mouth. Her tongue pushed past my lips. I sucked on it. She flattened her palm against my chest, splayed her fingertips over my collarbone.

I pulled my hands out of my pockets so I could put my arms around her waist. When I tightened my grip, she fell forward. Her T-shirt was rough and warm against my bare chest. I pushed my hands under the shirt, slid them up. Her skin was smooth, soft. I traced the planes of muscle and bone.

It wasn't until we hit the bed that I realized we had moved. I fell back and she landed on me. Her thigh slid between mine, pressed excruciatingly for a moment, then shifted. I tugged at her shirt. Together we wrestled her out of it. She stretched on top of me. Her skin against mine was exquisite. She kissed my neck, down to my chest, then back to my lips. I rolled until I was on top. She grabbed my ass and held me against her.

The front door opened. The faint creak was enough to make us freeze, then jump away from each other. Laurel backed away from the bed.

"Cash? Kallen?" Nate called.

Why the fuck had I given him a key?

Laurel grabbed her shirt and pulled it on. I found my bra and yanked it over my head.

"Back here. I'm getting wired," I called back.

His footsteps stopped, then the sound shifted direction. I glanced at Laurel to make sure she wasn't wearing a sign that said, hey, I almost just fucked Braddock. She wasn't, but her shirt was inside out. I pointed at it.

"What?" she whispered.

"Inside out. Your shirt." I stood to go intercept Nate.

"Fuck," she muttered. She tugged the shirt back over her head.

I went into the hallway and almost ran into Nate.

"Whoa, hey." Nate grabbed my shoulder to stop us from colliding.

"Sorry. I was just going to ask if you wanted a beer or something," I said.

"I'm good. So we're getting wired?"

"Yeah, it's apparently quite the process." We moved back into the bedroom.

"Fun." Nate looked at the array of supplies Laurel had spread on the bed. They weren't in a neat little line like before, but he didn't know that. "So why are we getting wired this time?"

Laurel shrugged like a casual person because she was super casual. "This environment is hard to predict. We are going in at different times and can easily be separated."

"That makes sense."

"You mind unbuttoning your shirt?" Laurel asked.

Nate looked at my state of undress and shrugged. We were just bros being asked to strip. No big. He unbuttoned the shirt and shrugged it off in solidarity. It was a vintage polyester number straight out of grandpa's closet. We sat side by side on the bed.

Laurel repeated her explanation of wires. Nate nodded along. I was fine. Even when she asked me to take off my bra again, I was totally cool. It wasn't until her fingertips were tracing over my skin again that I wasn't cool. My heart rate sped up. I was convinced that she and Nate could see the rapid beats. But no, Nate just kept staring straight ahead, asking questions about who was stationed where. Because protocol was important. Yep, I was a big fan of protocol.

CHAPTER TWENTY-TWO

Laurel cranked her engine. I slid back a little farther in my seat to accommodate the not entirely comfortable plastic transmitter in my underwear. We had ten, twenty minutes tops before we arrived at the party. We'd given Nate a fifteen-minute head start so our arrivals would be staggered.

"Did you turn on your wire yet?" Laurel asked.

"No, I assumed you would tell me when to do so."

She nodded and took a deep breath. "I should apologize."

"Are the mics in here on?" I pointed at the ceiling.

"No. This light shows when it's active." She pointed at a tiny little bulb next to one of the many defunct knobs on her dash.

"Cool. So you were trying to apologize for our apparent lapse into teenage hormones?"

"For crossing a slew of ethical lines."

"You don't have anything to apologize for," I said.

"I literally just explained what I have to apologize for." She tapped impatiently on the steering wheel.

We crossed under the freeway. There was some foot traffic by the hospital, but otherwise this stretch of town was silent. The address we were going to was on the east side of the Fab Forties. It was close to Sac State, but far enough away that someone's daddy wanted to make it clear that junior was better than living just off campus. We turned off Folsom Boulevard. We would be there soon.

"Last time, I didn't know all of the information. This time, I did. That matters," I said.

"But there's a power imbalance." She wasn't wrong.

"There is. But I have yet to feel like you're exploiting that imbalance. If anything, I'm using your guilt to garner special treatment."

"So the real ethical violation is that, despite being susceptible to your influence, I haven't asked someone else to take over working with you," she said.

"You could. Ionescu would want to know why. You'd have to tell him it's because you want to fuck me again." I grinned at her. She grinned back. We were downright dangerous. "And then I'd get some asshole who would probably break a whole bunch of different ethical violations—'cause, let's be honest, your colleagues aren't known for their impeccable ethics."

"Hey."

"You really wanna get into that one?"

She shrugged. "No."

I resumed my litany. "So you would lose your credibility, your mother would be so pleased—"

She laughed. "Low blow."

"And I'd still get taken advantage of."

"My parents would love you," she said.

"I feel like that wasn't a compliment?"

We turned onto the street where the party was being held. Cars lined the road. In a few hours, it would be open season on DUI arrests. Hopefully, those patrol cars knew they needed to stick around once we wrapped this mess up. Laurel slowed more than necessary. Guess we were finishing this talk.

"It wasn't. That took some argumentative gymnastics. And you made it relatively compelling. Juries would love you."

"Except I'm not wrong." I was carefully glossing over the debate about sleeping with Laurel. There were a thousand reasons why we shouldn't. So why did I still want her?

"You're not entirely right either. Your logic is flimsy. Charming, but flimsy." She parked the car, though I got the impression she would have rather circled the block a few more times.

"So we're going to deal with this in our usual way?"

"Having a discussion that resolves nothing, then ignoring the problem and hoping it will solve itself?"

"With high fives." I put my hand up.

Laurel turned and looked at me hard. She lasted about ten seconds before she smiled, shook her head, and high-fived me. "This is going to be a disaster."

"This evening or our life decisions?"

"Life decisions. Which, for the record, I used to be pretty good at."

I hadn't ever been good at life decisions. But I was pretty fun and I gave great life advice to other people so I figured it was a wash. "I don't know. I saw your haircut when you were fifteen so that's debatable."

Laurel rolled her eyes. "Turn on your wire. Let's get this party started."

We both stuck our hands in our underwear. "This certainly is a party."

"Shut up. Reyes, can you hear us?" Her phone buzzed with a text. She checked it. "Cash, you talk."

"My name is Cash and I love pedicures."

Laurel shot me a look. Her phone vibrated again. "Reyes says you're a damn liar. I don't even want to know, do I?"

"Nope."

We got out and approached the house. It was a small bungalow. Looked like a cheery yellow, but between the darkness and warm glow of streetlights, I couldn't really tell. Voices and music carried over from the backyard. The front door was open. Two straight kids were making out on the stoop. Damn heteronormativity. It was pervasive.

The interior of the bungalow was beautifully restored. A fireplace took up most of the outer wall. The Spanish tile glimmered in the low romantic lighting. To really finish out the ambiance, a frat boy was playing bartender behind a bar made out of cinderblocks and a scarred piece of plywood. It looked like his repertoire mostly consisted of opening beer bottles and pouring from a legit tower of boxed wine.

Laurel shook her head. "Do we know where the guys are?"

"Nate said they were out back."

"Good. I can't watch this."

The frat boy was juggling beer caps. I did a final check, but couldn't see a single bottle of booze. He really had set up a bar for beer and boxed wine. I decided that I would challenge Dawson to order a martini just to see what would happen.

The backyard had a fountain. That was neat. California was in a constant drought so a fountain had absolutely been a good idea. And it was on. Not wasteful at all.

Nate and Dawson had commandeered a table. They lounged around it with five other guys. All of them looked roughly the same. One kid was Asian—Jimmy, I thought. Or James. But they had all clearly been made from similar molds. As we approached, Laurel slowed.

"What's up?"

"See the kid behind Dawson, about fifteen feet to the left? He's wearing the Navajo patterned short shorts and striped T-shirt."

"You just described two different guys." It was true. There were two dudes wearing cultivated, clashing patterns. I had a feeling I could predict the contents of the most recent Urban Outfitters catalogue with disturbing accuracy.

Laurel sighed. "The Latino one. Baby face. Awkward facial hair."

"Yeah. I see him."

"That's Duarte."

I nodded. He did have a baby face, but I was betting that was mostly a result of being a baby. He would only be able to pull off this particular undercover beat for a few years. I realized Laurel could get away with playing young while undercover because she looked like a pretty boy. What was it about androgynous and masc of center chicks that made them read younger?

"Does he know who Nate and I are?" I asked.

"Yeah."

We stopped in front of the boys' table and waited for their conversation to slow. Dawson saw us first.

"Cash, Laurel!" Dawson jumped up. We both got one-armed bro hugs. "Guys, Cash is here." As if they hadn't noticed. "And Laurel. Have you guys met Laurel?" The guys all shook their heads. "Okay, so, Laurel, meet Raleigh." Ironic mustache. "Brando." Ironic name? "Mike." Nothing ironic there. "And James and Jimmy, of course." They nodded simultaneously.

Laurel shook each of their hands in turn. They all looked pretty similar to the last time I'd seen them except Jimmy and James. At the beginning of summer, James had shoulder length, dirty blond hair. But he had cut it to his ears and parted it down the center like a nineties heartthrob. Jimmy had grown his hair out. It was parted on the side also like a nineties heartthrob.

Dawson dragged over a couple more chairs for us. Nate and Laurel sat next to each other. Their body language was open, engaging. They were damn good actors for people who didn't particularly get along. Dawson sat next to me. We were buddies now.

"So when's our guy get here?" I asked.

"He's inside," Dawson said. I hadn't seen any Aryan Nations types inside, but maybe I'd missed him. "I didn't know how you wanted to do this. I mean, this is your territory, so like you and Nate are in charge."

I nodded very seriously because we were taking this very seriously. "Thanks, man."

"So do we just jump him? I can get him to go outside if you want." He was so helpful.

"We will probably talk to him first, you know? What if he's the wrong dude?" Or what if the police want to speak to him?

"But he's dealing pills and shit. That's your thing. Don't you want to kick his ass for that?" Dawson was so sweet and innocent.

"I'm not usually an ass kicking type of dealer, you feel me?"

"But—"

"You remember last spring when you guys had that party and you and Raleigh took all that Vicodin and painted each other into animals?"

Dawson laughed. "I was a lion. Rawr." He flexed. "I won all of the wrestling matches. King of the jungle."

Raleigh looked up. "King of the jungle." He pointed at Dawson and laughed.

"Yeah, but you didn't pay us. You just snagged it from Nate's messenger bag," I said.

"But we had the money. You knew we had the money," Dawson said.

"We did. So when we went to collect and found you guys asleep, we just let it go. Nate came back the next morning."

"And we paid him."

"Bro, that's not the point. We know you guys are cool," I said. He was really focused on the wrong part of this story. "A lot of other dealers would have woken you up or taken photos of you snuggling while in your underwear painted like cats or kicked your asses. We just let you sleep it off and came back in the a.m."

"Yeah, that was dope. You guys are the best."

"I know, man. But you get it, right?" I asked.

"Yeah, yeah. You're a pacifist."

"Exactly."

"But if it's him, we're gonna fuck his shit up massive," Dawson said.

"Totally. Way going to fuck his shit up." I couldn't take myself remotely seriously.

"So you guys want me to point him out?"

"Yeah, we can go in and get a beer or something."

"Why?" Dawson asked.

"Because he's inside."

"He came outside like five minutes ago. He's over there." Dawson nodded across the patio.

I took a deep breath. I'd known going into this that Dawson wasn't bright. It wasn't okay to get frustrated with him for something he couldn't help. Like being an idiot. "Which guy is it?" I looked for white-blond hair, but didn't see any.

"He's got the kinda round glasses and he's real skinny."

That eliminated half the guys. I kept studying faces, wondering if he was sitting or wearing a hat, anything to make it harder for me to spot. "Identifying features? Clothing?"

"Dark hair, curly. He's wearing the cutoffs and gray button up with the pink bow tie."

I would have led with pink bow tie, but that was just me. "Got it." I leaned over to Laurel. "Pink bow tie, glasses, dark hair." I tried to swallow my disappointment that he clearly wasn't the guy from the lab. There were a lot of potential ramifications there. Maybe the guy making the pills wasn't the guy selling the pills. Maybe this was the wrong kid. "Should we approach?"

"I'm not sure yet. Give me a minute." Laurel leaned her head on my shoulder like we just needed to be touching at all times. Really, I think it just gave her an unobtrusive view of bow tie boy. She smelled really good. Which wasn't important right then. "Nate should talk to him."

"Okay. Why Nate?"

"He just sold to a straight couple. Completely ignored the girl even though she had the money."

"Solid. It's a man's world. Hey, Nate." I reached over Laurel to poke him. He turned away from what had to be stimulating conversation with Mike. "You're up."

"I'm going solo?"

I nodded. "Pink bow tie." I looked in his direction so Nate could follow my gaze.

Nate looked back, his lips pressed in a tight line. He had also noticed that this kid did not scream white nationalist. "I'll be back."

If Aryan was distributing through this kid, he might have a whole network of clueless nineteen-year-old bow tie wearing guys. Tracking them all down would be a nightmare. Plus, we would just look like assholes rounding up rosy-cheeked boys.

CHAPTER TWENTY-THREE

Laurel and I went back to our covert watching slash cuddling in public. Neither of us was the public type, but there was something subversive in acting against our basic instincts in order to serve the man, yet getting to make out with a hot chick I wasn't supposed to be into in the process. I listened to the college bros' conversation. Dawson wasn't speaking at all. I spared him a glance. He was blatantly watching Nate.

"Dawson, be cool, man."

He jerked and looked at me. "Oh, right." He jumped into Raleigh and Jimmy's discussion about the virtues of Voltron. Which was a thing I totally understood.

"I think I want a beer," Laurel said. "You should probably go with me, then get distracted by Nate."

"I do get distracted easily."

We stood. I was mildly concerned that bow tie would have noticed our blatant staring, but he seemed completely oblivious.

"Hey, what's the deal?" I asked Nate as we got closer.

"I'm grabbing a beer." Laurel kissed me briefly. It was unnecessary for our cover, which made it more enjoyable. "You cool?"

"Yeah, I'm gonna stay with my boy." I clapped my hand on Nate's shoulder.

Laurel nodded and went inside.

"Hey, man. This is Tony. Tony, Cash."

Tony looked mildly concerned. "Cash?"

"Yeah." I shook his hand. Harder than necessary. This kid knew who I was.

"I was just getting some Molly. You want?" Nate asked.

I grimaced. "Not feeling it. Anything else?"

Nate shook his head. "No, just that and acid. I know you hate acid."

I really did hate acid.

"That's all I sell. I swear," Tony said.

"Yeah?" I asked. He nodded. "You sure?"

"Look." He fumbled in his chest pocket and pulled out a painted Altoids tin. He popped it open and showed me the contents. It was a couple dozen tabs of acid and about five white pills. "I'm not trying to take over from you. I know you've been kinda off the radar, but that's not my game. I swear."

Laurel came back in time to catch the tail end of Tony's speech. She glanced at the open tin in his hand and sighed. "How's it going?" She leaned against me.

"Good." I leaned over and kissed her cheek. "It's not him." I kept my voice low so only she could hear. Well, the wire probably was picking it up just fine.

"I'm getting that." Laurel turned to the guys. She took a drink of her beer and stared hard at Tony. "Get out of here."

"Huh?" Tony tucked away his drugs. He must have finally realized he wasn't going to make a sale.

"Just go home." Laurel shook her head at Tony. "I'll be with Dawson," she said to me.

"Yeah, okay," I said. We watched her rejoin Dawson and his boys.

"What's her deal?" Tony asked.

"You heard the lady," I said.

"She can't tell me what to do." He had looked young before. With that, he lost about ten years. This kid was in the wrong game.

I decided to do him a favor. I shoved him in the direction of the fountain, which I suddenly found an appreciation for. He stumbled backward and I shoved him again. When he was next to the fountain with its glorious running water, I grabbed the front of his shirt and pulled him close to my face. "Listen, kiddo. You're done."

"Let me go." He sniffled, which didn't help his case.

"No." I shook him for good measure. "You're over your fucking head."

"No, I'm not. I can handle myself."

Nate stepped up close behind him. Tony was so focused on my face that he didn't notice until he was pressed uncomfortably close between us.

"You really can't handle yourself," Nate said.

"You guys are assholes." Tony was whining now.

"We are. And this is just the beginning." I yanked the tin out of his shirt pocket.

"Hey." He tried to grab the tin back, but Nate grabbed his wrists and twisted them behind his back. Tony struggled against the sudden constraint. "Hey, let me go."

I opened the tin and upended it over the fountain. The pills dropped straight to the bottom of the pool. The tabs of paper with their cute little designs drifted down to the surface of the water. They floated for a moment before swirling and sinking. The colors bled into the water, briefly turning it pink and green.

Tony hung his head. He stopped struggling against Nate.

"Who is your distributor?" I asked. Probably should have asked that before I dumped the evidence, but I was pretty confident his distributor wasn't Aryan Nations.

"I don't have to tell you."

"Get your head out of your ass, kid," I said.

"I'm not telling you shit." Someone found his big boy pants. Nate pulled his arms up.

"Oww, fuck. Stop it." Tony's voice seemed to be getting higher. Nate didn't stop. "Fine. Fine." He looked around. A fair number of people were watching, but they were giving us a wide berth. "My aunt. She's like a total old hippie chick."

"Your aunt gave you LSD to sell?"

Tony stopped struggling again. He was staring pretty intently at my feet. "I stole it from her," he muttered.

"What?"

"I was visiting her property up in Tahoe. And I found her stash and I stole some."

"What about the Molly?" Nate asked.

"I traded for it at a rave."

Nate and I looked at each other. We were benevolent as fuck. Nate shook his head and grinned. This kid was lucky.

"We're watching you. You're out. If you start back up, we'll know," I said.

"But—"

Nate yanked Tony's arms again. "Listen to her."

"We will know and we will fuck you up." I almost believed me when I said it.

"Okay." Tony went back to sniffling. Nate let go of the kid. He stretched like he was trying to regain his dignity, not just full movement. "You guys can suck my dick." He turned to walk away.

I grabbed his shirt and pulled him back. "Your dick is not a weapon."

"Let me go."

I released him. He shoved me and ran away. I laughed. Nate laughed. Dawson, Raleigh, Brando, Mike, James, and Jimmy all stood and applauded as he ran past. Nate and I rejoined the little group. Laurel nodded at me and smiled.

"He wasn't the guy was he?" Dawson asked.

I shook my head. "Sorry. We'll find him though."

"Yeah, okay." Dawson sat down. The other boys followed suit.

"You guys keep asking around. That will help, all right?" I squeezed Dawson's shoulder.

"Totally." They all nodded their heads.

"I heard it was an opiate, which makes sense if it was an OD. Did you guys hear that?" Nate asked.

"Yeah, that's what P's brother told me," Brando said.

"Oh, yeah." Mike pointed at Brando and nodded emphatically. "He said it was Fan...Fant...Fate..."

"Fantasia," Brando said triumphantly.

"Fantasia isn't a fucking drug, dipshit." Raleigh hit Brando.

"Farma...Flail..." Mike was getting real good at sounding out words.

"Fentanyl?" Nate asked.

"Yes," Mike and Brando said simultaneously.

"Got it. So when you're asking around, see if anyone is dealing fentanyl," I said.

"What's fentanyl?" Dawson asked.

They all looked at me. I was the expert, after all. "It's a synthetic opioid. Like hydrocodone." Blank looks. "Like Vicodin or Norco, but it's a lot stronger." They nodded in understanding.

"Like a lot stronger," Nate said.

"Like sometimes they use it to cut heroin," I said.

The boys all went wide-eyed. "Why would Pedro take that?" Jimmy asked.

I really didn't have an answer for that one. "He might have thought it was something else. Or he was told it wasn't as strong as it actually was."

We all sat in silence for a moment. They were all maintaining a decent facade, but it was clear they were still struggling. I would have been more worried if they were fine.

Laurel held up her beer. "To Pedro."

They collectively reacted like college boys. There was a brief hesitation like they had never seen a toast, followed by an emphatic hoisting of bottles and Solo cups. They all took long drinks, then broke back into their small groups of two or three.

Laurel leaned over and showed me her phone screen. We were being called back to the van. In all caps. That probably wasn't good.

"Is it that late already?" I asked just loud enough for everyone to hear.

Raleigh giggled. "You getting old, Cash?"

"If by old you mean able to rent a car without my parents, then yes."

The other guys hooted and high-fived.

"Okay, okay." Raleigh put up his hands in surrender.

I laughed. They weren't terrible kids. "Actually, we're supposed to work another party tonight." Dawson and James perked up. I really didn't need them trying to tag along. "It's in Davis." They both deflated a little.

"Sorry to be a buzzkill," Laurel said.

The boys waved that off. Nate, Laurel, and I stood to leave. We got hugs and slaps on the back and high fives and fist bumps. It was overwhelming, but sweet. They were trying. Once we got out of the house, Laurel turned back to us.

"We're being asked to go to mobile headquarters. They're moving to a parking lot a couple blocks north of here. Nate, do you know where they are?"

"Yeah, Reyes texted me the location. I'm parked down the street." He nodded the opposite direction of Laurel's truck. "So I'll see you guys in a sec."

The door of the little bungalow opened again. Officer Duarte came out and walked past us. He barely made eye contact. Just enough to acknowledge our presence.

Nate took off down the street. We did the same. As soon as we got in the truck, Laurel reached into her pants, presumably to turn off her wire.

"You can turn yours off too," she said.

"Cool. When can I pull off the mic? It's annoying as hell." I turned off the transmitter.

"I'd wait until you can wash off the adhesive. That's what bugs me." Laurel pulled onto the street.

"So it wasn't the guy."

"No. Not even a little bit." Laurel was gripping the steering wheel tight.

"I'm sorry."

She shrugged. "This happens in every investigation."

"But we didn't even get a viable lead."

"But you did that kid a favor." She smiled at me briefly. "That was kind of you."

"He will probably do some other equally dumb thing to make a quick buck." I didn't think I was better or more enlightened than little Tony. I just had a deeper understanding of the world. A kid like him would get eaten alive trying to deal drugs. But the same logic that led him to dealing would probably hurt him in some other way.

"Possibly. Or this will be the one truly dumb thing he ever does and everything else will be a pale imitation of this stupidity."

"We can hope, right? At least this gives him a chance."

Laurel parked behind the very obvious surveillance van. She spared a moment to stare at me. "You give a lot of people a lot of chances. For a cynic, you're shockingly optimistic."

I stared at her. I didn't know how to respond. Simple seemed best. "Thanks."

She nodded at me, then got out of the truck.

Nate approached from the other direction and pulled into a parking space. Duarte got out of his car too. Otherwise, the lot was empty. About half the streetlights were operational, so that was a win. We knocked on the back of the van. The back door swung open and Gibson jumped out.

"What the fuck were you thinking?" He grabbed the front of my T-shirt and slammed me back into the grill of Laurel's truck.

"Jesus fucking Christ." Laurel hooked her arms under Gibson's biceps and hauled him backward. Which was kind of hot.

Michelson and Reyes jumped out of the van. Gibson threw Laurel off. She stumbled back and Reyes caught her. Gibson came right back at me. I was prepared enough this time to brace myself for impact, but that was about all I could do. Gibson was a big dude.

"Detective, you need to stand the fuck down," Agent Michelson said. He waited a full second to see if Gibson would respond before yanking him off me.

"That bitch needs to answer my goddamn questions." Gibson wrestled with Michelson. Michelson shoved him into the side of the van and held him there. Duarte stepped up close behind Michelson like he wanted to help but didn't know how.

Nate moved into my field of vision. Then Kallen and Reyes stepped in front of him. That was kind of nice. Three people protecting me.

"Cool off, man," Reyes said.

Gibson stopped fighting Michelson, but he didn't relax. "I will cool off when this bitch tells me why she let our best lead go."

"She didn't. I did," Laurel said.

Gibson laughed. "That better be some quality tail, Kallen. You sure it's worth your career?"

"Excuse me?" Laurel said.

Nate started laughing. He looked back at me so I followed suit. "You think Cash would fuck a cop?"

"Okay, everyone, stop talking." Reyes stepped between Laurel and Gibson with his hands up. "Let's not say things that we will regret later."

"This isn't your fucking hippie therapist, Reyes. We all need answers. It's not just me. Your goddamn CI is obstructing justice and your goddamn cunt of a partner is fucking her so she's colluding—" Gibson suddenly stopped talking because Michelson's forearm was across his throat. Gibson started turning red.

"Reyes is doing you a favor so shut the fuck up and listen to him." Michelson's voice was low. It reverberated through the parking lot.

Belatedly, I realized that Laurel was also turning red. I'd seen plenty of emotion from her, but I'd never seen this level of anger. She stepped up close behind Michelson and spoke over his shoulder.

"My CI isn't obstructing justice. You're just a shit detective. Don't blame your incompetence on other people. We can't manufacture evidence to indulge your poor instincts." That was as far as she got before Reyes pulled her away and stepped in front of her again.

Nate leaned against the truck next to me, his body vibrating with silent laughter. I wanted to join in, but Gibson's fixations had officially moved from obnoxious to violent. And he was wrong about the case, but he wasn't exactly misinterpreting my relationship with Laurel. The disconnect between truth and imagination was too dramatic for my comfort.

Michelson finally let go of Gibson. He clenched his jaw, his hands, his biceps, but didn't try to assault anyone. After a moment, he climbed back in the van.

"Ms. Braddock, Mr. Xiao, I think it would be prudent to conduct this interview down at the station," Michelson said.

"Yeah, okay," I said. I was afraid if I didn't respond, Nate would and he was definitely going to laugh if he opened his mouth.

"I'm sorry if that's inconvenient," Michelson said.

It really was. Especially considering we had four hours before we needed to be in our own van in a UC Davis faculty lot.

"Why don't you two head home, get some rest, and we will schedule an interview in the morning?" Reyes said.

Michelson started to say something, but Gibson let out a bark of laughter from inside the van. Michelson shook his head and moved toward the open door.

"Nate, do you mind driving Cash home? I should probably stay and sort this out," Laurel said.

"Sure." Nate grinned and shrugged. He was gaining far too much pleasure from this whole exchange.

"You guys have a super fun night," I said. Kallen and Reyes shot me looks that suggested their night was not going to be fun. "And remember, it's not okay to be respectful toward a CI, but making wild, unfounded accusations is totally fine."

A low stream of curse words began emanating from inside the van.

"You were one of those kids who liked to light things on fire just to watch them burn, weren't you?" Reyes asked.

I shrugged. Nate threw his arm around my shoulders and directed me to his car. He was still quite amused with the turn our evening had taken.

CHAPTER TWENTY-FOUR

When I'd picked Nate up ninety minutes before, he'd climbed in the van and reverently, triumphantly set up a shrine on the dash for a bag of purple grapes. An hour into our stakeout, the grapes had lost their appeal, the shrine had lost its humor, and I'd lost the ability to focus. Nate had been going on for twenty minutes about his Amazon-for-drugs seller and I hadn't processed a word of it.

"Start over. What are you suggesting?"

Nate huffed. "Okay, the reason we got the drugs so cheap is that this seller is known for inconsistencies. Like their pills are always a grab bag of dosage."

"That's not worrisome." That was totally worrisome.

"Shut up. There was a whole section of reviews and descriptions I didn't know about, okay?" He held out a bag of almonds and I took a handful.

"Remember a couple weeks ago when I was all pissed about this?"

"Yeah." He said it real slow.

"I'm over it. I've realized that we are just fucked, so this is our new reality. It's cool." I tossed a couple almonds in my mouth and tried to find a more comfortable position.

"It's cool that we are fucked, got it."

"Good. So you ordered from a bad seller." I waved my hand for him to continue.

"Not a bad seller, a notoriously inconsistent seller. People order from them to sell at raves, just like we talked about. If you want consistency, the price goes way up."

"So we need to order from one of the expensive ones? Which means we need to reevaluate all our costs. Again." I held out my hand. Nate poured in more almonds.

"Or we can keep using Mateo," Nate said. I cocked my head. "It would still be cheaper. And we get the added bonus of him checking every single shipment so we don't accidentally sell adulterated product."

"Well, that's interesting, isn't it?"

"It is."

We stared at each other.

"Is there any downside here?" I asked.

"There's a longer delay. So if we run out, it could be a couple weeks," Nate said. I held out my hand again. Out of the corner of my eye, I saw movement across the quad. "And we are adding a third party—" I shushed Nate and pointed. The almonds he was pouring hit the floor. "Hey."

"Nate," I whispered. As if we could be heard. I slid down in my seat.

Aryan crossed the courtyard. The shadows surrounding him melted away as he approached the building entrance. The moon was blinding against his hair.

"Oh, shit," Nate whispered. He slid down too.

At the building entrance, he paused long enough to swipe a keycard, then pulled open the door.

"This is happening. We found him," I said.

"Duh. What did you think was going to happen?"

I shrugged and watched the windows. I knew there wouldn't be any movement, but my sudden vigilance needed a focus. "I kinda thought he would never show up again. Or it would be like weeks."

"Shit. Yeah. He was just here Wednesday. How much product is this asshole blowing through?"

"A fuckload."

"Okay, so we need to follow him."

"Yeah, but he will probably be up there for a while. How long until dawn?"

Nate checked the time. "An hour."

"So we chill."

Chilling proved to be very difficult. It was very tempting to just call Kallen and Reyes and tell them to arrest this asshole. Or go punch him hard in a soft place. But Laurel had driven her point home about evidence. I didn't want this guy to get off on a technicality. We'd make sure it got done right. And that meant patience.

With fifteen minutes to go, Nate pulled on a gray hoodie and zipped it up. He climbed into the back of the van and carefully opened the back door. I followed him and helped him lift his bike out. He set the bike down, gave me a thumbs up, and rode toward the line of trees at the edge of the parking lot. I pulled the doors shut as quietly as possible.

Two minutes later, my phone rang. I put in an ear bud and answered.

"Hey, I'm in place," Nate said.

I scanned the trees that spilled from the lot into the courtyard to make sure he wasn't visible. "I can't see you."

"Good. I'm going to circle the building, see if the light is still on."

"Cool."

I could hear faint white noise of the breeze in Nate's mic as he rode. A few minutes later, he spoke again. "It's still on."

I pulled up my weather app. "We have ten minutes until sunrise."

"I'll be here. Keep the line open."

"If you're going to say shit like 'keep the line open,' we're going to need call names."

"We do not need call names."

"You're a real downer, you know that?"

"Yeah, I know."

We waited. Nate whistled. The light slowly shifted to the watery blue of dawn. The abundance of light felt overwhelming after straining to see in the dark. I caught movement behind the wavering glass.

"He's heading out," I said.

"Is he coming my direction?"

"I'll let you know."

Aryan pushed open the door. His purposeful steps echoed across the quad. Or maybe that was the unnecessary combat boots. It was the end of summer. Who was this guy kidding?

"Cash?" Nate whispered.

"He's going back the way he came. You in position?" I lost sight of our target.

"Mmm-hmm."

If he was resorting to noises, that meant he was close to Aryan. After a couple minutes, I could hear the air movement again. Aryan was well out of my sightline. I climbed into the back of the van and properly closed the doors. Then I properly closed the passenger door Nate had left partially open on his first sweep of the building. I waited. I really didn't like waiting.

"He just went into a parking structure. I'm dropping a pin."

"Cool." I opened Nate's text as it came in. They were halfway across campus. I hit navigate and started up the van. "Are there multiple exits? What if he leaves and you can't see him?"

"No, I used to park here. Both exits put you on the same road."

"What if someone else is in there and leaves?"

"Stop asking questions and get your ass over here."

I turned the final corner. A quick glance at my phone showed that I was on top of the pin. "Where are you?"

"Here." Nate emerged from a walkway and waved.

I crawled in the back and opened the door. He lifted the bike in. I heard an engine and turned. A light gold minivan pulled out of the lot. Not the vehicle I was expecting, but okay. "Time to go." I left Nate to deal with the bike and climbed back in the driver's seat. The minivan turned. I glanced back at Nate.

"I'm fine. Drive."

I pulled onto the road. At the intersection I turned to follow the minivan. Nate dropped into his seat. "Any idea where we are heading?" I asked.

"There are a ton of neighborhoods out here. Hopefully, he's going home." He tugged off the sweatshirt and pulled on a baseball cap. "Here." He handed me the Massey Ferguson cap I'd tucked into our duffel bag.

"Thanks." I put it on.

We turned on a main road, then got on the freeway. There were some early risers on the freeway, but not enough for any sort of decent cover.

"He's getting off the freeway," Nate said.

"I see it." I took the West Sacramento exit and wondered who chose to live in West Sac when Sac was right across the river. It was like diet soda. It tasted like ass, was worse for your health, and cost just as much.

We merged onto a main road. There were a few cars out. We weren't the only van, which was a plus. It was clearly the time to make deliveries.

"He's switching lanes." Nate pointed.

"I see it." The van turned into a neighborhood, just like Nate had predicted. Suburban mostly, but older. It was that strange blend of a neighborhood built in the middle of a semi-urban area. The type of place that didn't quite know how to define itself. We followed Aryan through one turn, but on the second Nate pointed straight.

"Just pull over and I'll grab my bike again. He's driving slow." He climbed into the back.

I didn't love that plan, but it still had merit. I pulled to the curb. "You have your phone?"

"Yeah." He jumped down and hauled the bike out.

"Be careful," I said, but he was already gone. I shut the doors and climbed back behind the wheel. The neighborhood was starting to wake up. I could hear cars starting and see lights flicking on. Nate would have coverage. I put my ear bud back in and called him.

"Hey, I'm still following him, but he's driving slower than I'm riding, which is an issue."

"Can you stop and adjust something on your bike?"

"Yeah, I guess I could throw the chain. I'm sending you a pin to track me. Don't follow me though. We've been on the same street for half a mile. I don't want him to spot you."

"Okay." The text popped up at the top of my screen. I punched the pin to see where Nate was. Almost exactly a half a mile away. He was weirdly good at spatial relationships.

"All right. I've played with my chain enough. And he just put on his blinker."

"At least he's a responsible driver. The blinker usage really makes it easier to track him," I said.

"Yeah. He probably killed five guys with his lack of foresight, but at least he uses a blinker."

"Exactly."

"Okay, he just pulled into a driveway. I'm riding past. It looks like he's heading up the driveway. Yeah, he just went inside. Come get me. But try not to drive down his street."

My phone lit up with another pin. I shifted navigation to avoid the road connecting Nate's two pins. A few minutes later, I pulled up across from Nate. He walked the bike over and took his time lifting it into the van.

"Is he still inside?" I asked when he got in his seat.

"Yeah. I'm guessing he's home for now. What do you want to do?"

"Well, if he does live there, he's probably going to bed. If he's making a delivery or anything, then he will leave soon. I think we should park and watch for a while."

"Works for me." Nate ditched his cap and pulled on a new sweatshirt. This one was bright blue. "Take off your hat too."

I tossed the cap back in the duffel. Nate handed me sunglasses. It was barely sunny enough to warrant them. We pulled back onto the street Nate had just left. "Which house?"

"It's that seventies style ranch house. The lower half is red brick. The top is eggshell. There." He pointed. "The minivan is parked out front."

I parked about five houses down. There was plenty of movement on the street itself, but the house we were watching was still. The windows were covered by standard white blinds. There was a two-car garage, but he had parked in the driveway. Did that mean someone else parked in the garage? Or was something else in there?

A guy emerged from the place two houses down. He grabbed the newspaper off the lawn and went back inside. These people were up way too early for a Sunday. Aside from that, there wasn't much information to be gleaned here.

We wrote down the address and his license plate. Not that we could do much with that information, but it was better than nothing.

"I'm exhausted," Nate said.

"Yeah, same. Bedtime?"

"Yes, please. If he's been up all night, he will want sleep too."

I started the van back up. "We can come back around noon. Plenty of time to catch him and follow, right?"

"Totally. If you're really feeling crazy, we could order another one of those trackers. You know, the ones we put on Jerome's boys."

"Yeah. I like that."

"Okay." Nate got out his phone and typed a bit. "It will be here Tuesday."

"Cool."

We escaped the awkwardly suburban neighborhood and got back on the freeway. I got off in Davis and headed toward Nate's much more imaginative neighborhood. The traffic held steady. I wondered when church started. People still went to church. I was sure of it. At Nate's place, we decided to keep the bike in the van. It had proved more than useful. He climbed the stairs to his apartment, leaned over the wrought iron railing, and waved before going inside.

I got back on the freeway and headed home. I was way too old for all-nighters. At best, I was about to get four hours of sleep and I was pretty damn happy about it. Nate and I were going to need to work out a better system now that we had figured out where Aryan lived.

Robin's car was parked out front. She'd be on her way to the hospital soon. I parked the van behind my SUV. I was almost to the porch when I saw the Crown Vic at the curb. The doors flung open. Gibson and Michelson got out. This was bad.

"Can I help you guys?" I asked.

Michelson stopped in front of me. His face was carefully neutral. Gibson was grinning as he stepped into my space.

"Cash Braddock, you're under arrest."

CHAPTER TWENTY-FIVE

The good news was they didn't bring me to County. The bad news was they brought me to the station and stuck me in an interview room. Not one of the nice ones with a couch and an unlocked door. My ass was sore from sitting and doing surveillance all night. My back was sore from lack of movement. My eyes were gritty and itchy. So I put my head on my arms and fell asleep. I woke up to an even more sore back and a grumbling stomach. Without my phone, I had no concept of how much time had passed, but it felt like a while.

I stood and stretched. Stretching was awesome. When I finished that, I knocked on the glass.

"You guys mind calling my lawyer?" Shockingly, there was no response. "Okay, great. That's very kind of you. I'll just wait here." I pointed at the chair I'd just vacated, then gave my reflection a thumbs up.

An indeterminate amount of time later, the door opened. Gibson and Michelson let themselves in.

"Ms. Braddock." Michelson nodded at me.

"I assume my lawyer is on her way," I said.

"Oh, do you want a lawyer?" Gibson smirked.

"Yeah, that's kind of why I told you guys on the drive here that I wanted a lawyer. And also why I told whoever is behind the glass that I wanted a lawyer. And also why I literally just said, 'I assume my lawyer is on her way.' All of that was to indicate that I want my lawyer. Was that unclear?"

Gibson achieved a look that was half smirk and half scowl. It was very impressive. Michelson nodded and sat across from me. Gibson hesitated, then sat as well.

"Of course. I'll make sure we contact your lawyer." Michelson motioned at the glass. "May we ask you some questions?"

"Not without my lawyer present."

"Okay." Michelson stood back up. Gibson reluctantly followed suit. They left.

I was tired. And hungry. I had a slew of other needs, but those two were really duking it out for the top place. I put my head back down and tried to sleep. My stomach grumbled. Eventually, I dozed.

The door opened again. This time it was Joan Kent in a suit and tie.

"Hey, favorite lawyer." I grinned. "Don't you love when I call on weekends?"

Kent smiled. "I think these guys only arrest you on weekends to make you sweat. They aren't very nice."

"I agree. Any idea what time it is?"

She looked at her watch. It was a hefty leather number and I immediately decided to start wearing watches. "Just after eleven."

"Damn."

"You have somewhere to be?"

"I'm supposed to pick Nate up at eleven," I said.

"Well, that isn't going to happen." She set her briefcase on the table and sat across from me.

"Any chance you have food in there?"

She shook her head. "Sorry. I'll ask an associate to bring you something." She picked up her phone.

"I'd sell an organ for a cup of coffee."

"Let's hold off on that. You may want all your organs."

"So they are charging me with manslaughter, which is neat," I said.

"You're being very calm about it."

I shrugged. "I haven't killed anyone so that helps a lot. Plus, I've got a super lawyer. But mostly, I've only gotten like three hours of sleep. And all three hours were in this very room." I spread my arms wide. "At this point, if they want to give me a bed, they can charge me with whatever the fuck they want."

"I thought you hated partying all night." Kent took a notepad and pen out of her briefcase.

"I really do. Cameras and audio are off in here, right?"

"Yep."

"Cool. Nate and I are pretty sure we found the guy making pills that are killing people. We spent the wee hours of this morning following him."

Kent stared at me wide-eyed. She wasn't taking notes. "Is there any reason you haven't told the detectives that?"

"Our evidence isn't remotely solid."

"Expand, please."

"Long version? Short version?"

"Cash, tell me what is happening." Oh, lawyer voice. That was scary.

I launched into the long version. Mateo, Aryan boy, Gibson. I neglected to mention my make out session with Laurel. It wasn't relevant. Probably.

Kent started taking notes. There was something rhythmic and comforting in the glide of her pen. I was reasonably certain my words started to slur halfway through, but she kept prompting me with little questions until we had the whole story out.

"What are you going to tell them when they ask about your whereabouts between leaving the detectives last night and arriving home this morning?" she asked.

"I'll stick to the truth and leave out the good bits."

"Meaning what?"

"I'll tell them we had a lead, but we followed the guy and it was nothing," I said.

Kent nodded. "You realize the longer you wait, the higher the possibility that someone else will die?"

"Yes. But that's why we gave Kallen and Reyes the description of our guy. Now I'll give them his address and license plate."

"Kallen and Reyes aren't the lead on the case as of this morning," Kent said.

Blood rushed in my ears. The rapid pounding made it hard to concentrate. "What?"

"I couldn't gather much information, but I got the impression that the sixth death forced Ionescu to make some changes in the investigation."

"Sixth death?" My vision got spotty. Everything was loud.

"You knew another young man died this morning, right?"

"What? No. How would I know that?"

"They charged you with his death."

I couldn't comprehend what she was saying. I understood the words, but they didn't make any sense. "I'm fucked, aren't I?"

"No. You didn't kill anyone."

"Yeah. True. That's good." I was straining for the surface, but coming up with lungfuls of water.

There was a knock at the door.

"They are waiting to interview you. I need you to get it together for that," Kent said. I nodded. "Cash."

"Huh?" I looked at her.

"Can you keep it together for an interview?"

I blinked. "Yes."

"Are you sure?"

Another knock before the door opened. It was Michelson. "Ms. Kent, Mr. Thompson is here. Can I let him in?"

"Yes, thank you."

Michelson stepped aside and a young black guy entered. He was dressed much the same as Kent, except his tie was more conservative.

"Cash, this is Rory Thompson. He's a junior associate at my firm. Rory, Cash Braddock."

Rory set a large cup and a paper bag on the table before reaching across to shake my hand. "Good to meet you."

"You too. Sorry for ruining your weekend as well."

He grinned. "Ms. Kent relishes ruining my weekends. At least this time I'm not in the office."

"Then you're welcome." There was something calming about normal conversation. Or maybe he was the second person I'd seen today who wasn't treating me like a killer.

"Eat your breakfast, Cash. Rory and I will review a few things before we let in the detectives," Kent said. Rory pulled out a seat.

I pulled the bag toward me. "Detective and agent."

"Excuse me?" Kent said.

"The guy who let Rory in was an FBI Agent. Since half the boys died in Yolo and half died in Sac, the FBI is involved." I looked inside the bag. Breakfast burrito. I unwrapped the foil.

"But the angry detective is Sac PD, right?" Rory asked.

"Tall and kind of muscled? Almost fat, but not quite yet. Mid forties. Looks like he just found out that he can't use his penis and his whiteness in lieu of his badge to intimidate everyone?"

Both lawyers leaned back a little. "That was a disturbingly accurate description," Rory said.

"Yeah, we've been getting up close and personal recently." I took a bite of my breakfast. Breakfast burritos were my new favorite food.

"How so?" Kent asked.

I shrugged. "Last night he threw me against a truck. That was fun. Oh, and then he suggested that I was obstructing justice. Which is his favorite thing to accuse me of. Well, it was until manslaughter." Another bite. There was a disgusting amount of cheese and peppers in this thing. It was beautiful.

"Cash, at any point did you consider that I might need to know about a police detective assaulting you?" Kent asked it real slow.

"I did point out my lack of sleep, right? I'm not firing on all cylinders here." For good measure I took a healthy gulp of coffee.

"Anything else potentially relevant?"

"He suggested that Kallen and I have a sexual relationship and that she is helping me obstruct justice slash kill people. He made some vague accusations about Reyes too, but without the whole sexual exploitation thing, they just don't have the same impact, you know?"

Kent massaged her temple. Rory took furious notes.

"Who else was present for Gibson's assault and accusations?" Rory asked.

"Kallen is the one who hauled Gibson off me. Reyes stopped Gibson from assaulting Kallen. Nate thought the whole thing was hilarious and helped no one. But Michelson is the one who forced Gibson to get under control. Duarte was there too, but that's kind of like saying there was a puppy there. Cute, but no substance."

"Nate is Nathan Xiao, your associate, correct?" Rory asked. I nodded. "And Michelson is the FBI lead on the case?" I nodded again. "Is there any other information you have that might demonstrate Gibson's inappropriate fixation on you?"

I pressed my lips together. I really buried the lede here. "I filed a formal complaint against him a couple weeks ago."

Kent took a deep breath. "Why?"

"I was brought in presumably to offer expertise on a case. He tried to bully me into answering a bunch of questions. I asked that either of my handlers or lawyer be present and he refused."

"Which case?"

"This one."

"Anything else?"

"He also suggested then that my relationship with both Kallen and Reyes was unprofessional."

The lawyers made some eye contact. Kent briefly read over the new notes. "Will you excuse us for a moment, Cash?"

"Sure." I ate my final bite of burrito.

Kent stood first. Rory scribbled something new, then stood as well. Kent knocked on the door to be let out.

Their moment lasted a lot longer than a moment. I finished my coffee, considered another nap, but I knew I'd never be able to get back to sleep. I wanted to know who the seventh victim was. Even if I didn't know the kid, it was still a tragedy. I wanted to go track down that Aryan Brotherhood-looking fuckwad and drag his ass in.

Twenty minutes later, the door opened. Michelson propped the door. "You're free to go, Ms. Braddock."

"Excuse me?"

Kent slid past Michelson. "You're free to go. It sounds as though Agent Michelson wants to interview you about an operation last night, but he has agreed to wait until tomorrow."

I stood. "So I'm not being charged with manslaughter?"

"Not at the moment, no." Michelson handed me a manila envelope. "Your things."

I pulled out my cell phone and tried to turn it on. It was dead. That was probably good. It meant they hadn't been able to read my messages as they came in. "I'd say thanks, but you guys are dicks."

Michelson shrugged. "Reyes is downstairs. He offered to give you a ride home."

"Come on. I'll walk you out," Kent said.

I nodded and followed her. We didn't speak until we had exited the lobby. "'Thanks again for coming down."

"Of course." She held out her hand. I shook it. "You might want to consider telling your handlers what you know. Otherwise, you'll be looking at a legitimate obstruction charge."

"I know," I said.

"Braddock," a voice called from the curb.

I looked in the direction it had come from. Reyes was leaning against a Crown Vic and waving at me. I was grateful for the lift. I was. But I couldn't help but think about the last ride I'd gotten post-arrest. Kallen had told me she loved me. She hadn't actually said it, I guess. But that was where she was going. I wondered how I'd gotten Reyes this time. I wondered where Laurel was.

"I'll let you go. Good luck," Kent said.

"Thanks." I headed for Reyes.

"You need a ride?" Reyes asked.

"Yeah, that would be nice." I got in the passenger side.

Reyes went around the car and got behind the wheel. He didn't say anything until we were on Freeport Boulevard.

"Are you okay?"

"I'll survive." I dug out my dead phone. "Do you have a charger in here?"

He dug between the seats until he came up with a cable. "This should work."

"Thanks." I plugged in the phone. It lit up.

"You should probably call Nate. He's worried about you."

"Yeah, I was supposed to pick him up at eleven."

"You're a bit late," Reyes said.

"I know." The phone started up. Half a dozen messages from Nate, two from Robin. I sent Robin a quick text to let her know I was okay. I called Nate.

"What the fuck happened?" was how he answered the phone.

"I was arrested for manslaughter."

"What?" he shouted.

"And then apparently the charges were dropped. Or something."

"Jesus Christ."

"And someone else died," I said.

"Shit. Who? Do we know them?"

"I don't know. Just a sec." I put the phone down. "Who died this morning?"

Reyes tapped on the wheel while he debated. In the end, I apparently won. "Chaz Rapaport. You know him?"

I felt relief. Then guilt for the relief. "No." I lifted the phone back up. "Chaz Rapaport."

"Doesn't sound familiar," Nate said.

"I'll see if I can get a picture for you."

"Cool."

"So I think it's time to tell them," I said.

He sighed. "Yeah, okay. But we should gloss over Mateo."

"Totally. So where are you?"

"Outside Aryan Brotherhood's house. When you didn't show and didn't call, I called Reyes. He told me you were unavailable so I just went for it myself."

"Do you want me to wait for you?"

"No. Go ahead. Maybe one of them can take over this shit show when you're done."

"Yeah, maybe." I hung up. "Nate and I have decided to give you everything." Well, that wasn't true at all.

Reyes nodded slowly. "Good."

"Are you available today? Like now-ish?"

"Sure. Do you want to call Kallen?" Reyes turned onto my street.

I didn't really. But I couldn't very well tell him that. I tapped Laurel's name on my screen.

"Hey, are you okay?" She almost sounded breathless.

"I'll live."

"I'm so sorry. I—We tried to stop it, but our hands were tied."

"It's fine. I just need to wash these clothes twice and take a shower and I'll be good."

She laughed briefly, stifled it. "Are you sure? I can come over."

Too late, I realized Reyes could probably hear. Which was fine. It was an innocent request.

"Actually, that's why I'm calling. Reyes and I are headed to my place. I need to tell you guys some stuff. Are you available?"

"Of course." Her tone shifted dramatically. "Now?"

"Yes."

"I'll see you soon." She hung up.

"She's on her way." I looked up and realized we were parked in front of my house.

"Cool," Reyes said.

"So this car."

He nodded. "I should park it a couple blocks away, right?"

"If you don't mind."

"It's all good. I'll just walk back. You've had too many cop cars hanging around."

"I'm going to jump in the shower. I'll leave the door unlocked."

Reyes nodded and I got out of the car. "Hey, Cash?"

I leaned back down. "Yeah?"

"You sure you're okay?"

"You kidding? I love erroneous early morning arrests. It's right up there with ignorant people and strobe lights."

CHAPTER TWENTY-SIX

When I got out of the shower, I could hear voices. I quickly got dressed. Reyes and Kallen were sitting on my couch. They'd helped themselves to beer, which didn't upset me. Mostly because there was an unopened bag of food on the table that looked like it came from Burgers and Brew. Laurel saw me standing in the hallway and jumped up. It seemed involuntary.

"I brought lunch," she said as if it was a reason to stand so suddenly.

"I see."

"Lucas said we weren't waiting for Nate." She went into the kitchen and started unpacking the food.

"Yeah, he's on a stakeout."

Laurel stopped unpacking and came out of the kitchen to stare at me. Reyes looked up from his phone.

"A stakeout?" Reyes asked.

"For you guys."

"Thanks?" Laurel said.

"It's your perp." They both nodded like they were following, but they weren't following. "In fact, he would probably appreciate some help. We should get moving."

Laurel shook her head and went back in the kitchen. Reyes followed her. I let them distribute food while I set up the appropriate video. That was probably the best starting point.

I was still skipping through the video when they came back. Laurel handed me a sweating beer. Reyes set a plate on the coffee table for me.

"Okay. What the hell is going on?" Laurel asked.

"We got a tip that someone was making pills in a lab at UC Davis." I blew right past Mateo's involvement. That was good. "There's really only one lab with the right equipment, so Nate and I installed cameras one night."

They exchanged a look. "You know that won't be admissible in court," Laurel said.

"Yes, but that's your problem, not mine."

Reyes grinned. "So what did you find?"

"This." I sat next to them on the couch and hit play. At normal speed, the video of Aryan took a long time. I fast forwarded through the slow parts. I knew they would end up taking the video and watching it on repeat until they caught the bastard. Even with fast forwarding, I managed to finish my burger and fries and move on to Laurel's fries before it was over.

"We need to ID this guy," Reyes said to Laurel.

She nodded and turned to me. "We tried with the images you gave us before, but we couldn't find anything."

"Here's his address and license plate. That will help." I handed a slip of paper to Laurel. She scanned it rapidly, then showed it to Reyes. He read it and nodded. She pocketed it.

"How did you find this?" she asked.

"We watched the building at four a.m. until Aryan Nations showed, then followed him home. You're welcome, by the way."

"Is that where you were this morning before Michelson and Gibson arrested you?" Reyes asked.

"Yeah. This video is from Wednesday morning. With today, that adds Sunday morning. Still no idea if that's a standing engagement or if it's random."

"What time did you start watching the building?"

I shrugged. "Just after three." They exchanged a look. "Jesus Christ. Just ask what you want to ask."

Reyes looked sheepish. "Can you account for your whereabouts after leaving the party last night?"

"I went home and showered. That adhesive was a bitch to wash off, by the way," I said to Laurel. "I read for about an hour. Then I left around two a.m. Stopped at Safeway for snacks because Nate only brings candy on stakeouts. Picked up Nate, drove to UC Davis."

"So we can't prove where you were at all?" Reyes asked.

"We can probably account for the grocery store trip," Laurel said.

"What the hell do you think I was doing?"

They exchanged another look. "I think you were doing exactly what you said. I just want to account for as many of your movements as possible," Reyes said.

So we were opting for lying. That was cool. "Aside from the grocery store, I can't really prove much."

"That's fine. It's not a big deal." Laurel was reassuring one of us, but I wasn't sure who.

"Okay." Reyes motioned between himself and Laurel. "One of us needs to go to the station and get a name for...Aryan Nations?" he asked me. I grinned and nodded. "Remind me not to say that in front of Ionescu."

"We also call him Aryan Brotherhood," I said.

Laurel shook her head, but she was smiling. "Yeah, no one is allowed to call him either of those names."

"Cops are very sensitive to the whole white supremacist thing," I whispered to Reyes.

"White people are very sensitive to the whole white supremacist thing," he whispered back.

I nodded emphatically. Laurel cleared her throat.

"You also said Nate needs someone to help him out?" she asked.

"Yeah. Another body would probably be helpful. And if you guys want to continue this stakeout business, we should work out a schedule or something," I said.

"Is there anything else we need to do?"

I shrugged. "Not really. Nate probably wants some food. We should bring him some. I need a nap, but last time Reyes told me a bedtime story, I woke up with a pedicure. It was weird."

Reyes started laughing.

"Okay, what is with the pedicure thing?" Laurel asked. We just shook our heads at her. She rolled her eyes and gave up. "Whatever."

"All right. I'll bring Nate a sandwich and follow the Brotherhood around. You go to the station." Reyes nodded at Laurel. "You take a nap so that you can take over the stalking in a few hours."

"Works for me." I loved naps.

"Yeah, sounds good," Laurel said.

I collected the remains of our lunch. Reyes collected bottles and followed me into the kitchen.

"You need help?" he asked.

"No. Get out of here. Keep us updated."

"Will do." Reyes took off.

Laurel picked up the bottles Reyes had set on the counter and started rinsing them to put in recycling. "So you sure you're okay? After this morning, I mean."

"Yeah. I'm irritated, but I'm not worried." I tossed out the Styrofoam containers stacked on the table. "How many bullshit charges can he try to throw at me?"

Laurel watched the water run into the bottle she was holding. She slowly turned off the faucet and poured out the bottle. "I don't know." She sound distracted.

"Laurel."

"Yeah?"

"Why are you being weird?"

She set down the bottle and turned around. "I'm trying to figure all this out. Last night, another kid died. Did you hear that?"

"I was charged with his death, so yeah."

"Right. Well, he collapsed at a party. His friends debated getting him help for a while before someone else finally called an ambulance. Allegedly, he bought the pills at the party."

"Kids are assholes." I sat at the table. "I'll never understand that logic. If your friend collapses, why would you hesitate to get help?"

"It baffles me too."

"So did you interview his friends?"

She sat across from me, settled into her narrative. "Some of them. One of the EMTs was on the call that brought Blake Welter in. He made the connection in time for us to round up people at the party."

"That's good, right? Did you get anything?"

Laurel grimaced and shrugged. "The most common description of the dealer was a Caucasian woman with short hair. About five eight, hundred and twenty-five pounds. Some of the partygoers claimed there was a tall, slim guy working with her."

With each piece of evidence, my heart rate climbed. She was describing me. "Fuck."

"There were some conflicting reports." Her voice went up like she was trying to be upbeat.

"Oh, yeah?" I tried to match her tone. It didn't work out.

"Some people said that the woman was blond. Some said that she was wearing a low-cut top with a whole lot of cleavage. No one mentioned that the guy was Asian. Just that he was handsome."

I grinned. That didn't sound like me and Nate. "That's good, right?"

"In my opinion, yes."

"But your opinion isn't the one that matters here."

"No. The current theory is that you could very easily put on feminine clothing and match the description," she said.

"But I don't have boobs. I mean, not like that."

Laurel's eyes dropped to my chest, then rocketed back up. "I know." She looked panicked at having been caught.

"So basically, it could go either way."

"There's also the timing. We left the party with Dawson around eleven. So five law enforcement officials can attest to your and Nate's whereabouts until fifteen after. Two young women we interviewed claimed to have seen the dealers arrive at ten thirty."

"Okay, another point in my favor."

"Yeah." Laurel nodded. "Absolutely."

"But?"

"Gibson suggested that you put them up to lying."

"Wow. I can see why he's running this investigation. A real detective."

Laurel laughed. It was halfway between release and mirth. "Welcome to my world."

"Thanks for telling me." I knew she was sharing privileged information. I was the only suspect in an ongoing case and she had just given me everything they had. She'd probably broken a whole slew of rules in the last five minutes.

"Yeah, of course. You deserve to know what we are up against."

We. I felt the weight of her trust settle around us. We were in this together. I reached across the table and put my hand over hers. She smiled halfway and nodded.

The sound of the back door opening woke me up. It was still light out, but barely. I could just make out the gray shape of my furniture. A light flipped on in the kitchen. Someone shook Nickels's food container. Next to me, Nickels put her head up. The container was shaken again.

"Nickels, where are you? It's dinner time," Robin called.

Nickels liked that idea a whole lot. She jumped off the bed and ran down the hall. I rolled out of bed, pulled on my jeans from earlier, and followed her.

"What are you doing here?" I asked.

Robin jumped and almost dropped the food container. "Goddamnit, Cash."

I laughed and took the cat food from her. She started laughing too. Nickels stopped eating long enough to stare at us. Then she went back to her dinner.

"So you're feeding the cat?"

"Yes. You jerk. I thought you were in jail. I saw them arrest you this morning," she said.

I started putting together the coffee maker. "I was released. I mean, they might arrest me again, but they need to manufacture a lot more evidence." I hit the burr grinder.

Robin sat at table and waited for the noise to stop. "I was worried my whole shift. Why didn't you let me know?"

"I did. I texted you as soon as I was out."

"Oh." She laughed again. "I may have forgotten to charge my phone. It died while I was at work. In my defense, I was very distraught over seeing my friend arrested this morning."

I shook my head and sat across from her. "You're a mess, woman." The coffee machine gurgled and started to brew.

She sighed. "I know. So what happened?"

"There's a dealer selling fentanyl pills. Seven guys have overdosed thus far. Six died. One is in a coma."

"Oh, no. Are you wrapped up in that?"

"How do you know about it?" I asked. Robin was one of those moms who magically knew everything, but this was a bit extreme.

"I was on shift when two of them were brought in."

"That's rough," I said. We both nodded. It was rough.

"So what's your involvement?"

"I'm being charged in their deaths."

"What?" Robin shouted.

"There's some sketchy circumstantial evidence. A dealer who might fit my description. The victims have all fit the profile of my clients. It's bullshit, but there's a detective who is convinced I'm behind it."

"It's not Laurel, right? Because she must know that's not how you operate."

"Yeah, she knows. There's a whole bunch of politics involved. The lead detective is convinced that Laurel and her partner are at least protecting me. Worst case, he's convinced they're helping me. It's a whole thing. He's a complete idiot."

"Is Laurel going to clear your name?" Robin asked.

"We're working on that."

"How's all of that going?"

I shrugged. "I don't know. I might be in love with her."

Robin's eyes got wide. "Okay."

"I might not. It's very confusing."

"I was mostly just talking about working with her, but that's good information too. Kind of important."

"That's the thing. The more I work with her, the more I respect her. I understand her in ways I didn't before." Behind me the coffee pot beeped. I stood and pulled a mug from the cabinet. I held it up in Robin's direction and she nodded.

"Does she know?"

"Probably." I poured coffee and set one of the mugs in front of Robin. "She's still way into me too."

Robin nodded slowly like she was trying to absorb all of the information. "Andy said that too."

"She said what?" I sat back at the table.

"That you guys were madly in love. And she called you stupid." That was a tame version of what Andy had told us.

I shrugged. "That's fair."

"They've been talking, you know."

"Oh, yeah. I wondered if Andy would work up the courage."

"When you first told me, I was a bit wary. I thought Laurel might use Andy to get information about you."

That was a new angle. I hadn't thought of that. "Why did you let me give her Laurel's number?"

"I could have been wrong." She lifted one shoulder. "Turned out I was."

"You're brave." My phone vibrated. I wrestled it out of my pocket.

"Most parents of teenagers are brave. And stupid."

We laughed. I unlocked the phone and looked at my messages. One was from Nate an hour earlier.

There's two. He included a fuzzy photo. It looked like Aryan behind the wheel of a sedan. There were two cars?

There was also a message from Laurel. I opened it.

There are two Aryans.

"Christ," I whispered.

"What?" Robin asked.

"Nothing. We just got a lead. I need to call Laurel."

Robin stood. "Okay. Be careful."

"Thanks for feeding Nickels." I grinned. Robin rolled her eyes at me.

As soon as the door closed, I called Laurel.

"You got my message," she said.

"Yeah. What the hell does that mean?"

"Exactly what I said. There are two of them. Siblings. Tyler and Alyssa Hirsch."

"Jesus fucking Christ." Even their names were white bread.

"There's more. Tyler perfectly matches the image from the video. He's twenty years old. He's six one. The minivan is registered to him at that address. So that corroborates everything you guys brought us. I reached out to campus security for Tyler's keycard usage, but it could take them days to get back to me. If they even bother to."

"I doubt he used his own keycard anyway."

"You're not wrong."

"What about the girl?" I really just wanted to ask if she fit my physical description, but I was too afraid that asking outright would curse it somehow.

"Alyssa is twenty-three. She's five seven. Has short hair. License photo shows a more shag-like cut, but Reyes just sent me an image from the house. The girl they saw was driving the Chevy Malibu registered to Alyssa. She matches the description, but her haircut is almost identical to yours now."

"This is fucking fantastic."

"It is, but now we need something concrete. Unlike Gibson, I like to gather evidence."

"Such high standards."

"I'm crazy that way."

"So we need to continue the stakeout?"

"Yeah. Nate and Lucas split up. Nate is on Tyler. Lucas is on Alyssa. Watching two of them means our lives just got complicated."

"Can you call in backup?" I barely trusted Kallen and Reyes. I was reluctant to include anyone else. But if it got my name cleared faster, I'd make my peace with it.

"I'll have to. Are you still down to help tonight?"

"I'll pick you up in my stalker van at ten."

"Someone sure knows how to woo a lady."

"Yeah. I get that a lot."

CHAPTER TWENTY-SEVEN

Tyler Hirsch was the most unimaginative college student I'd ever seen. He went to class, he worked out in the gym on campus, he went home. I couldn't see inside his house, but I was certain that he took his vitamins and went to bed at nine o'clock. The only remotely interesting thing about him was that he had killed at least six people.

Granted, I was judging him after watching for only a day, but I felt secure in my assessment.

Alyssa had marginally more personality. She didn't keep a strict schedule like her brother, but she wasn't exactly fascinating. Monday morning, she had gone grocery shopping where she apparently paid with cash. I wasn't judging, but I was the only person I knew who paid with cash at the grocery store. That afternoon, she started dealing.

Duarte had spent the better part of the day shadowing her. He had some crystal clear photos of her exchanging a paper-wrapped package for a wad of cash with the bouncer at Club Et Les Filles in midtown. Laurel had to coach the hell out of Duarte to stop him from arresting them on the spot. He was so excited about the entire exchange that I got to hear him retell the story for two hours straight when I took over for Laurel.

We were leapfrogging our coverage. It was wildly ineffective, but it was the only way to cover two perps with only five people.

Including Ionescu or Michelson would have resulted in warm bodies, but it was also a guarantee that Detective Gibson would be one of those bodies.

It was a relief when Nate called to report that he was ready to take over for Duarte. I didn't mind puppy dogs, I just didn't want to drive around with one all day. We made the switch when Alyssa stopped for frozen yogurt. Dealing drugs was hard work. I mean, I never stopped mid-delivery for frozen yogurt, but she was new to the game.

"How was junior detective?" Nate asked as he settled into the passenger's seat. We were in my SUV today. It was less conspicuous than the van for daylight hours, but mostly I was excited to be sitting in a comfortable seat.

"More junior than detective."

Nate laughed. "Has Lady Aryan Nations done anything since selling to that bouncer?"

"Ran errands. She went to the bank. She went to Target. This girl is all over the place."

"Well, buckle up, buddy. It looks like we are going to the pet store." He pointed as Alyssa turned in the lot for Petco. "I'll take this one."

I groaned. "I'll let you have it."

Nate clapped his hand on my shoulder. "You're a true friend."

"I know." I pulled into a spot at the edge of the lot. "You should try to tag her car on the way in." I grabbed the tracker out of my glove box.

"You got it." Nate took the tracker and jumped out of the SUV.

We had ventured outside of midtown into Natomas. I understood it. Running errands was a lot easier in suburbia than midtown. But of all the suburban options, Natomas was nowhere near the top of my list.

Nate strode toward the entrance to the store. He stopped to tie his shoe behind Alyssa's car. It was a tried and true method. He stood and continued into the store. I pulled up the tracker app. The second dot on the map was stationary.

I drummed my fingers on the steering wheel. I drank some water. I watched the entrance of the pet store intently. This was Olympic level boring. Alyssa finally emerged. The reusable bag that had been tucked under her arm on the way in now held something. She climbed in the Malibu and spent a few minutes rummaging in the front seat. Nate emerged from the store and wound his way through the lot toward me. She finally got back on the road. We followed her.

"So Alyssa has a fish and the fish now has food," Nate said.

"That is absolutely relevant information. I'm glad we were able to confirm that detail."

"Same. We are going to blow this case wide open."

Alyssa turned into a neighborhood without warning. She did not drive as safely as her brother. We made the turn, but I pulled into a driveway a few houses down. When she turned again, Nate gave me the go-ahead to follow her. We went a whopping quarter mile before we spotted her car parked in a driveway. The house was a cookie-cutter single level built in approximately 1997. It looked exactly like a house across the street. Next door was a mirror image of the house. On the other side there was a two-story version. We parked on the street and watched. Nate handed me a pair of binoculars. He got out Duarte's camera with its impressive telephoto.

There was no movement in the house. To be fair, it was two o'clock on a Monday afternoon. There wasn't much movement in general. Twenty minutes later, I wasn't sure if I was still awake. I wasn't entirely sure I was still alive. The door finally opened. Alyssa stepped out. She stopped in the middle of the walkway and turned back. A guy stepped out. He was mid-twenties, a little chubby, and had no chin. His hair was almost to his jaw, but it looked lank and heavy. It had been at least three years, but Benji looked the same as he always had.

"You have got to be fucking kidding me," Nate said.

"Is this happening?" I asked.

"Yes." The shutter went crazy as Nate took photos.

Alyssa continued down the walkway and climbed in her car. Nate redirected the camera to take a picture of the address. I grabbed my phone and dropped a pin for good measure.

"Hey, Nate?" I asked as I started to follow Alyssa again.

"Yeah?"

"We just found Benji Nelson."

"Yeah, we fucking did."

We high-fived.

Benji was a generally useless human. Smart, but just enough that he could see the truth in the world. He really didn't like seeing the truth so he did his damnedest to be high most of the time to keep himself from seeing said truth. Some people turned to activism. Some people ran for office. Some people just worked on their listening skills. But not Benji. He built a blanket fort and crawled inside.

Last time we'd seen him, he had grabbed my messenger bag at a party. It had about five hundred bucks and an equal amount of pills. And I liked that bag. Nate and I gave chase. I was pretty sure Benji had no idea he could run that fast.

"Text Kallen. Tell her we might have a lead and we need someone to take over," I said.

"On it." He started typing.

"We are getting back on the freeway. Might be headed back to West Sac." Traffic was just starting to pick up. Highway 80 was a nightmare anytime after three. We were dangerously close to three. At least the traffic gave us plenty of cover.

"Reyes is still on Tyler. He's home already," Nate said.

"Maybe we can just ditch Alyssa there?"

"Totally."

Alyssa threw us for a loop when she pulled off the main drag, but she was just getting gas. As expected, she drove straight home after that.

"Verdict?" I asked.

"Kallen is on her way in case Reyes needs her. She says to go follow our lead." That was worth another high-five. "I can keep an eye on her tracker too. You know, in case she leaves." Nate pulled out his phone and started the app.

"You're so tech savvy."

"Maybe I'm not." He held up the phone, but I was driving so I couldn't focus on it.

"What am I looking at?"

"The tracker is on the freeway and it's not moving. It must have fallen off. Dammit."

"Shit."

Nate grumbled and tapped his phone, but that didn't miraculously reattach the tracker. At least we still had another. We retraced our steps back to Natomas. Halfway there, Nate accepted the fate of the tracker and tucked his phone away.

We got lost in Benji's neighborhood briefly, but in our defense, everything looked beige. I parked in front of the house. Nate triple checked the address. We were in the right place.

"You ready?"

"I've been ready for this moment for a long time. That little shit outran me," Nate said.

We got out and went up the walkway. Nate rang the doorbell. There was a delay and then we heard footsteps. The door swung wide. Benji looked lost for a moment, then his eyes went wide and he stumbled backward.

"Hey, Benji," I said.

Benji stuttered but couldn't seem to land on a word.

"Thanks, we'd love to come in." Nate took a step inside and threw his arm around Benji's shoulders. "How's it going, buddy?"

I followed and closed the door. Nate led Benji through the house. There was a formal dining room with a hutch. Benji didn't live alone. Just off the kitchen at the back of the house, there was a living room. The large screen TV displayed a paused video game. Nate sat Benji down on the couch in front of the TV.

"Is there anyone else home?" I asked.

Benji shook his head.

"You want to go check?" Nate asked me.

"I'll be back. You two get acquainted again."

I went back through the house. There was a hallway that led to a couple of bedrooms and an office. It looked like Benji lived with one of his parents. I opened a couple of drawers in the master bedroom. There were a lot of polo shirts and size 42 khakis. The bathroom held Barbasol, drug store shampoo, and an expired Viagra prescription. I felt pretty confident in betting he lived with Dad.

Benji's room was surprisingly neat for a twenty-four-year-old who lived with his father and had the luxury of video game playing on a Monday afternoon. It smelled clean and the bed was made. He still had posters stapled haphazardly to the walls. Some were more sun faded than others, but all of them appeared to advertise Xbox games. In the center of his bed was a paper-wrapped package. It was a lot smaller than the one Alyssa had given to the bouncer at Club Et Les Filles. I really wanted to open the package, but stupid Laurel had impressed upon me the power of evidence. Dammit.

I went back to Daddy's bathroom and searched under the sink until I found a pack of latex gloves. I pulled on a fresh pair and opened the package. It was plastic baggies of black pills. I left it on Benji's bed, retrieved a Ziploc from the kitchen, and bagged the entire package. That was way easier than trying to orchestrate a buy.

"So, boys, have you caught up?" I leaned against the counter that separated the living room from the kitchen.

"We're sure trying," Nate said.

"Cash, listen, dude, I'm so sorry," Benji said.

"For what?"

"For umm, ripping you off. That wasn't cool. But it wasn't my fault. I had a problem. A real addiction, you know?"

I turned to Nate. "Drugs are addictive?"

"According to this guy." Nate pointed at Benji. We laughed. We were funny.

"So you had a problem? Like past tense?"

"I'm doing a lot better now. I have focus, you know. Friends."

"I want to believe you, buddy. I do. But you're playing video games in the middle of the day and I just found a package of drugs on your bed. So..." I weighed my hands up and down. "You can see why I'm having trouble here."

"I can pay you back. I swear. Just give me till the weekend."

"What's on the weekend?"

"It's this coding event. I'm going with a bunch of my boys. We are starting a company. A friend of mine was supposed to sell those pills, but like he dropped out and moved home. So if I sell those, our debt will be gone." He snapped his fingers. "And we will get some startup capital."

"And if you pay me the two grand, you'll still have enough startup capital?" I asked.

His eyes bugged out. "Two grand?"

"I'd say that's fair interest. What do you think, Nate?"

"Two grand is downright generous. You're so kind, Cash. I've always admired that about you." Nate smiled dreamily at me.

"Thanks, man."

"You betcha."

Benji whimpered. "I can't afford two grand. My boys are counting on me. Please, cut me a break here." This kid had no stamina. I was a little ashamed that we hadn't managed to catch him.

"Why would I cut you a break?"

"Because I just need one." And Benji started to cry. "I finally got clean, dude. It was hard and my dad was so nice to me and we're just starting to really, you know, get along. And I got these friends. Real friends. They like me. They get me." He gave a long, wet sniffle. "We met playing games, you know? And we just got a plan together to start our own gaming company. How cool would that be?" Another sniffle. "And then Will just disappeared. Like gone. And he had spent our money and we didn't even know it." He started to rock. "It was so good and then it got so shitty. You gotta believe me. I just need a win." He buried his face in his hands and sobbed.

Nate patted his shoulder awkwardly and mouthed, "wow."

"Hey, Benji, calm down. It's cool. We're going to figure this out."

"There's nothing." He gasped for air. "There's nothing to figure out." More rocking.

I went back to the bathroom and brought out a box of tissues. When I handed them to Benji, it just made him cry more.

"Just take some deep breaths, okay?" Nate said calmly.

"You're being so nice," he wailed.

This was getting us nowhere. Nate shrugged at me. I decided to try a new tactic.

"Benjamin Nelson, you need to calm the fuck down. Right now." I used my most authoritative voice, which wasn't saying much. But Benji responded to it. He stopped sobbing and took a long, deep breath.

"Sorry. I'm sorry." More shuddering breaths.

"Don't be sorry. I need you to focus."

He started nodding and didn't stop. "Yeah, okay. Focus."

"If I open that package, what will I find?"

"Pills."

So far so good. "What kind?"

"Fen—Fentanyl," he stuttered.

"Are they black?"

He stopped gasping, stopped rocking. "Yes." It apparently hadn't occurred to him that I could have opened the package already.

"And your friend Will. Is that William Seldin?"

The rocking was back full force. "Yes."

"When's the last time you heard from Will?"

Benji shrugged. "A couple months ago."

I really didn't want to tell him. But someone had to. I glanced at Nate. He nodded once. "Benji, Will died."

"No." He shook his head. "You're wrong."

"I'm not. I'm really sorry."

He started crying again. I hadn't handled that well. Nate put his hand on Benji's shoulder again, but the kid didn't even notice.

"Maybe it's time to call your girl," Nate said.

"Yeah, are you okay here?"

Nate shrugged. "We're good."

I stepped out of the room and called Laurel.

CHAPTER TWENTY-EIGHT

We were forty-eight hours, seven vehicles, and five bodies into our stakeout and I was infinitely bored of the spectacle.

Monday had suggested that Alyssa at least had a plan. But Tuesday, she didn't even go out. The Hirsches lived lives of tedium. Or maybe I became less tolerant the more time I spent sitting in a car staring at a tract house.

It had been thirty hours since we brought in Benji. Ionescu had blocked Gibson from the interrogation, which hadn't gone over well. Michelson had spent fifteen hours interrogating Benji and the only thing he learned was Benji was absolutely terrified of Alyssa Hirsch. Enough that he was willing to take a distribution charge over immunity. So all we had done was suck a scared kid back into the system he had finally escaped. All of the cops seemed stoked that we'd gotten black pills to test. But that wasn't enough to feel like a win for me. And it hadn't gotten us out of this stupid stakeout.

Nate continued to check the clock compulsively. He must have been aiming for every fifteen minutes because he had checked at exactly fifteen for the last hour.

"What time do you want to go for it?" I asked.

"I'm thinking midnight. The Hirsches are obviously asleep and have been since seven o'clock." That was untrue, but only just.

"These two give drug dealers a bad name."

"It's disgraceful," Nate said.

"So Duarte and Reyes went home already?"

"Right before you got here. And Kallen is taking over for me at three. You think you can manage to share such a small space without ripping each other's clothes off?"

I rolled my eyes. "I think we will manage."

"Did you see that?" Nate asked.

I watched the house. There was nothing. "No. What am I looking for?" I studied the windows for movement.

"Four houses down. They just turned off the light in the front room." Nate tipped his chin toward the house.

"What about it?"

"That's the last one on the street. And it's almost midnight." He would know.

"Suburbia is weird," I said.

"Yes, it is."

"Shall we do this?"

"Sure." Nate reached behind the seat and grabbed his duffel bag. He rummaged and pulled out a tracker. A small green light on it blinked periodically. "Is your phone reading it?"

I pulled out my phone and launched the app. It used to have six little dots on the map to track Jerome St. Maris and his merry band of idiots, but the batteries on those trackers had died a while back. Now there were just two dots. Why was my business partner such a geek?

"Do you want to install it or do you want me to?" I asked.

"I think we both know I'm your bitch."

I shrugged and laughed. "I'm not going to dispute that."

"Asshole." He climbed out of the van, then leaned back in. "If I don't make it back, tell my mother I love her."

"Mama's boy."

He grinned and jogged across the street. We were a couple houses down. Nate slowed to a stroll. He glanced over his shoulder at me when he got to the Hirsches' driveway. I gave him a thumbs up out the open window. He took a single step off the sidewalk and bent to tie his shoe. I didn't even catch him sticking the tracker to the minivan's undercarriage. And I was looking for it. He continued his walk until he was at the end of the block, then crossed the street again and circled back. That seemed unnecessary. Anyone watching him might have missed the application of the tracker, but his behavior was still weird.

"How did I do?" he asked.

"You're basically a spy. The CIA will recruit you any day now."

"My teenage boy life dreams have been fulfilled."

"So we have a tracker on Tyler, who might be the most boring person I've ever witnessed."

"So that we can watch him go to class and come back home," Nate said.

Oh, good. I wasn't the only one who had noticed. "What about sister Alyssa? Wouldn't it have been better to put the tracker on her?"

Nate smiled. "Remember how I'm smarter than most people?"

"I think about it constantly. Some nights, I just lie awake wondering what it's like to be so smart."

He nodded sagely. "Yeah, I can see that."

"It's nice to know you understand me."

He put his hand on mine and stared deeply into my eyes. "I do understand."

I rolled my eyes. "Okay, so you're smart?"

"Right. Well, I ordered three trackers. As soon as we get another chance, sister Alyssa will also be on our radar. Literally. Get it? 'Cause they are GPS trackers."

"Terrible jokes aside, you're my favorite employee."

"I know."

I gasped. "Who told you?"

"I'm just intuitive." More wise nodding. "Plus you just paid my tuition. It's one hell of a bonus."

"Oh, yeah. How did that go? You just texted and said everything was good."

"Not much to tell." He pulled his bag into the front seat again and started digging again. "Patricia is a good actor. I almost believed we had never met. And I was there when we met."

"The checks went through fine? And you got tuition paid?" I waited to see whatever he was about to take out of the duffel to back his narrative, but he pulled out a bag of jelly beans.

"Yeah, everything went just like it was supposed to. Except sweet shopgirl Natalie asked me out." He poured a handful of jelly beans into his mouth.

"Aww, sweet shopgirl Natalie."

"She's confident, I'll give her that. And gorgeous, but also she is about twenty. Once you pass twenty-five that just seems skeevy."

"It is skeevy. And, you know, you were there to launder money."

"Okay, yes, there's that too. Anyway, I had to tell her no and I felt terrible."

"Such a heartbreaker."

"It's the burden of beauty," he said. I reached over and took his jelly beans. "Hey."

"Sorry. This sugar is clearly going to your head." I ate a handful of jelly beans.

"It's what makes me sweet."

I groaned. "Okay, moratorium on talking."

"You'll be so bored without me talking."

I checked the time. "I think I can survive two and a half hours of silence. In fact, I'm looking forward to it."

Nate huffed and took back his jelly beans.

❖

Laurel brought coffee when she took over for Nate. If I'd had any doubts about being in love with her before, that kinda cemented the whole thing,

"I love you. You're like snuggles and happiness. When I hold you, it's like nothing is wrong in the world."

"Stop talking to your coffee, you freak," Laurel said.

"I'm trying to express my feelings."

"You've been expressing your feelings for five minutes. Besides, I'm the one who brought you the coffee."

"You want me to express my feelings to you?"

"Will it get you to stop expressing your feelings to your coffee?"

I shrugged and turned to Laurel. "I love the gift you brought me. It's like snuggles and happiness, and when I hold it, it's like nothing is wrong in the world."

"You are the most obnoxious person I've ever met. And that includes my sister who spit up on me every Christmas morning for the first four years of her life."

"She spit on you?"

"No, spit up. Like babies do."

"Like vomit?"

"Yeah. I'd unwrap exactly two presents and then my mother would hand me baby Lane so she could take pictures of us. And baby Lane would proceed to spit up on me. Every year. For four years."

I started laughing. "That's tragic."

"No, the sad part was I'd go clean up and change clothes, and by the time I came back downstairs, the boys would have finished unwrapping their presents. Lane would be asleep. Dad would be making breakfast. So Mom would awkwardly sit there and watch me open presents." She lowered her voice. "Quietly, so I wouldn't wake the baby."

"That's so bizarre."

"Is it? Everything was chaotic growing up. I forget that it isn't normal."

"No, I mean, I think it is normal. I'm the one who had the strange upbringing."

"How is Clive?"

I shrugged. "I don't know."

"Oh, okay." She leaned back.

"I don't mean it like that. I really don't know. Last time we spoke was weeks ago."

She furrowed her brow. "What happened?"

I stared out the windshield and willed movement from the dark house. "I think Henry is entitled and misogynistic. He thinks Henry is a misunderstood good guy. We are at an impasse."

Laurel said nothing. I finally looked at her and she was staring at me intently. Her lips were pursed and her brow had moved well beyond furrowed. "Misunderstood?" She rubbed at her bicep. It looked involuntary. She was wearing a navy baseball shirt so I couldn't see her arm, but I knew it was still healing.

"Sorry. I didn't think. I shouldn't have brought it up."

"What?" She looked down and realized she was massaging her bullet wound. "Oh, no. I'm fine. I'm just thrown. I didn't think Clive was one of those guys."

I shrugged. "Same."

She reached across the seats and squeezed my shoulder. I caught a whiff of crisp cedar. "I'm sorry."

"It is what it is."

"Okay, new subject. How's this stakeout going for you?" she asked.

"It's not bad. I'd give it an eight out of ten right now."

"Only a eight? I'm hurt."

"Reyes was probably a six. I was only with Duarte for a few hours after that, but he was a solid, neutral five. That kid needs a personality."

Laurel laughed. "In his defense, you terrify him."

"Because I'm a scary drug dealer?" I asked. She nodded. "I'll take it."

"What about Nate? Tell me I rank higher than Nate."

"With Nate it was a two. So an eight is quite a bump."

She smiled. "My company pushed it up six points? I'll take it."

"You did bring coffee. You don't appear to want to talk about how good-looking Nate is. And you smell really good."

"I do?"

I waved her off. "Don't get cocky. It's biological."

"The way I smell is biological?" She pulled her foot up on the seat and set her chin on her knee. The movement stretched her pink chinos tight.

"Yeah. You just smell good because I'm attracted to you. It's not like you did anything to earn it."

Laurel grinned at me. "Yeah, don't try to argue your way out of this one. Just let me have it."

"Fine. But you're attracted to me too."

"Cash?" Her tone shifted.

"What?" I looked around, but then I saw Tyler. He pulled the front door closed and walked purposefully toward the minivan.

"Don't start the engine yet." Laurel slowly put her foot down and buckled her seat belt.

I also pulled on my seat belt. "I think I know how to follow someone without them seeing me." I reviewed what I had just said. "Or something less creepy."

Laurel chuckled. Tyler backed out of the driveway. I waited to start the van until he turned down the next street. When we got out to the main road, I dropped back. He got on the freeway. It would have been a hell of a lot easier to just rely on the tracker, but Nate and I had agreed to give the detectives plausible deniability if at all possible. The best way to do that was not tell them.

"He's definitely going to the college," Laurel said.

"Yep." I changed lanes and did my best to be as unobtrusive as possible. We got off the freeway in Davis. He reversed the exact directions he had used to leave the college on Sunday morning. Tyler made it way too easy to follow him. The hard part was not being seen. Other than Tyler, we were only sharing the road with one other vehicle. Apparently, college students didn't drive much at four in the morning midweek. "If he parks in the same structure, do you want to follow him on foot? Or do you trust that he is probably going to the lab?"

"How close are we to the parking structure? Is that it?" Laurel pointed out the garage.

"Yeah. That's where he parked last time."

"Just pull over here and I'll follow him. Didn't you say both the exits are on the same road?" she asked. I nodded. "So if you follow him all the way there, he will see you."

I pulled to the side of the street. "All right, Detective. You are the expert, after all."

"I'll see you in a couple minutes." Laurel hopped out and went around to the back. She pulled Nate's bike toward her.

"You got it?"

"I'm good." She closed the back door and kicked off.

I didn't watch her ass as she rode away.

CHAPTER TWENTY-NINE

Tyler had probably parked already. I didn't want to risk him seeing me. And I wanted to have already parked by the time he got to the lab. I flipped a bitch and cut through the school. The other car on the road followed me through campus. I imagined I was being followed until they turned toward the dorms. It took under five minutes for me to get in place. I cut the engine and watched the break in the trees where I expected Tyler to appear. He didn't disappoint. He strode to the building and slid his keycard like before. If nothing else, he was confident. Then again, why wouldn't he be? He'd likely been doing this for months. There was no indication of resistance.

About a minute after he disappeared inside, Laurel appeared at the edge of the parking lot. She coasted to the van. I climbed in the back and opened the doors. She lifted the bike up, then left me to situate it while she climbed back in the passenger seat.

"So you survived?" I asked.

"There was a tense moment with a squirrel, but I stood my ground."

"Any issues?"

"Nate is a lot taller than I am. Remind me to lower the seat next time. Aside from that, no."

"Cool."

We watched the building. Like before with Nate, it was pretty damn boring. We couldn't see the windows to the lab, which meant Tyler couldn't accidentally see us, but it made for a lot of nothingness.

"You're right, you know."

I forced myself to continue looking at the building. "What do you mean?" I damn well knew what she was talking about.

"I am attracted to you. And I think you smell really good too."

"Damn biology."

"It might be more than physiological."

"What do you want to do about it?" I asked.

"Want?" She chuckled, but it sounded rough. "I want to take you home and not leave my apartment for about a week."

My heart started to pound. "I could be okay with that."

"Just because we want it, doesn't mean that we should."

I finally turned to look at her. She slowly mirrored the motion. "You afraid of breaking the rules, Detective?"

She shook her head. "I'm afraid that you won't love me."

It felt like infinity sitting there and staring at her. Like I was on the edge of the worst game of truth or dare. Both of them could devastate me.

I waited too long to speak. Laurel turned away.

We waited in excruciating silence for Tyler to return. The first blue tendrils of dawn started to frame the trees. Tyler finally appeared in the doorway. He was framed perfectly. The automatic lights in the building gave him a halo.

"That kid couldn't blend in a room of white men," Laurel said.

I laughed. It only felt slightly forced. "You see why we call him Aryan Brotherhood."

"Oh, I saw it all along. I just didn't realize he glowed in moonlight." Laurel hefted the camera and started taking pictures.

"Why do you bother taking photos? He's just walking."

She shrugged, but didn't stop. "Compulsive need to document, aggregate."

"Were you one of those kids who collected butterflies?"

Laurel laughed, but it sounded real. "No. It's only compulsive because the academy drills it into you."

Tyler strode across the quad. His white-blond hair shone. He was probably going to shift into a werewolf at any moment. Or start to fly. Suddenly, he went stiff.

"What the fuck?" I whispered.

He slowly turned. It felt like a horror movie where we were frozen and powerless. He looked directly at the van. He squinted, then seemingly realized that two people were watching him. "Don't do it," Laurel whispered. "We're so close."

Tyler sprinted away.

"Fuck. What the fuck just happened?" I cranked the engine.

"Cash, wait." Laurel reached over and put her hand on my arm. With her other hand, she raised the camera again and blindly pressed the shutter. "There. In the trees next to that bench."

I stared hard at the shadows under the trees. When my eyes adjusted, I could make out the outline of someone. There was a glint of light catching on glass, almost as if he had a camera. Based on bulk and height, I would have sworn it was Gibson.

"There's no way he could be that stupid, right?" I asked.

"I had no idea you were so optimistic about people. Gibson is a shit human being, a shit detective. This is exactly what I would expect."

"Do you want me to try to follow Tyler or do you want to arrest that person?"

"Fuck. I don't know. Tyler, I guess. We can't afford to lose him."

"What if, hypothetically, his minivan had a tracker on it?" I asked.

Laurel shot me a look. "To my knowledge, no one involved in this investigation has gotten a warrant to put a tracker on Mr. Hirsch's minivan."

"But we could still track him down."

"Stay here. I swear. Do not get out of this vehicle."

"Yes, ma'am."

"And photograph as necessary."

"I promise. Go." I took the camera and lifted it to eye level.

Laurel got out of the van and strode across the quad toward her quarry. He started to turn away, to run, but Laurel was faster, more fit. They collided. She got in two solid punches before he turned and she saw his face. She grabbed his shirt and threw him away from herself. Gibson stumbled into the open quad. He looked pissed. She looked more pissed. He started shouting at her. She returned to the van and climbed in.

"Let's get out of here. Follow Tyler," she said.

I backed out of the space. We cut through the school, but he had already left the parking garage. I pulled out my phone and checked the track app.

"It looks like he's headed home," I said.

"Seriously?"

"Yeah, he's on 80 and he just passed the split."

"Head that direction. Maybe we just got lucky." Laurel shifted uncomfortably. "Or we just got fucking screwed over by a member of our own team and this might salvage our utter shit investigation."

I glanced at my phone. Tyler was off the freeway in West Sac. "What are you going to do?"

"I want to kill that motherfucker." Her fists were clenched around the seat belt. She was clearly not talking about Tyler.

"I fully support this plan," I said.

"Can you believe him? He wasn't following you. He was following me." Laurel planted her foot on the seat and leaned against the door to look at me. Her posture suggested relaxation, but every muscle was stretched tight.

"You don't know that." Not that I wanted to defend Gibson, but I didn't want her to get unnecessarily angry either.

"No, I do know that. He just told me."

"Huh?"

"That's what he was shouting at me. He said he knew if he just followed me he'd catch me with you. I don't think he even registered that our perp was ten feet from him."

"You need to call Ionescu and Michelson like right now. Gibson is straight up negligent."

Laurel took a deep breath and nodded. "I will. I want to make sure Tyler is tucked in his bed first."

"Well, the tracker shows him heading home still."

"But the tracker is on his car, right? So he could easily park it and run away," she said.

I accelerated. "I don't suppose anyone else is in the vicinity?"

Laurel shook her head. "Duarte starts watching the house at seven. But it's twenty till."

"Call him." I switched lanes and rocketed onto the exit ramp.

Laurel pulled up Duarte's phone number. "Hey, any chance you're at the Hirsches' already?" Duarte's voice rumbled through the line, but I couldn't understand him. Laurel relaxed into her seat. She gave me a thumbs up. "No, you're right. Tyler went to school. We were on him, but then we got made." Duarte's yelp carried to me. "Just lay low. We think he is headed to the house. We are on our way." She hung up.

"Thank God for overachieving junior detectives."

Laurel grinned. "He's been there for half an hour. He didn't see us, but he didn't want to call and compromise our position."

"I think someone deserves a gold star today. Maybe even a lollipop."

"I will buy that boy two lollipops." She held up two fingers to make sure I really got how many lollipops Duarte was getting.

"Wow. Someone is feeling generous."

❖

I had been sitting in the world's most uncomfortable chair outside of Ionescu's office for ten minutes. Around minute seven, I'd lost all ability to feel so I was doing okay.

The shouting from within the office carried. I found that if I leaned my head back so it was touching the wall, the voices carried better. I had also found that their discussion was nothing new or surprising.

Kallen was angry that Gibson had jeopardized the entire operation.

Reyes was pissed that Gibson was so distrustful of his colleague that he had jeopardized the entire operation.

Ionescu was not happy that he had been cut out of his own department's investigation after handing the reins to Gibson.

Gibson was still angry that Kallen and I were involved. He was under the impression that his photographs of us sitting in a van were proof of that fact.

Michelson was silent, but he didn't seem to enjoy playing mediator.

Inside the office, a cell phone rang. It was silenced. There was some growling. Ionescu's office phone rang. He picked it up and slammed it on the cradle. That seemed ineffective as far as running a unit of detectives went. Maybe that was why his detectives kept going off book. My phone went off. I pulled it out. It was Officer Duarte.

"Hey."

"Cash? Hi, it's Jeff. Jeff Duarte."

"Yeah, your name is stored in my phone."

"Oh, yeah. Got it." He laughed nervously. "Umm, someone is watching the Hirsch house, right? Like it's not just me?"

"I think there are two FBI agents there as well now."

"Good. Because Tyler is on the move again. I kinda left Alyssa because I didn't want to lose Tyler. He just got on 80 going west. I'm following him."

"Shit. Okay. Stay on him. I'll make sure one of the detectives follows you."

"Cool. Cool. Thanks. I tried calling Kallen. And Reyes. And Ionescu. But none of them picked up. Well, Ionescu did, but then he hung up on me." His voice got higher the more he talked.

"Duarte."

"Yeah?"

I stood. "You're doing great. I'm hanging up. Stay on Tyler. If he drives past UC Davis, call me again. Do not let him out of your sight." We hung up and I knocked on Ionescu's door. It wasn't immediately opened and I was tired of cop politics so I opened it myself.

"Can we help you, Ms. Braddock?" Ionescu shouted.

I was reasonably certain that he hadn't meant to shout. That was just the volume he was currently operating at. "You could answer your goddamn phones." Kallen, Reyes, Gibson, and Michelson all pulled out their cell phones. "Tyler Hirsch just got on 80 west. Your junior detective is currently following him."

"Kallen, Reyes, go." Ionescu waved them out, which was good because they were already moving. I stepped back. "Daniel, I want regular updates." He really hit the word regular. Michelson nodded stoically. "Gibson, call your fucking union rep and get the fuck out of my sight." The office emptied.

Laurel and Reyes headed for the stairwell. Michelson fell into step behind them. I followed because I didn't know what else to do. Michelson was speaking rapidly into his cell phone. Laurel and Reyes were walking so close together, they were basically becoming the same person.

"Cash, any word from Duarte?" Laurel asked over her shoulder.

"Nothing yet. He was only supposed to call if Tyler went past Davis." I shot off a text to Duarte. He wrote back immediately. "They're approaching campus."

We pounded down two flights of stairs. Reyes's and Michelson's dress shoes tapped in perfect rhythm as we descended. We spilled into the parking lot. Michelson had an FBI lackey waiting at the curb. He pulled the phone away from his face long enough to exchange some vague instructions with Kallen. She nodded and he climbed in the black sedan. Reyes ran off to retrieve the Crown Vic. Laurel guided me to follow him. I hated running.

"Why the hell would Tyler go back to campus?" I asked.

Laurel shrugged. "Maybe he still has drugs stashed. Maybe there's a contact we don't know about. Maybe he just wants to go to class."

"Are you guys going to arrest him?"

"Probably. The lab emailed this morning. The pills from Benji Nelson are a match. That's enough to detain the Hirsches."

"Why didn't you guys do it when they were both home this morning?"

"Politics."

"That's dumb. What if he runs?"

"He might. At this point, we're all pretty curious where he is headed." Laurel was amped. She hadn't even been this wired when Henry tried to kill her. Maybe it was the lack of sleep or residual anger, but either way it was tiring to watch.

Reyes popped the locks and climbed behind the wheel. I got in the backseat. Then I questioned why I had gotten in the backseat. I really didn't need to accompany them. My phone buzzed with another text. I checked it.

"Duarte says they are circling the garage, looking for parking right now," I said.

The detectives nodded in acknowledgment and continued with whatever game plan they were working on, something about consulting with Davis PD. Duarte sent regular updates as we drove. They were walking across campus when we got off the freeway. Tyler entered the building with the lab as we drove onto campus. Laurel directed Reyes to the lot we had been watching from. He parked at the curb. Advantage of police plates.

Laurel had gotten Duarte on the phone. He was apparently narrowing down which room Tyler had entered, but couldn't confirm what the suspect was doing. At that, Reyes made a call to let someone know they weren't doing a room by room search.

"Guys?" I asked. They barely acknowledged me. "Guys, I can access the cameras in the lab." Laurel and Reyes turned and stared at me. "If he is doing something dangerous, you need to know before you go in, right? And if he is grabbing a stash of fentanyl, then you can nab him with evidence. But if he is just attending class, you'll want to wait for a less volatile arrest location." I'd been listening just enough to figure out the pertinent issues.

"What do you need from us?" Reyes asked.

"I need someone to clear out a men's bathroom," I said.

They exchanged a look that was part praise and part incredulousness.

"Let's go." Reyes got out of the car.

As they walked, both detectives adjusted their holsters and badges. Reyes had everything attached to his belt, but Laurel was wearing a shoulder holster cinched over her loose shirt. Her badge was slung around her neck. Their serious conversation was gone. Now they appeared to anticipate each movement the other would make as they ascended the stairs.

On the second floor, Reyes let me lead the way. I found the right bathroom and pointed it out. Reyes went in. A minute later, a guy came out, then another. Reyes finally emerged with one straggler who seemed quite annoyed.

"Thanks." I passed Reyes on my way in.

"Anytime."

The door closed and I locked it. I climbed on the counter and popped out a ceiling tile. The laptop was where Nate had left it. That was good. It was warm so it was still on. I opened it and launched the right program. The videos started streaming. The camera over the door just showed a lab in session. There were ten kids moving around, talking. They all gave a wide berth to Tyler who clearly didn't belong.

The camera over the center workstation showed Tyler calmly pressing a new batch of pills.

I opened the bathroom door. Laurel and Reyes stepped forward.

"He's making more. He probably knows this is his last chance."

"Seriously?" Reyes asked. He glanced at the screen. "That arrogant little shit."

Laurel was already on the phone listing off information about the approximate size of the room, the number of people inside, the perpetrator's location. Two minutes later, Michelson ran up. He had changed clothes. Instead of his suit, he was wearing black fatigues and a T-shirt. Laurel was still in her stakeout outfit: chinos and a baseball tee. Reyes was dressed for work in slacks, a dress shirt, and tie. They all looked out of place, both for a college and each other's company. Two agents dressed the same as Michelson flanked him. Laurel and Michelson spoke rapidly, quietly, then they all moved toward the stairs. I realized a cadre of uniformed police were following Agent Michelson.

At the last second, Laurel turned back to me. "Stay here. Do not intervene."

As if. "Sure thing." What else was I going to say? Have fun? Be careful?

I found a bench and watched the silent videos. The door opened. The agent twins went in first. They tapped students on the shoulder and motioned them out of the lab. They got eight kids out before Tyler noticed them.

Michelson, Reyes, and Laurel filed in. They spread in front of Tyler. Michelson moved toward the front of the room, Laurel the back. Reyes approached dead-on. Tyler faced Reyes. He seemed panicked. His neck and scalp started to turn pink. Reyes stepped closer. Tyler shouted something and Reyes stopped moving. Tyler started mumbling, seemingly to himself. Reyes looked like he was straining to hear, to understand.

Then Tyler swept everything off the table into his satchel. He reached behind his back. I saw the gun, the flash of fire. Distantly, a gunshot echoed through the building. One of the FBI guys drew on Tyler. I heard another gunshot, then another. I couldn't follow the action anymore. Around me, kids were running for the stairs. People were screaming. There were sirens.

But on the very edge of the camera above the workbench, I could see Laurel holding Reyes. Blood was spreading everywhere. Their clothes were sodden with it. She moved in and out of the frame, but her hands were unmoving. They pressed into his chest, gathering material, twisting it tighter against him. A body moved into the frame. He blocked my view, then crouched next to Laurel. He moved her hands long enough to slap a white square over the hole. Laurel put her hands back in place. He put his hands over hers and helped her press.

Reyes watched Laurel's face until he passed out.

CHAPTER THIRTY

Duarte told me the waiting room had been packed all night. I hadn't come because I wasn't sure of my place. I had no claim on Laurel. No matter how much I disagreed with her blue brotherhood, I knew that space wasn't mine to intrude on. So I had settled for texts from Duarte. It wasn't until long after midnight that I decided that was fucking stupid. Despite our strange circumstances, Reyes was my friend.

I drove to the Med Center and followed Duarte's instructions to the right waiting room. The waiting bodies had dwindled to two guys and Laurel. I stood in the doorway and watched her. She was still wearing her blood-soaked shirt. It looked stiff. White lines across the shoulders showed where her holster had been. She slouched with her elbows on her knees, her head close to the other two officers. Their conversation seemed to float, to fill the space with muttering.

"Kallen?" I said.

Laurel and one of the guys turned. It was Lance.

"Hi." Laurel stood slowly, like she'd forgotten how.

Lance and the other guy stood as well.

"I hope you don't mind. I wanted to see how he's doing," I said.

"Why don't we see if they will let you in?" Lance clapped his hand on the other officer's shoulder and pulled him toward the door.

I stepped inside. "Isn't it way after visiting hours?"

Lance grinned cockily. "We're cops. They never keep us from visiting each other."

"Right." I didn't even bother getting irritated. I was over cops.

Lance and his buddy left. I took another step toward Laurel. She wrapped her arms around my waist and buried her face in my neck.

"I was so fucking scared," she mumbled.

"I know. I was too."

We stood there. I could feel the cadence of her heart pressing into my chest. She radiated heat through the thin, stiff cotton of her shirt. I dug my hands into her shoulders, tightened my grip. She took deep, shuddering breaths. Her exhalations were warm against my skin. She still smelled like cedar and salt.

I heard footsteps approaching. Laurel stiffened when she heard them too, but she didn't let go.

"All right, Cash, we got you two minutes with the man himself. He's asleep, but you can stare at his dumb face."

I let go of Laurel with one arm, but kept the other firmly around her shoulders. Lance was leaning in the doorway with half a smile on his face.

"Thanks," I said.

"Anytime. Well, not anytime. I try to avoid situations like this." Lance waved us forward. "Come on."

Laurel tightened her grip on my waist and took a step toward her brother. "Let's go."

"Oh, introductions," Lance said as he led us down the hallway. "This is my brother, Seth." He nudged Seth with his shoulder.

Seth reached over Lance. "It's good to meet you, Cash."

"You too." I shook his hand. "I thought your brother was Logan?"

"That dickwad?" Lance laughed. "Sure, if blood counts. Seth is my bro, though. We were in diapers together."

Laurel squeezed my waist. "He means that literally. They once found a package of Grandma's diapers, stripped off their underwear, and climbed into one big diaper together. It was disgusting and weird."

"Wow." I shook my head. "That's way more information than I ever needed."

Lance leaned closer to me. "There are pictures."

"Is there any way to get him to stop talking?" I asked Laurel.

"Not that I've found," she said.

I looked over at Lance, but he had rapidly sobered. He stopped outside a door. "We will be out here."

Laurel and I went in. Laurel twisted her fist in my shirt. Reyes was asleep like Lance had said. Other than being astonishingly pale, he looked normal. White bandages peeked out at the neckline of his hospital gown.

"So what happened?" I asked.

Laurel hesitated like she didn't know what I was asking. "Michelson's guys got Tyler. He's in custody somewhere in the hospital. Two gunshot wounds. One major, one minor. They expect a full recovery."

"Okay. That's good, right?" I knew all of that, but there was no point in telling her. Nate and I had tricked Duarte into giving us information. He was very confused about what we should be privy to. We also learned that Alyssa had disappeared. The Hirsch house was currently being ransacked and catalogued. It was probably good that our tracker had fallen off her undercarriage on the freeway. Its presence in the garage would have raised some uncomfortable questions.

"Yep."

"What about Reyes?" Which was the question I really wanted an answer to.

She took a deep breath. "The bullet didn't hit any important structures in his chest. It clipped an artery or vein…I don't know. One of the big ones."

"That's why he bled so much." And why he was so pale.

She nodded a few times. "Yeah. Michelson helped me slow the bleeding."

"He going to be okay?"

More nodding. "Assuming he doesn't get an infection or anything, they said he will recover just fine."

"Good. That's good."

Laurel leaned her head on my shoulder. Reyes slept on. The gentle rise and fall of his torso was a reliable comfort.

"Can you take me home now?" Laurel asked.

"Yes."

We left the room. Lance and Seth were leaning against the opposite wall. They pushed up and came toward us.

"Everyone good?" Lance asked.

"Yeah," Laurel said.

"I'm going to take her home," I said.

Lance clapped his hand on my shoulder. "Cool. See if you can get her to eat or shower. I'm not holding out for a miracle so either one would be pretty chill."

I laughed. Laurel shook her head. We got to the elevator. Lance hit the button because he was clearly the guy who liked to hit elevator buttons. Lance and Seth kept up a running commentary the whole way to the first floor. We walked out to the parking lot together. When we got to my SUV, Laurel let go of me for the first time. She hugged Seth and called him little bro. Then she hugged Lance and called him idiot bro.

In the car, she pulled one foot up on the seat and stared out the window. When I parked outside her apartment, she looked mildly surprised. She turned toward me and rested her cheek on her knee.

"Will you come up?"

"I did promise your brother I would try to get you to shower."

Laurel smiled, but there was a hint of disappointment in it. "You don't need to feel obligated."

"I'm not." I reached over and squeezed her leg. "I want to be here with you."

"Because my partner got shot and I'm broken?"

"Because your partner got shot and you're still not broken."

Some of the disappointment slipped away. We went upstairs. Laurel unlocked the door and led me through the apartment, flipping on lights at random as she went.

"Go take a shower. I'm making you food."

She sighed and went down the hallway on the right toward the bedroom and the bathroom. The shower turned on. I went through the doorway on the left into the kitchen. I hated that I knew my way around Laurel's apartment because I had broken into it before. Then again, if we were analyzing our past behavior, neither of us would fare well.

I opened the fridge. She had more food than I did, which wasn't saying much. I opened cabinets and drawers at random until I found enough supplies to make scrambled eggs. The shower turned off. I stuck my head around the corner in time to see Laurel walking away from me, buck naked, running a towel over her hair. I groaned. She turned and grinned sleepily.

"Got a problem?" she asked.

"No, Detective. Put something on and come eat."

She shrugged.

I went back in the kitchen and washed the pan out. Laurel leaned against the doorframe. She was wearing short boxer briefs and a threadbare T-shirt with a bear on it. Dangerous. I handed her the plate of scrambled eggs and pointed at the kitchen table where there was a glass of juice. She ignored my instructions and ate standing at the counter.

"These are crazy good. Why are they so good?"

"Partially because I put a fuckload of cheese in them. But mostly because you probably haven't eaten all day."

"Oh, yeah." Laurel drained the glass of juice, then closed her eyes and leaned her head against the cabinet behind her.

I took the empty plate out of her hands. She would have dropped it in about three seconds.

"I got this." I washed the plate and put it on the dish rack. "Go get in bed." She didn't move. "Hey." I squeezed her hand. Her eyes flickered open. "Wouldn't you rather sleep not standing up?"

Laurel grinned sleepily. "I think I'd prefer if you came to bed with me."

"Yeah?" I was full of great lines.

She leaned forward and kissed me slowly. It reminded me of the first day we had kissed. There was something chaste, yet vulnerable in it. She grabbed the tail of my T-shirt and dragged me around the corner, down the hallway to her bedroom. I kicked off my shoes. She unbuttoned my pants and shoved them down. We crawled in bed. Laurel was asleep before I even hit the light. She curled up against my side. Her damp hair smelled clean and sweet.

It was just after dawn when I woke up. Laurel was pressed back against my stomach. My hand was under her shirt, splayed across her rib cage, which might have been invasive if not for her fingers intertwined with mine. My face was pressed between her shoulders. She smelled like skin and heat and sleep.

I tightened my hold on her. She made a contented noise. I dozed. When I woke up again, her foot was curled around my ankle. The movement forced my thigh between hers. I traced my fingertips over the ridges of her ribs, dug into her smooth flesh. She woke up when I kissed the back of her neck. She arched into me and sighed. I continued my line of kisses up her neck to her ear, back down to the juncture of her shoulder.

Her shoulder blades were outlined perfectly under her thin T-shirt. They arced and swooped like wings. I kissed the rough cotton covering them. Laurel reached back and buried her fingers in my hair, yanked me closer to her body. I shifted my weight until I was half on top of her. She pressed her ass back into my crotch. My hand was halfway down her body before I realized what I was doing. I wanted to go, to move, to feel her thrum beneath me, but we had done that. It had demolished us. I stopped with my fingertips against the elastic of her underwear.

"Do you want me to stop?" I asked.

"Do you?" She tugged on my hair until my lips were against her cheek.

"No." I kissed her cheek, the corner of her mouth.

She kissed me back. "I can't make you any promises."

"Neither of us can."

"But you want this?" she asked.

"Badly." I pressed my hips against her ass.

She groaned. I drew lines against her skin until she grabbed my hand and shoved it into her underwear. I dragged my fingertips between her lips. Her breathing went ragged. She reached back again and cupped my neck, pulled me tight against her. I traced around her clit, dipped a fingertip into her cunt. She rolled her hips into the bed, tried to trap me against her.

I licked and sucked at her neck, bit the soft skin. She rubbed herself against my hand. Her cunt was warm and slick. I forced myself to keep still, to make her work for it. When her movements became erratic, I pressed lower. She lifted her hips to give me room. I slid inside her. She gasped at the invasion. I moved slowly at first, then built a rhythm.

Laurel let go of my neck and reached for my ass instead. She held me tight against her. I pressed down with my hips, braced her against the bed. She ground her clit into my palm. Her body felt solid, real against mine. I groaned. She pushed her hand inside my underwear. I tried to focus on my fingers buried inside her, the wet press of her clit, but she cupped me and squeezed and everything refocused. I angled my hips into her harder.

She was mumbling nonsense now. Gasping and groaning at each movement of my hand. When she came, everything was perfectly still for a moment. She arched back, pressed her fingers into my clit with bruising accuracy, held on that edge, then fell. Her breathing came in a rush. She exhaled, went limp. I started to move off her, afraid I was crushing her, but she twitched her fingers just right.

"Stay. I like you here," she said.

"Okay." I forced myself to keep still, waited for the final press that would let me come.

She turned her face toward me. Kissed, licked my jawline. I knew she was taunting me. Hell, I was enjoying it thoroughly. When she had lulled me into a soft, sweet expectation, she began to move against my clit with deep purpose. The trembling pressure made me jerk, beg, come.

Laurel shifted under me, flipped. She pulled my head down to her chest. My breathing finally evened out.

"If that's bad at decision-making, then maybe we've been making decisions wrong for a long time," she said.

I laughed. "I blame you and your cop morals."

She groaned and started laughing too. "Same."

CHAPTER THIRTY-ONE

A ndy was a shitty driver. She had no concept of the subtleties of steering a vehicle. As a result, she was all over the place. She ran into walls and other drivers and basically every banana peel she could. It was uncanny, her ability to hit every single banana peel, but completely miss the road itself.

"Did you just fucking shrink me?" Andy shouted.

"No. You just shrank me," Laurel said.

"It was Peach, guys." I was shooting for innocence, but fell short of the mark.

"You're Princess Peach, asshole." Laurel nudged me with her shoulder.

"Oh, right. I guess I am." I sailed across the finish line. "First place, bitches."

"Third, dammit." Laurel dropped her controller in her lap.

Andy grunted and scowled and tried real hard. "Seventh is better than eighth, right?"

Laurel laughed at her. "Sure, bud."

My phone lit up on the table again. I'd ignored it the first time because winning was important. I grabbed it. Unknown number. Super.

"Hello?"

"Hey, umm is Cash there? I'm looking for Cash."

"This is her."

"Cash! It's Raleigh."

"And Brando," a voice in the distance shouted.

"You know, Dawson's friends?"

"Yeah, hi guys. How's it going?" I resisted the need to shout to match their volume.

"We are high as fuck right now so that's pretty dope." There was a heavy EDM track playing so I felt pretty confident in assuming they were at a rave or club.

"It sounds real dope."

"It's so dope," Raleigh said.

"Hey, where you at right now?" This was either a misguided we've been roofied call or an even more misguided come party with us call.

"Kadi Parti," he shouted.

"Huh?"

"Kadi Parti," they both shouted the second time.

"Where is Kadi Parti?"

"Club Plastics," Raleigh, Brando, and Andy all answered.

I shot Andy a look. She shrugged and mouthed, "What?"

"Listen, Cash. Cash, listen. Listen," Raleigh said.

"What's up, man?"

"Cash, there's a chick here selling fentanyl."

I tapped Laurel's shoulder. She gave me a look, then went back to ignoring me. "No way. Tell me about this woman."

"What woman?"

"The one selling fentanyl," I said. Laurel's head shot up.

"She's a scary lady," Raleigh said.

"How do you know it's fentanyl?"

"We don't!" he said triumphantly.

"Why do you think it's fentanyl?"

"Because Becca said this chick was selling fentanyl." As if I knew who the hell Becca was.

"You didn't take any though, right?"

"Cash, we took a lot of pills. I don't know what they were," Raleigh said very matter-of-factly.

"Were any of the pills black?"

Laurel began repeating a litany of curse words. She grabbed her phone and started making calls.

"Yo, how did you know?" Raleigh started singing along with the music. It was EDM so there weren't any lyrics, but that didn't stop Raleigh.

"Because the fentanyl pills are black."

"Are you sure?"

"Yes." Laurel tossed my Converse at me. I sat on the couch and pulled them on.

"Are you sure the fentanyl is bad?"

"Yes. Fentanyl is bad."

"Uh-oh," Raleigh said.

"What's uh-oh?"

"Maybe it's bad to take pills when people give them to you?"

"Probably," I said.

"Come on," Laurel whispered. "Backup is meeting us at the club."

Andy waved as we left. I gave her a head nod and followed Laurel to her truck.

"They took fentanyl?" Laurel asked.

"Of course they did."

"I'll assign someone to get them out and bring them to a hospital. You want me to text Nate too?"

I nodded at her before going back to my inane phone call. "Hey, Raleigh, man. I need you to focus. Laurel and I are going to come get you. Can you point out the chick selling fentanyl?"

"I can try, but like we didn't buy it. Becca did. She said the chick was so mean. You know those girls in high school who are like really, really mean?"

"Mean girls?" I asked.

"Yes! She was just like that," Raleigh said.

"Got it. She was mean."

"Hey, Cash? Did we just take the same kinda drugs that killed Pedro? I don't want to die," Raleigh said.

"We're going to die?" Brando asked. I could hear their voices as they argued over possession of the phone and dying.

"Guys, Raleigh, Brando," I shouted.

"Yo," Raleigh said.

"Can you tell me where you are in the club?"

"By the bar. By one of the bars."

"By one of the bars?" I repeated.

Laurel huffed and parked on the street in front of Club Plastics. Duarte, Michelson, and three plainclothes cops were waiting for us. A couple of cruisers waited across the street. The detectives put their heads together and started planning. I got to listen to half of Raleigh and Brando's argument. Nate jogged up.

"What's going on?" Nate whispered to me.

"Alyssa is inside. So are Raleigh and Brando and they took fentanyl. And probably quite a few other drugs."

"Super."

I looked up at the facade of the building. It was two stories high. The front of the building was barely tinted glass. On the bottom floor, you could only see movement and bright lights. Up top, people danced against the glass.

"Cash." Laurel waved me over. "Do you have a picture of Raleigh and Brando?"

I covered the mouthpiece on my phone. "No, but I can get one." Laurel looked at me like I was crazy. I uncovered the mouthpiece. "Raleigh, can you send me a selfie?"

"Hell yeah. We look dope." Two minutes later, my phone vibrated. I clicked open the image. They didn't look dope. They looked tired and high. I texted it to Laurel. She nodded in thanks. She and Michelson continued giving orders. An ambulance parked behind the cruisers across the street.

Laurel waved Nate over to join us. "Okay, we are all going to fan out. Everyone knows what the perp looks like. Everyone knows what the vics look like. There are probably other potential vics so watch for symptoms of fentanyl overdose."

"What are the symptoms?" Nate asked.

"I just texted both of you a list," Laurel said.

Nate pulled out his phone and showed me the screen. It was basically a list of every overdose symptom: confusion, poor circulation, difficulty walking and talking, drowsiness, seizure. At the bottom of the list, the final symptom was death. I felt like it was a little unnecessary to include that one.

"You two are eyes only," Michelson said to me and Nate. "We're including you because you may have contacts we can use. Focus on finding those boys and getting them out."

I was totally cool with that plan.

We moved en masse toward the entrance. The bouncer tried about ten tactics to keep us out, but he wasn't much of a match for half a dozen law enforcement officials. Plus, Michelson and Kallen were loudly debating if they should shut the whole club down.

The inside of the club was basically my worst nightmare. People everywhere, deafening music, colorful lights. The cops all fanned out. Nate and I stuck together. There were two bars that I could see, so we aimed for the closer one. I studied faces, but it was difficult to make out features in the low, undulating light. Raleigh still had his horrific mustache, but that was his most identifiable feature. In the photo, Brando was wearing a bright purple shirt with two unicorns fucking. So I was basically just scanning for that.

We walked the length of the bar, looking at faces, watching for obscene mustaches and obscene T-shirts. We worked our way to the bar itself and leaned over to check the people waiting for service. A girl checked out Nate, then checked out me, then checked out Nate again. She motioned at one of the bartenders. He came over. She ordered shots that sounded terrifying. I tried to say no, but then she called me a handsome boy. Nate clapped his hand on my shoulder, thanked her profusely, and downed the neon shot. She smiled. He smiled. It was gross. Just when I'd given up on the foundation of our friendship, Nate pulled out his phone.

"Have you seen these guys?" He showed her the photo of Raleigh and Brando.

"Have I?" Her tone was ambiguous.

"Have you?" Nate tried again.

"They were dancing on a platform a little while ago. They're like a super cute couple. Are they your friends?" She touched Nate's bicep.

There were so many strange assumptions in that response. I didn't know if I was more offended that she thought we might be friends with them or that Raleigh and Brando might actually be one of my people. Queers had standards. They were not up to snuff.

I took a step back and let Nate worry about disentangling himself. From where I stood, there appeared to be seven dancing platforms. Four were high enough that the club could regulate who had access. The other three were a free-for-all. I studied each platform even though I knew they wouldn't still be there.

"You see them?" Nate shouted by my ear.

"Nope."

"You want to try the other bar?"

"Yeah. The stairs are over there." I pointed out the wide, deep staircase that flanked the DJ booth and stage.

We fought through the Friday crowds toward the staircase. I eventually gave up on asserting my dominance and just let Nate lead the way. He grabbed my hand and pulled me in his wake. Security kept the stairs relatively clear of dancers. I couldn't imagine what a liability that staircase was.

The second floor was no less loud, but marginally less crowded. It was essentially just a very wide balcony that ringed the entire club. The front balcony had that thick glass facing the street. Twenty-something-year-olds jockeyed for a good position to dance at the windows and provide free advertising for the club. I was certain they had no idea that the club was manipulating them, but they seemed pretty stoked for the opportunity. Opposite that, on the back wall, was a second bar. It was smaller and had a handful of tables and stools for the club goer who got tuckered out. Or was too high to stand. Nate scanned the room as he led us toward the bar. Which was how he ran into two guys buying drugs from Alyssa Hirsch.

The guys got angry at having borne the brunt of his bulk, but Alyssa completely, utterly lost it. She started screaming at Nate. I caught two racial slurs, one crack about his masculinity, and one insult to his mother. Nate just stared at her like he couldn't quite process the hateful tirade he had stumbled into.

I wrestled my phone out of my pocket and texted Laurel, Michelson, Duarte, Nate, and Reyes. The last two weren't intentional. We just had a group chat and that was how it worked out.

Alyssa upstairs bar.

That basically covered it.

Alyssa saw me staring at her and Nate and turned on me. I got a heterosexist remark, two about my gender presentation, my very own racist joke, and a violent threat.

I was starting to see what Raleigh and Brando had meant about Alyssa being a mean girl. I smiled to myself. Alyssa's vitriol kind of undermined everything she said. It was difficult to take someone seriously when their hate was so indiscriminate.

Alyssa didn't like it when I smiled. She stepped forward and grabbed my T-shirt. I tried to back away, but she pulled me closer and started screaming at me.

Laurel sprinted up the stairs with one of the plainclothes guys I didn't know. Alyssa's diatribe had cleared a nice little space in front of the bar. Laurel stepped into that space. There was a comfort in having Laurel so close. She wouldn't let Alyssa hurt anyone else.

"Alyssa Hirsch, you're under arrest. Let go of her. Keep your hands where we can see them." Kallen and the plainclothes guy slowly approached.

I saw movement behind Alyssa. Michelson was creeping behind the now empty bar to get in position at Alyssa's rear. Nate was about two feet to her right. He took a careful step away from her. I mimicked the movement, but Alyssa tightened her grip in my shirt.

"No." Alyssa reached back just like her brother had done.

"Gun," I shouted. Which was not a great thing to shout in a crowded club, but that was what I did. I frantically twisted away from Alyssa, but she put the gun to my temple. It was not a great feeling.

Kallen, plainclothes, and Michelson all lunged forward. Probably not the move I would have chosen.

"Stop." Alyssa turned us enough for them to get the visual of the gun and its proximity to my head.

"Put the gun down. You're just making this worse for yourself." Kallen lowered the gun I hadn't seen her draw, but didn't holster it.

"She's not wrong," I said.

"What the fuck did you say to me?" Alyssa pressed the gun harder.

"Oww, shit. Nothing." Maybe antagonizing the chick with a gun to my head was a bad idea. Then again, I wasn't entirely thinking straight. That gun was making me real sweaty and nervous. "Just, you know, she's not wrong. You're already fucked."

"Shut the fuck up, bitch." She pulled the gun back like she was going to pistol whip me.

I ducked. Nate coldcocked Alyssa. She went down.

"Jesus fucking Christ." I disentangled myself from Alyssa and stumbled backward. Nate grabbed my arm and hauled me upright.

Nate smiled. "That was really satisfying."

I laughed and tried to pretend I wasn't shaking. Kallen put cuffs on an unconscious Alyssa. She searched her thoroughly. There was the gun. There was also a fuckload of black pills. Michelson bagged each piece of evidence as Kallen pulled it off of her. A couple of uniforms joined the fray. The last officer to arrive was Duarte. He sidled up to me.

"I missed the action, didn't I?" he asked sadly.

"I was in the middle of the action. Be glad you missed it." I shrugged.

"Yeah, I guess." He shoved his hands in his pockets and sighed. "I got your friends out."

"Huh?"

"Raleigh and Brando. Brando was exhibiting quite a few overdose signs. Both of them are on their way to the hospital, just to be safe."

"Oh, great. Thanks." I nodded. They weren't my friends, but Duarte clearly wanted to impress me so I let him have it.

"I also found two girls in the bathroom who showed signs of overdose. The EMTs are loading them up right now." He shrugged like he was embarrassed.

"Was one of them named Becca?"

He looked hopeful at being able to answer a question. "Rebecca according to her ID."

I squeezed his shoulder. "That's some quality work."

"Is it? I feel like I'm just cleaning up. Not catching bad guys."

"But you probably saved four people's lives tonight."

He brightened. "Yeah?"

"Yeah."

"Thanks." Duarte shook my hand, then made his way over to Kallen.

I looked around for Nate. He was sitting at the bar, drinking a beer, with ice on his hand. I sat next to him.

"This is a twelve-dollar beer." Nate held up the bottle of Sierra Nevada. "The Coors were only eight, but I deserve a fucking twelve-dollar beer."

"You're goddamn right you do." I looked behind the bar, but no one was there. I knew I shouldn't have shouted gun. "How did you procure this twelve-dollar beer?"

"I went behind the bar and rang myself up. But I got to tell you, I am a lousy tipper. Who knew?" Nate grinned at me.

"I think that's fair. I feel like the bartender really didn't earn your tip." I followed Nate's instructions and got my own twelve-dollar beer.

"You cool?"

I shrugged. "I'm alive."

"This has been a night."

We both nodded. It had been a night.

The cops waded through a lot of tedious procedure after Alyssa had been taken away. We watched for quite some time before Laurel made her way over to Nate and me.

"I think I owe you, Xiao," she said.

"You totally owe me." Nate lightly punched her shoulder. "But if I'm being completely honest, I would absolutely do that again. I'm a pacifist like Cash, but punching that chick was deeply fulfilling."

"It looked deeply fulfilling." Laurel nodded.

"You deserve a reward. Would you like some twelve-dollar beer?" Nate held out the bottle.

Laurel laughed. "I really would. But I'm on shift until we wrap all this up. I wanted to tell you there's a uniform waiting to take you home."

"I drove here. I can take Cash home." Nate took a final swig and set his half consumed beer on the bar. "Oh, and I've had approximately one drink and a half in the last two hours, Detective Kallen. I'm quite certain of my ability to drive safely."

Laurel laughed. "Okay, I'll let them know not to expect you."

Nate headed for the stairs. I turned to Laurel.

"Are you okay?" she asked. I nodded. "I'm sorry I couldn't check earlier."

"No worries. I'm fine."

"Good. That's good." She reached out like she was going to touch me, but stopped herself at the last moment.

"You doing all right?"

She smiled halfway. "Yeah. It's the best-case scenario."

"Don't work too late."

Her smile widened. "I'll try not to."

Laurel wasn't home. I'd known she wouldn't be. It was after three in the morning. But I'd hoped that her duty would be done so I had come anyway. I sat on her porch and stared at the dark door.

Laurel was right. Arresting Tyler and Alyssa was the best-case scenario. It wouldn't give back what they had taken though. I wondered what I had taken. How many addicts had I fed? I was culpable in too many ways, for too many lives. It was time to tell Nate we needed a way out.

The deep rumble of her truck was audible from blocks away. I didn't move. There were a thousand reasons for me to run away, to hide, to be paralyzed by indecision. But I finally knew where I stood. I had no way to predict Nate's behavior or Laurel's or Clive's. The law was beyond my comprehension. Morality was perpetually up for debate.

The only thing I knew with any certainty was myself.

Laurel climbed the stairs and I stood.

"Cash?"

"Sorry. I know it's late."

"It's cool. I stopped by the hospital to update Reyes."

"He doing okay?" I asked.

"He's bummed he missed Nate punching that chick," she said. I grinned. "What are you doing here?"

"I needed to see you."

"Okay." She leaned against the post holding up the porch and slid her hands in her pockets.

"I still don't know anything. Not about who I am or who I want to be. I don't know when I'll figure that out." I didn't approach her. I knew I needed to speak first. "But you don't need to be afraid that I won't love you."

She straightened. Took a step toward me. "Cash."

"Wait." I held up my hand. "We need to work a lot out. I know that the middle of the night, in the dark, away from anyone who might actually see us is not the place to declare your love. But I really don't care." I shrugged. "So even if we resolve nothing, even if we never have answers, I'm here. With you."

"We may never sort out this mess." She grinned.

"I don't care."

Laurel nodded once, with finality. She unlocked the door. Then she reached out, took my hand, and led me inside.

About the Author

Ashley Bartlett was born and raised in California. Her life consists of reading, writing, and editing. Most of the time, Ashley engages in these pursuits while sitting in front of a coffee shop with her wife.

It's a glamorous life.

She is an obnoxious, sarcastic, punk-ass, but her friends don't hold that against her. She lives in Sacramento, but you can find her at ashbartlett.com.

Books Available from Bold Strokes Books

Change in Time by Robyn Nyx. Working in the past is hell on your future. The Extractor series: Book Two (978-1-62639-880-1)

Love After Hours by Radclyffe. When Gina Antonelli agrees to renovate Carrie Longmire's new house, she doesn't welcome Carrie's overtures at friendship or her own unexpected attraction. A Rivers Community Novel. (978-1-63555-090-0)

Nantucket Rose by CF Frizzell. Maggie Jordan can't wait to convert an historic Nantucket home into a B&B, but doesn't expect to fall for mariner Ellis Chilton, who has more claim to the house than Maggie realizes. (978-1-63555-056-6)

Picture Perfect by Lisa Moreau. Falling in love wasn't supposed to be part of the stakes for Olive and Gabby, rival photographers in the competition of a lifetime. (978-1-62639-975-4)

Set the Stage by Karis Walsh. Actress Emilie Danvers takes the stage again in Ashland, Oregon, little realizing that landscaper Arden Philips is about to offer her a very personal romantic lead role. (978-1-63555-087-0)

Strike a Match by Fiona Riley. When their attempts at matchmaking fizzle out, firefighter Sasha and reluctant millionairess Abby find themselves turning to each other to strike a perfect match. (978-1-62639-999-0)

The Price of Cash by Ashley Bartlett. Cash Braddock is doing her best to keep her business afloat, stay out of jail, and avoid Detective Kallen. It's not working. (978-1-62639-708-8)

Under Her Wing by Ronica Black. At Angel's Wings Rescue, dogs are usually the ones saved, but when quiet Kassandra Haden meets outspoken owner Jayden Beaumont, the two stubborn women just might end up saving each other. (978-1-63555-077-1)

Underwater Vibes by Mickey Brent. When Hélène, a translator in Brussels, Belgium, meets Sylvie, a young Greek photographer and swim coach, unsettling feelings hijack Hélène's mind and body—even her poems. (978-1-63555-002-3)

A More Perfect Union by Carsen Taite. Major Zoey Granger and DC fixer Rook Daniels risk their reputations for a chance at true love while dealing with a scandal that threatens to rock the military. (978-1-62639-754-5)

Arrival by Gun Brooke. The spaceship *Pathfinder* reaches its passengers' new homeworld where danger lurks in the shadows while Pamas Seclan disembarks and finds unexpected love in young science genius Darmiya Do Voy. (978-1-62639-859-7)

Captain's Choice by VK Powell. Architect Kerstin Anthony's life is going to plan until Bennett Carlyle, the first girl she ever kissed, is assigned to her latest and most important project, a police district substation. (978-1-62639-997-6)

Falling Into Her by Erin Zak. Pam Phillips, widow at the age of forty, meets Kathryn Hawthorne, local Chicago celebrity, and it changes her life forever—in ways she hadn't even considered possible. (978-1-63555-092-4)

Hookin' Up by MJ Williamz. Will Leah get what she needs from casual hookups or will she see the love she desires right in front of her? (978-1-63555-051-1)

King of Thieves by Shea Godfrey. When art thief Casey Marinos meets bounty hunter Finnegan Starkweather, the crimes of the past just might set the stage for a payoff worth more than she ever dreamed possible. (978-1-63555-007-8)

Lucy's Chance by Jackie D. As a serial killer haunts the streets, Lucy tries to stitch up old wounds with her first love in the wake of a small town's rapid descent into chaos. (978-1-63555-027-6)

Right Here, Right Now by Georgia Beers. When Alicia Wright moves into the office next door to Lacey Chamberlain's accounting firm, Lacey is about to find out that sometimes the last person you want is exactly the person you need. (978-1-63555-154-9)

Strictly Need to Know by MB Austin. Covert operator Maji Rios will do whatever she must to complete her mission, but saving a gorgeous stranger from Russian mobsters was not in her plans. (978-1-63555-114-3)

Tailor-Made by Yolanda Wallace. Tailor Grace Henderson doesn't date clients, but when she meets gender-bending model Dakota Lane, she's tempted to throw all the rules out the window. (978-1-63555-081-8)

Time Will Tell by M. Ullrich. With the ability to time travel, Eva Caldwell will have to decide between having it all and erasing it all. (978-1-63555-088-7)

A Date to Die by Anne Laughlin. Someone is killing people close to Detective Kay Adler, who must look to her own troubled past for a suspect. There she finds more than one person seeking revenge against her. (978-1-63555-023-8)

Captured Soul by Laydin Michaels. Can Kadence Munroe save the woman she loves from a twisted killer, or will she lose her to a collector of souls? (978-1-62639-915-0)

Dawn's New Day by TJ Thomas. Can Dawn Oliver and Cam Cooper, two women who have loved and lost, open their hearts to love again? (978-1-63555-072-6)

Definite Possibility by Maggie Cummings. Sam Miller is just out for good times, but Lucy Weston makes her realize happily ever after is a definite possibility. (978-1-62639-909-9)

Eyes Like Those by Melissa Brayden. Isabel Chase and Taylor Andrews struggle between love and ambition from the writers' room on one of Hollywood's hottest TV shows. (978-1-63555-012-2)

Heart's Orders by Jaycie Morrison. Helen Tucker and Tee Owens escape hardscrabble lives to careers in the Women's Army Corps, but more than their hearts are at risk as friendship blossoms into love. (978-1-63555-073-3)

Hiding Out by Kay Bigelow. Treat Dandridge is unaware that her life is in danger from the murderer who is hunting the woman she's falling in love with, Mickey Heiden. (978-1-62639-983-9)

Omnipotence Enough by Sophia Kell Hagin. Can the tiny tool that abducted war veteran Jamie Gwynmorgan accidentally acquires help her escape an unknown enemy to reclaim her stolen life and the woman she deeply loves? (978-1-63555-037-5)

Summer's Cove by Aurora Rey. Emerson Lange moved to Provincetown to live in the moment, but when she meets Darcy Belo and her son Liam, her quest for summer romance becomes a family affair. (978-1-62639-971-6)

The Road to Wings by Julie Tizard. Lieutenant Casey Tompkins, Air Force student pilot, has to fly with the toughest instructor, Captain Kathryn "Hard Ass" Hardesty, fly a supersonic jet, and deal with a growing forbidden attraction. (978-1-62639-988-4)

Beauty and the Boss by Ali Vali. Ellis Renois is at the top of the fashion world, but she never expects her summer assistant Charlotte Hamner to tear her heart and her business apart like sharp scissors through cheap material. (978-1-62639-919-8)

Fury's Choice by Brey Willows. When gods walk amongst humans, can two women find a balance between love and faith? (978-1-62639-869-6)

Lessons in Desire by MJ Williamz. Can a summer love stand a four-month hiatus and still burn hot? (978-1-63555-019-1)

Lightning Chasers by Cass Sellars. For Sydney and Parker, being a couple was never what they had planned. Now they have to fight corruption, murder, and enemies hiding in plain sight just to hold on to each other. Lightning Series, Book Two. (978-1-62639-965-5)

Summer Fling by Jean Copeland. Still jaded from a breakup years earlier, Kate struggles to trust falling in love again when a summer fling with sexy young singer Jordan rocks her off her feet. (978-1-62639-981-5)

Take Me There by Julie Cannon. Adrienne and Sloan know it would be career suicide to mix business with pleasure, however tempting it is. But what's the harm? They're both consenting adults. Who would know? (978-1-62639-917-4)

The Girl Who Wasn't Dead by Samantha Boyette. A year ago, someone tried to kill Jenny Lewis. Tonight she's ready to find out who it was. (978-1-62639-950-1)

Unchained Memories by Dena Blake. Can a woman give herself completely when she's left a piece of herself behind? (978-1-62639-993-8)

Walking Through Shadows by Sheri Lewis Wohl. All Molly wanted to do was go backpacking…in her own century. (978-1-62639-968-6)

A Lamentation of Swans by Valerie Bronwen. Ariel Montgomery returns to Sea Oats to try to save her broken marriage but soon finds herself also fighting to save her own life and catch a murderer. (978-1-62639-828-3)

Freedom to Love by Ronica Black. What happens when the woman who spent her lifetime worrying about caring for her family, finally finds the freedom to love without borders? (978-1-63555-001-6)

House of Fate by Barbara Ann Wright. Two women must throw off the lives they've known as a guardian and an assassin and save two rival houses before their secrets tear the galaxy apart. (978-1-62639-780-4)

Planning for Love by Erin Dutton. Could true love be the one thing that wedding coordinator Faith McKenna didn't plan for? (978-1-62639-954-9)

Sidebar by Carsen Taite. Judge Camille Avery and her clerk, attorney West Fallon, agree on little except their mutual attraction, but can their relationship and their careers survive a headline-grabbing case? (978-1-62639-752-1)

Sweet Boy and Wild One by T. L. Hayes. When Rachel Cole meets soulful singer Bobby Layton at an open mic, she is immediately in thrall. What she soon discovers will rock her world in ways she never imagined. (978-1-62639-963-1)

To Be Determined by Mardi Alexander and Laurie Eichler. Charlie Dickerson escapes her life in the US to rescue Australian wildlife with Pip Atkins, but can they save each other? (978-1-62639-946-4)

True Colors by Yolanda Wallace. Blogger Robby Rawlins plans to use First Daughter Taylor Crenshaw to get ahead, but she never planned on falling in love with her in the process. (978-1-62639-927-3)

Unexpected by Jenny Frame. When Dale McGuire falls for Rebecca Harper, the mother of the son she never knew she had, will Rebecca's troubled past stop them from making the family they both truly crave? (978-1-62639-942-6)